普通高等学校规划教材

Appreciation of British and American Classic Novels and Films Based on the Novels
英美经典小说及其影视赏析

陈才忆　主　编
肖建荣　谭言红　副主编

人民交通出版社股份有限公司
China Communications Press Co.,Ltd.

内 容 提 要

本教材精选了十三位英美著名作家的经典小说十五部,共分十五个单元,每单元涉及一位作家和一部作品(有个别作家被选了两部作品,在下一单元就只涉及作品本身),每单元由作家简介、小说故事梗概、原著选读、主要人物介绍和分析、主题分析、影视改编、影视对白选读和讨论题八个部分组成。在作家简介和影视改编中,配有从网络上下载的作家和作品图片以及从不同版本影视作品中截取的画面,这些图片便于读者对作家、作品和不同版本的影视都有一个从感性到理性的认识过程。

近些年,国内高校为了提倡大学生的综合素质教育,开设了不少通识课程,本教材可供非英语专业的大学生使用,也可以供英语专业大学生作为辅助教材使用,加深对英语经典作品的理解,提高对西方艺术电影的鉴赏能力,从而提高自身的西方文化修养。

图书在版编目(CIP)数据

英美经典小说及其影视赏析/陈才忆主编.—北京:人民交通出版社股份有限公司,2014.8
ISBN 978-7-114-11501-1

Ⅰ.①英… Ⅱ.①陈… Ⅲ.①小说—文学欣赏—英国 ②小说—文学欣赏—美国 Ⅳ.①I561.074 ②I712.074

中国版本图书馆 CIP 数据核字(2014)第 141227 号

书　　名:	英美经典小说及其影视赏析
著 作 者:	陈才忆
责任编辑:	刘永芬　潘艳霞
出版发行:	人民交通出版社股份有限公司
地　　址:	(100011)北京市朝阳区安定门外外馆斜街 3 号
网　　址:	http://www.ccpress.com.cn
销售电话:	(010)59757973
总 经 销:	人民交通出版社股份有限公司发行部
经　　销:	各地新华书店
印　　刷:	北京市密东印刷有限公司
开　　本:	787×1092　1/16
印　　张:	11
字　　数:	260 千
版　　次:	2014 年 8 月　第 1 版
印　　次:	2018 年 7 月　第 2 次印刷
书　　号:	ISBN 978-7-114-11501-1
定　　价:	27.00 元

(有印刷、装订质量问题的图书由本公司负责调换)

编委会

主　编　陈才忆

副主编　肖建荣　谭言红

编　者（以姓氏笔画为序）

　　　　　黄健平　李　敏　黄　鹏

　　　　　陈　婕　朱　林　刘安平

　　　　　舒红凌　陈江月

前　　言

　　为了满足当代大学生对知识的渴求和提高人文素质的需求,高校开设了不少供学生选择的通识课,其中"英美经典小说及其影视赏析"课程一直深受学生欢迎。

　　考虑到通识课一般只有三十个学时的授课时间,本教材只精选十三位英美著名作家的经典小说十五部(其中英国七部,美国八部),共十五单元,每单元涉及一个作家和一部作品(其中有两位作家各有两部作品),由八个部分组成:(1)作家简介;(2)小说故事梗概;(3)原著选读;(4)主要人物介绍和分析;(5)主题分析;(6)影视改编;(7)影视对白选读;(8)讨论。其中,在(1)和(7)部分中,有网络下载插图和影视截图。

　　在使用过程中,可以每周一单元,学生在课前先熟悉故事情节,观看影视;在课堂上细读原著选段,朗诵乃至表演对白,将人物、主题分析和讨论三者结合进行,并找出小说与影视之间的异同;课后写感想。

　　本教材资料一方面来源于网页上的原文作品,对作品的介绍和评论,另一方面来源于纸质原著、译本和影视。网址、作者和出版社名均列入参考文献。但正文中具体出处未标明,在此特对网页拥有者、涉及的作者和出版社表示感谢。也可能有些资料没有列入文献,凡涉及的作者,在此一并致以敬意。

　　本教材的出版除了受到重庆交通大学2012年校级规划教材项目资助和重庆交通大学2013年重点学科"中国语言文学"建设项目资助,还受到重庆交通大学外国语学院建院二十周年出版教材和著作计划的资助。

　　本教材虽然是在多年的教学经验下编写而成,但由于经验有限,对于书中存在的问题,敬请使用者批评指正。

编　者
2014年6月

CONTENTS

Unit 1   Daniel Defoe and *Robinson Crusoe* ······ (1)
Unit 2   Charlotte Brontë and *Jane Eyre* ······ (11)
Unit 3   Emily Brontë and *Wuthering Heights* ······ (25)
Unit 4   Jane Austen and *Pride and Prejudice* ······ (37)
Unit 5   Thomas Hardy and *Tess of the D'Urbervilles* ······ (48)
Unit 6   Charles Dickens and *A Tale of Two Cities* ······ (61)
Unit 7   Charles Dickens and *David Copperfield* ······ (73)
Unit 8   James Fenimore Cooper and *The Last of the Mohicans* ······ (85)
Unit 9   Mark Twain and *The Adventures of Huckleberry Finn* ······ (96)
Unit 10 Harriet Beecher Stowe and *Uncle Tom's Cabin* ······ (108)
Unit 11 Herman Melville and *Moby-Dick* ······ (119)
Unit 12 Theodore Dreiser and *Sister Carrie* ······ (128)
Unit 13 Scott Fitzgerald and *The Great Gatsby* ······ (137)
Unit 14 Ernest Hemingway and *A Farewell to Arms* ······ (148)
Unit 15 Ernest Hemingway and *The Old Man and the Sea* ······ (157)
References ······ (166)

Unit 1 Daniel Defoe and *Robinson Crusoe*

Daniel Defoe (1660—1731) was an English trader, writer, journalist, pamphleteer and spy, now most famous for his novel *Robinson Crusoe*(1719) and is among the founders of the English novel. A prolific and versatile writer, he wrote more than 500 books, pamphlets and journals on various topics (including politics, crime, religion, marriage, psychology and the supernatural). He was also a pioneer of economic journalism. *Robinson Crusoe* is a fictional autobiography of the title character—a castaway who spends 28 years on a remote tropical island, encountering cannibals, captives and mutineers before being rescued. Despite its simple narrative style, *Robinson Crusoe* was well received in the literary world and is often credited as marking the beginning of realistic fiction as a literary genre. It has become one of the most widely published books in history. By the end of the 19th century, no book in the history of Western literature had more editions, spin-offs and translations than *Robinson Crusoe*, with more than 700 such alternative versions, including children's versions with mainly pictures and no text.

Fig 1.1 Daniel Defoe

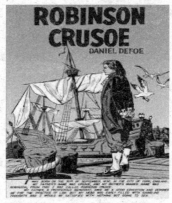
Fig 1.2 A Book Cover of *Robinson Crusoe*

Plot

Crusoe sets sail from the Queen's Dock in Hull on a sea voyage in August 1651, against his parents' wishes, who want him to pursue a career, possibly in law. After a tumultuous journey where his ship is wrecked in a storm, his lust for the sea remains so strong that he sets out to sea again. This journey, too, ends in disaster as the ship is taken over by Salé pirates and Crusoe is enslaved by a Moor. Two years later, he escapes in a boat with a boy. A captain of a Portuguese ship off the west coast of Africa rescues him. The ship is enroute to Brazil. With the captain's help, Crusoe procures a plantation.

Years later, Crusoe joins an expedition to bring slaves from Africa but he is shipwrecked in a storm about forty miles out to sea on an island near the mouth of the Orinoco River on September 30, 1659. The ship is bound for Africa to buy Negro slaves but out of the way of human commerce. Only he and three animals, the captain's dog and two cats survive the shipwreck.

Overcoming his despair, he fetches arms, tools, and other supplies from the ship before it breaks apart and sinks. He builds a fenced-in habitat near a cave which he excavates. By making marks in a wooden cross, he creates a calendar. By using tools salvaged from the ship, and the ones he makes himself, he hunts, grows barley and rice, and dries grapes to make raisins.

He learns to make pottery, raises goats. He also adopts a small parrot. He reads the Bible and becomes religious, thanking god for his fate in which nothing is missing but human society.

More years pass and Crusoe discovers native cannibals, who occasionally visit the island to kill and eat prisoners. At first he plans to kill them for committing an abomination but later realizes he has no right to do so, as the cannibals do not knowingly commit a crime. He dreams of obtaining one or two servants by freeing some prisoners. When a prisoner escapes, Crusoe helps him, naming his new companion "Friday" after the day of the week he appears. Crusoe then teaches him English and converts him to Christianity.

After more natives arrive to partake in a cannibal feast, Crusoe and Friday kill most of the natives and save two prisoners. One is Friday's father and the other is a Spaniard, who informs Crusoe about other Spaniards shipwrecked on the mainland. A plan is devised that the Spaniard would return to the mainland with Friday's father, bring back the others, build a ship and sail to a Spanish port.

Before the Spaniards return, an English ship appears. Mutineers have commandeered the vessel and intend to maroon their captain on the island. Crusoe and the ship's captain strike a deal in which Crusoe helps the captain and the loyal sailors retake the ship and leave the worst mutineers on the island.

Before embarking for England, Crusoe shows the mutineers how he survived on the island and states that there will be more men coming. Crusoe leaves the island on December 19, 1686 and arrives in England on June 11, 1687. He learns that his family believed him dead. As a result, he was left nothing in his father's will. Crusoe departs for Lisbon to reclaim the profits of his estate in Brazil, which has granted him much wealth. In conclusion, he transports his wealth overland to England to avoid travelling by sea. Friday accompanies him and, en route, they endure one last adventure together as they fight off famished wolves while crossing the Pyrenees.

With the success of the story, Defoe went on to write a lesser-known sequel, *The Farther Adventures of Robinson Crusoe*, in which Friday is killed in a sea battle.

Select Reading: Chapter 4

It happen'd one day about noon going towards my boat, I was exceedingly surpriz'd with the print of a man's naked foot on the shore, which was very plain to be seen in the sand: I stood like one thunder-struck, or as if I had seen an apparition; I listen'd, I look'd round me, I could hear nothing, nor see anything, I went up to a rising ground to look farther, I went up the shore and down the shore, but it was all one, I could see no other impression but that one, I went to it again to see if there were any more, and to observe if it might not be my fancy; but there was no room for that, for there was exactly the very print of a foot, toes, heel, and every part of a foot; how it came thither, I knew not, nor could in the least imagine. But after innumerable fluttering Thoughts, like a man perfectly confus'd and out of my self, I came home to my fortification, not feeling, as we see, the ground I went on, but terrify'd to the last degree, looking behind me at every two or three steps, mistaking every bush and tree, and fancying every stump at a distance to be a man; nor is it possible to describe how many various shapes affrighted imagination represented things to me in, how many wild ideas were found every moment in my fancy, and what strange unaccountable whimsies came into my thoughts by the way.

Heartening my self therefore with the belief that this was nothing but the print of one of my own Feet, and so I might be truly said to start at my own shadow, I began to go abroad again, and went to my country house, to milk my flock; but to see with what fear I went forward, how often I look'd behind me, how I was ready every now and then to lay down my basket, and run for my life, it would have made any one have thought I was haunted with an evil conscience, or that I had been lately most terribly frightened, and so indeed I had.

However, as I went down thus two or three days, and having seen nothing, I began to be a little bolder; and to think there was really nothing in it, but my own imagination: But I cou'd not persuade my self fully of this, till I should go down to the shore again, and see this print of a foot, and measure it by my own, and see if there was any similitude or fitness, that I might be assur'd it was my own foot: But when I came to the place, First, It appear'd evidently to me, that when I laid up my boat, I could not possibly be on shore any where there about. Secondly, when I came to measure the mark with my own foot, I found my foot not so large by a great deal; both these Things fill'd my head with new imaginations, and gave me the vapours again, to the highest degree; so that I shook with cold, like one in an ague: And I went home again, fill'd with the belief that some man or men had been on shore there; or in short, that the island was inhabited, and I might be surpriz'd before I was aware; and what course to take for my security I knew not.

译文： 一天中午，我去看我的船，极为震惊地发现海岸上一个光脚脚印，在平坦的沙地上，脚印一览无余。我像遭到雷劈或遇上了鬼似的僵直在那里。我侧耳倾听，四周环顾，什么也没听到，什么也没看见。除了这只脚印，其他什么痕迹也没有。我又一次走过去看看有没有别的脚印，去看看是否是我的幻觉。但不容我存任何侥幸，那儿确确实实是一个脚印——脚趾、后跟、脚的每一部位都俱全。这脚印怎么来的，我不清楚，也想象不出。我像一个失魂落魄的人，思绪如万马奔腾，一片混乱。我朝堡垒逃去，脚底软绵绵的，惊惧至极，每走两三步，就要回头望望，真是风声鹤唳，草木皆兵。恐惧激起各种想象，把事物幻化成千奇百怪的形状，荒诞不经的念头充斥我的脑海，数不清的魔幻意识阵阵袭来。

我相信那不过是我自己的脚印，我不过像被自己影子吓坏的人一样惊乍乍的，凭着这股信念，我又出门到乡村别墅为羊群挤奶。可是，我还是吓得发抖，频频回头，随时准备扔下篮子逃命。看到我的人一定认为我是鬼魂附体，或受了极度惊吓，我的确如此。

不过，连续出去两三天，什么也没发生，我胆子大了一些，又觉得这恐惧是自己的幻想，不必小题大做。但我还不能完全说服自己，我只有走到那片海滩，找到那只脚印，用自己的脚比画一下，看看是不是尺码相同，以此确定是不是自己的脚印，我到了那处——首先，我停船时显然不可能在那附近走动；其次，我比画了一下，我的脚没那么大。这两件事使我心中重新充满无数新的妄念,我忧悒无比,像害了疟疾似的颤抖不已。我奔回家,满脑子想的是,已经有人上岸,这岛上住上了人,也许我还未清醒过来就已遭到袭击。可该采取什么防卫措施,我茫然不知。

Analysis of Major Characters

Robinson Crusoe: He is no flashy hero or grand epic adventurer, but his perseverance in spending months making a canoe, and in practicing pottery making until he gets it right, is praiseworthy. His resourcefulness in building a home, dairy, grape arbor, country house and goat stable from practically nothing is clearly remarkable. He manages to make a fortune in Brazil despite a twenty-eight-year absence and even leaves his island with a nice collection of gold. He is never interested in portraying himself as a hero in his own narration. He does not boast of his courage in quelling the mutiny, and he is always ready to admit unheroic feelings of fear or panic, as when he finds the footprint on the beach. Crusoe prefers to depict himself as an ordinary sensible man, never as an exceptional hero. There are flaws in his character. He seems incapable of deep feelings, as shown by his cold account of leaving his family—he worries about the religious consequences of disobeying his father, but never displays any emotion about leaving. Though he is generous toward people, as when he gives gifts to his sisters and the captain, he reveals very little tender or sincere affection in his dealings with them. When he tells that he has gotten married and that his wife has died all within the same sentence, his indifference to her seems almost cruel. Moreover, as an individual personality, Crusoe is rather dull. His precise and deadpan style of narration works well for recounting the process of canoe building, but it tends to drain the excitement from events that should be thrilling. His insistence on dating events makes sense to a point, but it ultimately ends up seeming obsessive and irrelevant when he tells the date on which he grinds his tools but neglects to tell the date of a very important event like meeting Friday. Perhaps his impulse to record facts carefully is not a survival skill, but an irritating sign of his neurosis. While not boasting of heroism, he is nonetheless very interested in possessions, power and prestige. When he first calls himself king of the island, it seems jocund, but when he describes the Spaniard as his subject, it seems he really does consider himself king. His teaching Friday to call him "Master", even before teaching him the words "yes" or "no", seems obnoxious even under the racist standards of the day. Overall, his virtues tend to be private: his industry, resourcefulness, and solitary courage make him an exemplary individual. But his vices are social, and his urge to subjugate others is highly objectionable. In bringing both sides together into one complex character, Defoe gives us a fascinating glimpse into the successes, failures and contradictions of modern man.

Friday: Probably the first nonwhite character to be given a realistic, individualized, and humane portrayal in the English novel, Friday has a huge literary and cultural importance. If Crusoe represents the first colonial mind in fiction, then Friday represents not just a Caribbean tribesman, but all the natives of America, Asia, and Africa who would later be oppressed in the age of European imperialism. At the moment when Crusoe teaches Friday to call him "Master", Friday becomes an enduring political symbol of racial injustice in a modern world critical of imperialist expansion. Aside from his importance to our culture, Friday is a key figure within the context of the novel. In many ways he is the most vibrant character, much more charismatic and colorful than his master. Whereas Crusoe never mentions missing his family or dreams about the happiness of seeing them again, Friday jumps and sings for joy when he meets his father, and this emotional display makes us see what is missing from Crusoe's stodgy heart. Friday's expression of loyalty in asking Crusoe to kill him rather than leave him is more heartfelt than anything Crusoe ever says or does. Friday's sincere questions to Crusoe about the devil, which Crusoe answers only indirectly and hesitantly, leave us wondering whether Crusoe's knowledge of Christianity is superficial and sketchy in contrast to Friday's full understanding of his own god Benamuckee. In short, Friday's exuberance and emotional directness often point out the wooden conventionality of Crusoe's personality. Despite Friday's subjugation, Crusoe appreciates Friday. Crusoe does not seem to value intimacy with humans much, but he does say that he loves Friday, which is a remarkable disclosure. It is the only time Crusoe makes such an admission in the novel, since he never expresses love for his parents, brothers, sisters, or even his wife. The mere fact that an Englishman confesses more love for an illiterate Caribbean ex-cannibal than for his own family suggests the appeal of Friday's personality. Crusoe may bring Friday Christianity and clothing, but Friday brings Crusoe emotional warmth and a vitality of spirit that Crusoe's own European heart lacks.

The Portuguese Captain: He is presented more fully than any other European in the novel besides Crusoe, more vividly portrayed than Crusoe's widow friend or his family members. He appears at two very important junctures in Crusoe's life. First, it is the Portuguese captain who picks up Crusoe after the escape from the Moors and takes him to Brazil, where Crusoe establishes himself as a plantation owner. Twenty-eight years later, it is again the Portuguese captain who informs Crusoe that his Brazilian investments are secure, and who arranges the sale of the plantation and the forwarding of the proceeds to Crusoe. In both cases, the Portuguese captain is the agent of Crusoe's extreme good fortune. In this sense, he represents the benefits of social connections. If the captain had not been located in Lisbon, Crusoe would never have cashed in on his Brazilian holdings. This assistance from social contacts contradicts the theme of solitary enterprise that the novel seems to endorse. Despite Crusoe's hard individual labor on the island, it is actually another human being—and not his own resourcefulness—that makes Crusoe wealthy in the end. Moreover, the Portuguese captain is associated with a wide array of virtues. He is honest, informing Crusoe of the money he has borrowed against Crusoe's investments, and repaying a part of it immediately even though it is financially difficult for him to do so. He is loyal, honoring his duties toward Crusoe even after twenty-eight years. Finally, he is extremely generous, paying Crusoe more than market value for the animal skins and slave boys after picking Crusoe up at sea, and giving Crusoe handsome gifts when leaving Brazil. All these virtues make the captain a paragon of human excellence, and they make us wonder why Defoe includes such a character in the novel. In some ways, the captain's goodness makes him the moral counterpart of Friday, since the European seaman and the Caribbean cannibal mirror each other in benevolence and devotion to Crusoe.

Themes

Colonialism: Robinson Crusoe is the true symbol of the British conquest: "He is the true prototype of the British colonist. The whole Anglo-Saxon spirit is in Crusoe: the manly independence, the unconscious cruelty, the persistence, the slow yet efficient intelligence, the sexual apathy, the calculating taciturnity." In a sense Crusoe attempts to replicate his society on the island. This is achieved through the use of European technology, agriculture and even a rudimentary political hierarchy. Several times Crusoe refers to himself as the "king" of the island, while the captain describes him as the 'governor' to the mutineers. At the very end of the novel the island is explicitly referred to as a 'colony'. The idealized master-servant relationship between Crusoe and Friday can also be seen in terms of cultural imperialism. Crusoe represents the 'enlightened' European while Friday is the 'savage' who can only be redeemed from his barbarous way of life through assimilation into Crusoe's culture.

Religion: Crusoe is not a hero but an everyman. He begins as a wanderer, aimless on a sea he does not understand and ends as a pilgrim, crossing a final mountain to enter the Promised Land. The book tells the story of how Crusoe becomes closer to God, not through listening to sermons in a church but through spending time alone amongst nature with only a Bible to read. The Biblical story of Jonah is alluded to in the first part of the novel. Like Jonah, Crusoe neglects his 'duty' and is punished at sea. There is the Christian notion of Providence, penitence and redemption. Crusoe comes to repent of the follies of his youth. He learns to pray to God, first by randomly opening his Bible. He reads the words of Psalm 50 where he reads, "Call upon me in the day of trouble; I will deliver you, and you shall glorify me." Crusoe often feels guided by a divinely ordained fate, thus explaining his robust optimism in the face of apparent hopelessness. His various fortunate intuitions are taken as evidence of a benign spirit world. Defoe also foregrounds this theme by arranging highly significant events in the novel to occur on Crusoe's birthday. The denouement culminates not only in Crusoe's deliverance from the island, but his spiritual deliverance, his acceptance of Christian doctrine, and in his intuition of his own salvation.

Morality: When confronted with the cannibals, Crusoe wrestles with the problem of cultural relativism. Despite his disgust, he feels unjustified in holding the natives morally responsible for a practice so deeply ingrained in their culture. Nevertheless he retains his belief in an absolute standard of morality; he regards cannibalism as a 'national crime' and forbids Friday from practicing it.

Economics: In classical, neoclassical and Austrian economics, Crusoe is regularly used to illustrate the theory of production and choice in the absence of trade, money and prices. Crusoe must allocate effort between production and leisure and must choose between alternative production possibilities to meet his needs. The arrival of Friday is then used to illustrate the possibility of and gains from trade. Crusoe's experiences on the island represent the inherent economic value of labor over capital. Crusoe frequently observes that the money he salvaged from the ship is worthless on the island, especially when compared to his tools.

Film Adaptations

Robinzon Kruzo (1946) is a 1946 Soviet 3-D film directed by Aleksandr Andriyevsky, starring Pavel Kadochnikov as Robinson Crusoe and Yuri Lyubimov as Friday. The film is the first glass-free stereoscopic feature film, the first Soviet 3-D feature film, and possibly the world's first 3-D feature film partially in color.

Fig 1.3　Eating bread

Fig 1.4　Making a canoe

Fig 1.5　Measuring the print of a foot

Fig 1.6　Crusoe and Friday

Robinson Crusoe (1954) is a film directed by Luis Buñuel, starring Dan O'Herlihy as Robinson Crusoe and Jaime Fernández as Friday. This one is the most well-known in China.

Fig 1.7　Making pottery

Fig 1.8　Naming the captive

Fig 1.9　Robinson is reading the Holy Book

Fig 1.10　Leaving the Island

Man Friday (1975) is adapted from the 1973 play based on Daniel Defoe's *Robinson Crusoe*, but reverses the roles, portraying Crusoe as a blunt, stiff Englishman, while the native he calls Man Friday is much more intelligent and empathic. The film can be regarded as being critical of western civilization, against which it draws an idealizing picture of Caribbean tribal life. The film satirically portrayed Crusoe as incapable of seeing his dark-skinned companion as anything but an inferior creature.

Fig 1.11　　*Man Friday* Posters

Robinson Crusoe (1997) is directed by Rod Hardy and George T. Miller, starring Pierce Brosnan as Robinson Crusoe in the loose adaptation of Daniel Defoe's novel. Although titled "Daniel Defoe's *Robinson Crusoe*" in various releases, the film differs markedly from the book. In this film, Crusoe is portrayed as being a Scotsman with a love interest. The title of the novel states that its main character is from York, in Northern England. In the film Crusoe flees by sea to escape being hunted down by the family of the friend he killed. In the novel, Crusoe departs against his parents' wishes, due to a longing for adventure. In the film he initially spends less than a year at sea before being shipwrecked while Crusoe in the novel is stranded on multiple occasions and at sea much longer. He spends time on numerous ships in variety of places. In the film his ship founders near New Guinea in the vicinity of New Britain while the island in the novel is near Venezuela off the mouth of the Orinoco River. Crusoe's interactions with people— particularly Friday—vary considerably. In the film Crusoe comes to accept Friday's culture, which is the opposite of the theology of the novel, where Friday converts to Christianity. The film also avoids all instances of mutineers and European prisoners that lead to Crusoe's rescue in the original novel. Crusoe's rescue in the novel occurs when he helps the captain of a mutinous vessel in return for a passage home. The mutineers are left on the island instead. In the film, Crusoe is wounded by Friday's enemies and Friday takes him to his own island to be healed, but Friday's tribe has disowned him, and force Crusoe and Friday to fight to the death after saying they will allow the winner to go free. Just as Friday is about to kill Crusoe (after Crusoe tells Friday to take his life and be free), a slaver ship arrives and kills Friday before enslaving his tribe and razing their village. Crusoe then returns to England. In the novel, Friday is not killed and accompanies Crusoe on his return to England, where he begins another round of adventures.

Fig 1.12　A Poster　　　　Fig 1.13　Crusoe and Friday

A Wonderful Dialogue from the 1954 Film

Robinson and Friday smoke leisurely together and begin their talk.

Robinson: You understand, Friday. The devil is God's enemy in the hearts of men. He uses all his malice and skill to destroy the kingdom of Christ.

Friday: (*Smiling*) But master say God is so strong so great. Is God not much strong than devil?

Robinson: Yes, yes. Friday. God is stronger than the devil. He's above the devil. Therefore we pray to God.

Friday: But if God is much strong than devil, why God no kill devil, so make him no more wicked.

Robinson: (*Looking closely at Friday*) What's that Friday?

Friday: If God the most strong, why he no kill devil?

Robinson: (*Standing up and thinking*) Well we see Friday, without the devil, there would be no temptation and no sin. The devil must be there for us to have a chance to choose sin or resist it.

Friday: Is God let devil tempt us?

Robinson: Yes.

Friday: Then, why God mad when sin?

Robinson: (*Walking away, feeling puzzled*) Huh, ha, ha, ha. (*To the parrot*) You understand, don't you Poll? Friday can't get these things into his head. You understand, don't you?

He takes a look at Friday, who smokes very skillfully with satisfaction.

▼ Discussions

1. Since Robinson Crusoe builds a kingdom of his own on the island with his skills and efforts, can he be regarded as a hero?
2. Friday becomes a servant of Robinson Crusoe. As he says, he would rather be killed than leave Crusoe. How do you think of this person?

3. The Portuguese Captain is very kind, helpful and generous. Is this captain a believable character or an idealized one?
4. Is the novelist for imperialism or against it by portraying such a title character and his adventures?
5. There are several adaptations and each of them portrays Friday differently. Which one is the most faithful and acceptable according to our own understanding?

Unit 2　Charlotte Brontë and *Jane Eyre*

Charlotte Brontë(1816—1855) was the third of the six children of their parents. She went to school in Brussels with Emily in 1842. In 1846, the three sisters published a collection of their poems. The reviews were good and spurred on their further literary endeavors. In August of 1846, Charlotte began to write *Jane Eyre*, which was published in 1847. This success was followed up by tragedy. From September 1848 to May 1849, the only brother Branwell and the other two sisters, Emily and Anne, died of illness one after another. Charlotte's grief is plain in the last third of her novel *Shirley*, which she'd been working on when all the death started. Her father's curate, Arthur Bell Nicholls, proposed to her, whom she married in June of 1854. She died on 31 March 1855. *Jane Eyre* is described as an influential feminist text because of its in-depth exploration of a strong female character's feelings.

Fig 2.1　Charlotte Brontë

Fig 2.2　A Book Cover of *Jane Eyre*

Plot

The novel goes through five distinct stages: Jane's childhood at Gateshead, where she is emotionally and physically abused by her aunt and cousins; her education at Lowood School, where she acquires friends and role models but also suffers privations and oppression; her time as the governess of Thornfield Hall, where she falls in love with her Byronic employer, Edward Rochester; her time with the Rivers family, during which her earnest but cold clergyman cousin, St John Rivers, proposes to her; and the finale with her reunion with, and marriage to, her beloved Rochester.

Jane's Childhood: The novel begins with Jane Eyre living with her maternal uncle's family, the Reeds, as her uncle's dying wish. She is ten years old. Her parents died of typhus several years ago. Mr. Reed was the only one in the Reed family to be kind to Jane. Her aunt Sarah Reed does not like her, treats her worse than a servant and discourages and at times forbids her children from associating with her. Mrs. Reed and her three children are abusive to her, both physically and emotionally. The servant Bessie proves to be Jane's only ally in the household even though Bessie sometimes harshly scolds Jane. Excluded from the family activities, Jane is incredibly unhappy with only a doll to find solace. One day, Jane is locked in the red room where her uncle died. She had panics after seeing visions of him. She is finally rescued when she is allowed to attend Lowood School for Girls, after the physician Mr. Lloyd convinces Mrs. Reed to send Jane away. Before Jane leaves, she confronts Mrs. Reed and declares that she'll never call her aunt again, that Mrs. Reed and her daughters, Georgiana and Eliza, are deceitful and that she'd tell everyone at Lowood how cruelly Mrs. Reed treated her.

Lowood: Jane arrives at Lowood Institution, a charity school, the head of which (Brocklehurst) has been told that she is deceitful. During an inspection, Jane accidentally breaks her slate, and Mr. Brocklehurst, the self-righteous clergyman who runs the school, brands her a liar and shames her before the entire assembly. Jane is comforted by her friend, Helen Burns. Miss Temple, a caring teacher, facilitates Jane's self-defense and writes to Mr. Lloyd, whose reply agrees with Jane's. Ultimately, Jane is publicly cleared of Mr. Brocklehurst's accusations.

The eighty pupils at Lowood are subjected to cold rooms, poor meals, and thin clothing. Many students fall ill when a typhus epidemic strikes. Jane's friend Helen dies of consumption in her arms. When Mr. Brocklehurst's neglect and dishonesty are discovered, several benefactors erect a new building and conditions at the school improve dramatically.

Thornfield Hall: After six years as a student and two as a teacher, Jane decides to leave Lowood, like her friend and confidante Miss Temple. She advertises her services as a governess, and receives one reply. It is from Alice Fairfax, the housekeeper at Thornfield Hall. She takes the position, teaching Adele Varens, a young French girl. While Jane is walking one night to a nearby town, a horseman passes her. The horse slips on ice and throws the rider. She helps him to the horse. Later, back at the mansion she learns that this man is Edward Rochester, master of the house. He teases her, asking whether she bewitched his horse to make him fall. Adele is his ward, left in Mr. Rochester's care when her mother, who was once his lover and who betrayed him, abandoned her. Mr. Rochester and Jane enjoy each other's company and spend many hours together.

Odd things start to happen at the mansion, such as a strange laugh, a mysterious fire in Mr. Rochester's room, on which Jane throws water, and an attack on Rochester's guest, Mr. Mason.

Jane receives word that her aunt was calling for her, after being in much grief because her son has died. She returns to Gateshead and remains there for a month caring for her dying aunt. Mrs. Reed gives Jane a letter from Jane's paternal uncle, Mr. John Eyre, asking for her to live with him. Mrs. Reed admits to telling her uncle that Jane had died of fever at Lowood.

After returning to Thornfield, Jane broods over Mr. Rochester's impending marriage to Blanche Ingram. But on a midsummer evening, he proclaims his love for Jane and proposes. As she prepares for her wedding, Jane's forebodings arise when a strange, savage-looking woman sneaks into her room one night and rips her wedding veil in two. As with the previous mysterious events, Mr. Rochester attributes the incident to drunkenness on the part of Grace Poole, one of his servants. During the wedding ceremony, Mr. Mason and a lawyer declare that Mr. Rochester cannot marry because he is still married to Mr. Mason's sister Bertha. Mr. Rochester admits this is true, but explains that his father tricked him into the marriage for her money. Once they were united, he discovered that she was rapidly descending into madness and eventually locked her away in Thornfield, hiring Grace Poole as a nurse to look after her. When Grace gets drunk, his wife escapes, and causes the strange happenings at Thornfield. Mr. Mason found out about the bigamous marriage. Mr. Rochester asks Jane to go with him to the south of France, and live as husband and wife, even though they cannot be married. Refusing to go against her principles, and despite her love for him, Jane leaves Thornfield in the middle of the night.

Other Employment: Jane travels through England using the little money she had saved. She accidentally leaves her bundle of possessions on a coach and has to sleep on the moor, trying to trade her scarf and gloves for food. Exhausted, she makes her way to the home of Diana and Mary Rivers, but is turned away by the housekeeper. She faints on the doorstep, preparing for her death. St. John Rivers, Diana and Mary's brother and a clergyman, saves her. After she regains her health, St. John finds her a teaching position at a nearby charity school. Jane becomes good friends with the sisters, but St. John remains reserved.

The sisters leave for governess jobs and St. John becomes closer with Jane. St. John discovers Jane's true identity, and astounds her by showing her a letter stating that her uncle John Eyre has died and left her his entire fortune of 20 000 pounds. When Jane questions him further, St. John reveals that John is also his and his sisters' uncle. They had once hoped for a share of the inheritance, but have since resigned themselves to nothing. Jane, overjoyed by finding her family, insists on sharing the money equally with her cousins, and Diana and Mary come to Moor House to stay.

Proposals: Thinking she will make a suitable missionary's wife, St. John asks Jane to marry him and to go with him to India, not out of love, but out of duty. Jane initially accepts going to India, but rejects the marriage proposal, suggesting they travel as brother and sister. As soon as Jane's resolve against marriage to St. John begins to weaken, she mysteriously hears Mr. Rochester's voice calling her name. Jane then returns to Thornfield to find only blackened ruins. She learns that Mr. Rochester's wife set the house on fire and committed suicide by jumping from the roof. In his rescue attempts, Mr. Rochester lost a hand and his eyesight. Jane reunites with him, but he fears that she will be repulsed by his condition. When Jane assures him of her love and tells him that she will never leave him, Mr. Rochester again proposes and they are married. He eventually recovers enough sight to see their first-born son.

Select Reading: Chapter 37

"Ah! Jane. But I want a wife."

"Do you, sir?"

"Yes: is it news to you?"

"Of course: you said nothing about it before."

"Is it unwelcome news?"

"That depends on circumstances, sir—on your choice."

"Which you shall make for me, Jane. I will abide by your decision."

"Choose then, sir—HER WHO LOVES YOU BEST."

"I will at least choose—HER I LOVE BEST. Jane, will you marry me?"

"Yes, sir."

"A poor blind man, whom you will have to lead about by the hand?"

"Yes, sir."

"A crippled man, twenty years older than you, whom you will have to wait on?"

"Yes, sir."

"Truly, Jane?"

"Most truly, sir."

"Oh! my darling! God bless you and reward you!"

"Mr. Rochester, if ever I did a good deed in my life—if ever I thought a good thought—if ever I prayed a sincere and blameless prayer—if ever I wished a righteous wish,—I am rewarded now. To be your wife is, for me, to be as happy as I can be on earth."

"Because you delight in sacrifice."

"Sacrifice! What do I sacrifice? Famine for food, expectation for content. To be privileged to put my arms round what I value—to press my lips to what I love—to repose on what I trust: is that to make a sacrifice? If so, then certainly I delight in sacrifice."

"And to bear with my infirmities, Jane: to overlook my deficiencies."

"Which are none, sir, to me. I love you better now, when I can really be useful to you, than I did in your state of proud independence, when you disdained every part but that of the giver and protector."

"Hitherto I have hated to be helped—to be led: henceforth, I feel I shall hate it no more. I did not like to put my hand into a hireling's, but it is pleasant to feel it circled by Jane's little fingers. I preferred utter loneliness to the constant attendance of servants; but Jane's soft ministry will be a perpetual joy. Jane suits me: do I suit her?"

"To the finest fibre of my nature, sir."

"The case being so, we have nothing in the world to wait for: we must be married instantly."

He looked and spoke with eagerness: his old impetuosity was rising.

"We must become one flesh without any delay, Jane: there is but the licence to get—then we marry."

"Mr. Rochester, I have just discovered the sun is far declined from its meridian, and Pilot is actually gone home to his dinner. Let me look at your watch."

"Fasten it into your girdle, Jane, and keep it henceforward: I have no use for it."

译文:"哦！简。可我需要一个妻子啊。"

"是吗,先生?"

"是啊,难道你觉得这是新闻吗?"

"当然。你以前没有说起过呀。"

"这是个不受欢迎的新闻吗?"

"那得看情况了,先生,看您怎么选择了。"

"这得由你来给我选了。简,我坚决服从你的决定。"

"那就选择,先生—最爱你的人。"

"我至少要挑选—我最爱的人。简,你愿意嫁给我吗?"

"是的,先生。"

"一个到哪儿都得要你搀扶的可怜的瞎子?"

"是的,先生。"

"一个比你大二十岁、得要你伺候的残疾人?"

"是的,先生。"

"当真吗,简?"

"完全当真,先生。"

"哦! 我亲爱的! 愿上帝保佑你,酬报你!"

"罗切斯特先生,如果我这辈子做过什么好事,起过什么善念,做过什么真诚无邪的祈祷,有过什么正当的愿望,那我现在已经得到酬报了。对我来说,做你的妻子,就是我在世上所能得到的最大幸福。"

"因为你喜欢牺牲。"

"牺牲! 我牺牲了什么? 牺牲饥饿得到食物,牺牲渴望得到满足。有权拥抱我所珍视的人,亲吻我所挚爱的人,偎依我所信赖的人,这是做出牺牲吗? 要是这样,那我倒真的喜欢牺牲了。"

"还要忍受我的病弱,简,宽容我的缺点。"

"这对我来说算不了什么,先生,我现在更加爱你了,因为现在我可以对你真正有所帮助了,而过去你是那么傲慢,从不依赖别人,除了施予者和保护人之外,你不屑扮演任何其他角色。"

"以前,我一直讨厌让别人帮忙,让人领着走。今后,我觉得不会再讨厌了。过去,我不喜欢让给仆人牵着,现在让简的小手握着,感觉真是愉快极了。我以前宁愿孤零零地独自一人,不愿老是由仆人伺候着,可是简的温柔照料,却永远是件让人高兴的事。简合我的心意,我合她的心意吗?"

"我一丝一毫都没有感到不合我心意的地方,先生。"

"既然这样,我们还有什么可等的呢,我们得马上结婚。"

他的神态和说话都很急切,他那急躁的老脾气又上来了。

"我们应当毫不拖延地结为夫妇,简,只要领张证书,我们就可以结婚。"

"罗切斯特先生,我刚才发现太阳已经偏西了。派洛特已经回家吃饭去了。让我看看你的表。"

"把它系在你的腰带上吧,简,以后就由你留着,我用不着它了。"

Analysis of Major Characters

Jane Eyre: The development of Jane Eyre's character is central to the novel. From the beginning, Jane possesses a sense of her self-worth and dignity, a commitment to justice and principle, a trust in God, and a passionate disposition. Her integrity is continually tested over the course of the novel, and Jane must learn to balance the frequently conflicting aspects of herself so as to find contentment. An orphan since early childhood, Jane feels exiled and excluded at the beginning of the novel, and the cruel treatment she receives from her Aunt Reed and her cousins only worsens her feeling of alienation. Afraid that she will never find a true sense of home or community, Jane feels the need to belong somewhere, to find "kin". This desire tempers her equally intense need for autonomy and freedom. In her search for freedom, Jane also struggles with the question of what type of freedom she wants. While Rochester initially offers Jane a chance to liberate her passions, Jane comes to realize that such freedom could also mean enslavement—by living as Rochester's mistress, she would sacrifice her dignity and integrity for the sake of her feelings. St. John Rivers offers Jane another kind of freedom: the freedom to act unreservedly on her principles. He opens to Jane the possibility of exercising her talents fully by working and living with him in India. Jane eventually realizes that this freedom would also constitute a form of imprisonment, because she would be forced to keep her true feelings and her true passions always in check. The author may have created this Jane Eyre as a means of coming to terms with elements of her own life. She also struggles to find a balance between love and freedom and to find others who understands her. At many points in the novel, Jane voices the author's then-radical opinions on religion, social class and gender.

Edward Rochester: Despite his stern manner and not particularly handsome appearance, Edward Rochester wins Jane's heart, because she feels they are kindred spirits, and because he is the first person in the novel to offer Jane lasting love and a real home. Although Rochester is Jane's social and economic superior, and although men were widely considered to be naturally superior to women in the Victorian period, Jane is Rochester's intellectual equal. Moreover, after their marriage is interrupted by the disclosure that Rochester is already married to Bertha Mason, Jane is proved to be Rochester's moral superior. Rochester regrets his former libertinism and lustfulness. He has proved himself to be weaker in many ways than Jane. Since Rochester has been blinded by the fire and has lost his manor house at the end of the novel, he has become weaker while Jane has grown in strength.

St. John Rivers: He is a foil to Edward Rochester. Rochester is passionate, St. John is austere and ambitious. Jane often describes Rochester's eyes as flashing and flaming, whereas she constantly associates St. John with rock, ice and snow. Marriage with Rochester represents the abandonment of principle for the consummation of passion, but marriage to St. John would mean sacrificing passion for principle. When inviting her to come to India with him as a missionary, St. John offers Jane the chance to make a more meaningful contribution to society than she would as a housewife. At the same time, life with St. John would mean life without true love, in which Jane's need for spiritual solace would be filled only by retreat into the recesses of her own soul.

Helen Burns: She is Jane's friend at Lowood School, serving as a foil to Mr. Brocklehurst as well as to Jane. While Mr. Brocklehurst embodies an evangelical form of religion that seeks to strip others of their excessive pride or of their ability to take pleasure in worldly things, Helen represents a mode of Christianity that stresses tolerance and acceptance. Brocklehurst uses religion to gain power and to control others. Helen trusts her own faith and turns the other cheek to Lowood's harsh policies. Her submissive and ascetic nature highlights Jane's more headstrong character. Like Jane, Helen is an orphan who longs for a home, but Helen believes that she will find this home in Heaven rather than in Northern England. And while Helen is not oblivious to the injustices the girls suffer at Lowood, she believes that justice will be found in God's ultimate judgment—God will reward the good and punish the evil. Jane, on the other hand, is unable to have such blind faith. Her quest is for love and happiness in this world. She counts on god for support and guidance in her search.

Themes

Morality: Jane refuses to become Mr. Rochester's lover because of her impassioned self-respect and moral conviction. She rejects St. John Rivers' Puritanism as much as the libertine aspects of Mr. Rochester's character. Instead, she works out a morality expressed in love, independence and forgiveness. Jane does not want to be seen as an outcast to society by being a mistress to Rochester.

God and Religion: Throughout the novel, Jane endeavors to attain equilibrium between moral duty and earthly happiness. She despises the hypocritical Puritanism of Mr. Brocklehurst, and sees the deficiencies in St. John Rivers' indulgent yet detached devotion to his Christian duty. As a child, Jane admires Helen Burns' life philosophy of "turning the other cheek", which in turn helps her in adult life to forgive Aunt Reed and the Reed cousins for their cruelty. Although she does not seem to subscribe to any of the standard forms of popular Christianity, she honors traditional morality—particularly seen when she refuses to marry Mr. Rochester until he is widowed. Mr. Brocklehurst is a hypocritical Christian. He professes aid and charity but does the opposite by using religion as a justification for punishment. St. John Rivers is a more conventionally religious figure. Yet the author portrays his religious aspect ambiguously. Jane calls him a very good man but finds him cold and forbidding. In his determination to do good deeds, St. John courts martyrdom. Moreover, he is unable to see Jane as a whole person, but views her only as a helpmate in his impending missionary work. Mr. Rochester is a less than perfect Christian. He is indeed a sinner; he attempts to enter into a bigamous marriage with Jane and, when that fails, tries to persuade her to become his mistress. He also confesses that he has had three previous mistresses. However, at the end of the novel, he repents his sinfulness, thanks God for returning Jane, and asks Him for the strength to lead a purer life.

Social Class: Jane's ambiguous social position—a penniless yet moderately educated orphan from a good family—leads her to criticize some discrimination based on class, though she makes class discriminations herself. Although she is educated, well-mannered, and relatively sophisticated, she is still a governess, a paid servant of low social standing, and therefore relatively powerless.

Gender Relations: Jane attempts to assert her own identity within male-dominated society. Three of the main male characters, Mr. Brocklehurst, Mr. Rochester and St. John Rivers, try to keep Jane in a subordinate position and prevent her from expressing her own thoughts and feelings. Jane escapes Mr. Brocklehurst and rejects St. John, and she only marries Mr. Rochester once she is sure that their marriage is one between equals. Through Jane, the author opposes Victorian stereotypes about women, articulating her own feminist philosophy.

Conscience and Passion: Jane, extremely passionate yet also dedicated to a close personal relationship with God, struggles between either extreme. An instance of her leaning towards conscience over passion can be seen after it has been revealed that Mr. Rochester already has a wife, when Jane is begged to run away with Mr. Rochester and become his mistress. Up until that moment, Jane had been riding on a wave of emotion, forgetting all thoughts of reason and logic, replacing God with Mr. Rochester in her eyes, and allowing herself to be swept away in the moment. However, once the harsh reality of the situation sets in, Jane does everything in her power to refuse Mr. Rochester. Jane experiences an epiphany in regards to conscience. She finally comes to understand that all passion, as she had been living her life up until then, and all conscience, as she had leaned towards during her time at Lowood, is neither good nor preferable. She had allowed herself to lean too far in the direction of passion, and she is in danger of giving up all logic and reason in favor of temptation. Her struggles to find a middle ground between her passionate and conscience-driven sides frequently go back and forth throughout the novel. She has drawn the line as to where passion is taking too great a role in her life, and where she will not allow herself to forgo her moral and religious principles.

Atonement and Forgiveness: Mr. Rochester is tormented by his awareness of his past sins and misdeeds. He frequently confesses that he has led a life of vice, and many of his actions in the course of the novel are less than commendable. Readers may accuse him of behaving sadistically in deceiving Jane about the nature of his relationship with Blanche Ingram in order to provoke Jane's jealousy. His confinement of Bertha may bespeak mixed motives. He is certainly aware that in the eyes of both religious and civil authorities, his marriage to Jane before Bertha's death would be bigamous. Yet, at the same time, Mr. Rochester makes genuine efforts to atone for his behavior. For example, although he does not believe that he is Adele's natural father, he adopts her as his ward and sees that she is well cared for. This adoption may well be an act of atonement for the sins he has committed. The destruction of Thornfield by fire finally removes the stain of his past sins; the loss of his left hand and of his eyesight is the price he must pay to atone completely for his sins.

Search for Home and Family: Without any living family that she is aware of, Jane searches for a place that she can call home. The novel's opening finds Jane living at Gateshead Hall, but this is hardly a home. Mrs. Reed and her children refuse to acknowledge her as a relation, treating her instead as an unwanted intruder and an inferior. At Lowood Institution, a boarding school for orphans and destitute children, Jane finds a home of sorts, although her place here is ambiguous and temporary. Jane subsequently believes she has found a home at Thornfield Hall. She is relieved when she is made to feel welcome by Mrs. Fairfax. She feels genuine affection for Adèle (who in a way is also an orphan) and is happy to serve as her governess. As her love for Mr. Rochester grows, she believes that she has found her ideal husband in spite of his eccentric manner and that they will make a home together at Thornfield. Fleeing Thornfield, she literally becomes homeless and is reduced to begging for food and shelter. The opportunity of having a home presents itself when she enters Moor House. She is overjoyed when she learns that St. John and his sisters are indeed her cousins. She tells St. John Rivers that learning that she has living relations is far more important than inheriting twenty thousand pounds. However, St. John Rivers' offer of marriage cannot sever her emotional attachment to Rochester. In an almost visionary episode, she hears Mr. Rochester's voice calling her to return to him. After a long series of travails Jane's search for home and family ends in a union with her ideal mate.

Film Adaptations

Jane Eyre (1944) was directed by Stevenson, starring Orson Welles as Mr. Rochester, Joan Fontaine as Jane, and Elizabeth Taylor as Helen Burns. The end of the story is changed together with some other differences: At the beginning, the nine-year-old orphan Jane Eyre lives at the English estate of her cruel aunt, Mrs. Reed, who favors her spoiled son John over the spirited Jane. The other two cousins, Eliza and Georgiana, do not appear. On the way to Thornfield, Jane goes to the George Inn and is invited by a flirtatious young man to drink with him, which she refuses. This detail does not exist in the original work. After Rochester leads the wedding party to Thornfield and shows them Bertha, who is violently insane, Jane tells Rochester for the last time that she loves him and leaves the mansion, despite his pleas for her to stay. With nowhere else to go, Jane returns to Mrs. Reed, who has fallen ill, and nurses her until her death. Jane learns from Dr. Rivers that Rochester has been inquiring after her, but she asks him not to reply. One night, however, Jane believes that she hears Rochester calling her name in great torment, and she rushes back to Thornfield. There she is told by Mrs. Fairfax that Bertha set the mansion on fire and Rochester was seriously injured in an unsuccessful attempt to rescue her. Just then, Rochester enters the ruins of the mansion, and Jane realizes that he is blind. She is overjoyed to be reunited with him, and her passion convinces him that she feels more for him than mere pity. The Moor House experience is completely canceled. And Jane's reunion with Rochester is not set in Ferndean.

Fig 2.3 Young Jane, Mrs. Reed, John and Brocklehurstt

Fig 2.4 Jane and Adele

Fig 2.5 Rochester and Jane

Fig 2.6 Mrs. Fairfax and Jane among the ruins

Jane Eyre (1970) is a TV-film directed by Delbert Mann, starring George C. Scott and Susannah York, distributed by British Lion Film Corporation. This film was widely released in China in early 1980s with big success and was one of the most popular foreign films in China. There are differences from the novel: Jane's time at Gateshead Hall is only referenced and the tale starts with Jane arriving at Lowood School; events at Lowood School are mixed together and there is no outbreak of illness, only Helen's death; Mrs. Reed, Eliza, John and Georgiana do not appear at all. Neither does Bessie. Instead, Mr. Brocklehurst criticizes and immediately cuts Jane's wavy hair; Miss Scatcherd is shown as more cruel to Helen Burns, sending her out into the cold for punishments rather than simply humbling her in front of her classmates; The death of Mrs. Reed is cut, so Jane does not return to Gateshead Hall; Mr. Rochester and his guests at Thornfield Hall do not play charades; Mr. Rochester does not disguise himself as a gypsy woman; When Jane leaves Thornfield Hall, she quickly stumbles upon the Rivers, who take her in; Rosamond Oliver does not appear; Jane's kinship to Mary, Diana and St. John Rivers is not revealed; Jane does not inherit a fortune.

Fig 2.7　A Poster of *Jane Eyre*(1970)

Fig 2.8　Jane and Helen in Lowood

Fig 2.9　Jane and Rochester

Fig 2.10　Jane and St John Rivers

In Ferndean in the novel, the servants John and his wife Mary look after him. Jane has never been there. But in the film, Rochester once brought Jane there. So she can find him after she comes back to reunite with him. No servants appear around him.

Jane Eyre (1997) was directed by Robert Young, starring Ciarán Hinds as Mr. Rochester, Samantha Morton as Jane Eyre. This adaptation is notable for omitting the middle scenes with Mrs. Reed, the Rivers' relationship to Jane, and her uncle's inheritance but included classic lines from the novel. In the first part, Mrs. Reed has only one child, namely his son John. In the last part, St. John has only one sister living with him. Rosamond Oliver does not appear either. When Jane comes to Ferndean, it is Mrs. Fairfax who greets her, rather than his only servants John and his wife Mary in the novel. This is the most passionate of all the adaptations.

Fig 2.11　A Poster of *Jane Eyre* (1997)

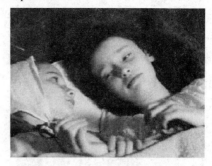

Fig 2.12　Jane and Helen at Lowood

Fig 2.13　Jane, Adele, Rochester and pilot

Fig 2.14　Jane and St. John Rivers

Jane Eyre (2006), directed by Susanna White, starring Lucy Welson, Toby Stevenson and distributed by British Broadcasting Corporation, is a four-part BBC television drama serial adaptation, which is generally considered a successful adaptation, garnering critical acclaim and a number of prestigious nominations from various award bodies. While for the most part a faithful retelling of the novel, the screenplay does contain minor deviations. These include the reduction of time devoted to the first third (Lowood School) and the final third (St. John) of the novel. The middle of the novel is instead developed and a few scenes from the novel are compressed or moved to different times and places in the narrative. The scenes surrounding Jane's flight from the Rochester estate until her gaining of health are treated as a brief flashback sequence: Many pages of text were condensed into a passage of a few minutes' length. Additional scenes were created for the screenplay which underscores the passionate natures of Jane and Rochester. One of the more significant plot changes occurs during the gypsy sequence as Rochester hires a gypsy rather than portraying one himself. Rochester also uses an Ouija board as a supplement to this game, a scene which was written specifically for the screenplay. The new BBC version shows that it is possible to make successful drama by telling the story straight. It features an excellent performance from Toby Stephens, who manages to make Rochester simultaneously macho and vulnerable, and also from Ruth Wilson as a quizzical, strong and un-neurotic Jane. The new adaptation doesn't add new colors to the author's romantic novel. It brings out all the shades and hues of the original portrait, restoring it to its full glory. The story is splendidly retold from sweeping shots of the English countryside through all seasons to intimate scenes in the recesses of the manor house. In the other adaptations, how Bertha Mason burned Thornfield and jumped off is only narrated as in the novel, but in this adaptation, this is vividly reproduced with motion pictures. Bertha sees a bird flying freely away. She jumps with the implication that she also wants to be free from this place, which is her prison. What young Jane says to her aunt when she leaves Gateshead for Lowood is cut off.

Fig 2.15   A Poster of 2006 Film

Fig 2.16   Jane in the red room

Fig 2.17   Jane and Rochester

Fig 2.18   St. John Rivers

Jane Eyre (2011) is a British romantic drama film directed by Cary Joji Fukunaga, starring Mia Wasikowska and Michael Fassbender, produced by Focus Features. It is a splendid example of how to tackle the daunting duty of turning a beloved work of classic literature into a film, which tells its venerable tale with lively vigor and an astute sense of emotional detail.

Fig 2.19   A Poster of the 2011 Film

Fig 2.20   Jane and Rochester

A Wonderful Dialogue from the 2006 Film

Rochester and Jane are walking outside Thornfield. Jane has heard from Fairfax that Rochester will have a wedding soon. Jane is sad.

Rochester: Thornfield is pleasant in the summer, isn't it, Jane?

Jane: Yes, sir.

Rochester: You have become attached to the place?

Jane: Yes, sir.

Rochester: And you'd be sad to leave?

Jane: Yes. Must I leave, sir? Must I leave Thornfield?

Rochester: Yes. I'm sorry. But I'm afraid you must.

Jane: You're to be married?

Rochester: Exactly. Precisely. As you, with your usual acuteness, have already predicted, when I do marry. Adele must go to school and you must find a new situation.

Jane: Yes, sir. I will advertise immediately.

Rochester: No, you won't. I have already found you a place.

Jane: Ireland is a long way away, sir, from Thornfield. It is a long way away from you, sir.

(They sit down under a tree.)

Rochester: We have been good friends, haven't we, Jane? It is difficult to part from a friend and know you will never meet them again. And you and I, it's like we're a pair of Eshton's twins, bound together in some unworldly way, sharing a spirit we've so alike. When we are parted, when you leave me, I believe that bond will snap and I will bleed inwardly. But you will forget me after a while.

Jane: I would never forget you! (*Standing up, facing Rochester and crying*) How can you imagine that? What do you think I am? Oh, I wish I'd never been born! I wish I'd never come here. I wish I'd never grown to love Thornfield. I love Thornfield. I love it because I have lived a full life. I have not been trampled on. I have been treated as an equal. You have treated me as an equal. You are the best person I know. And I cannot bear the thought of having to leave you.

Rochester: Must you leave me, Jane?

Jane: Why, of course. I must because you have a wife.

Rochester: What do you mean?

Jane: Blanche Ingram of course. You, you are as good as married to her. You have promised her.

Rochester: I have not promised Blanche anything.

Jane: …to someone who is inferior to you, someone who you have no sympathy with. Of course, I must go. Do you think that I am a machine that I can bear it. Do you think, because I'm poor, plain, obscure and little that I have no heart that I am without soul? I have as much heart as you and as much soul! And if God had given me some beauty and wealth, I would make it as hard to leave me as it is now for me to leave you.

Rochester: (*Standing up and holding Jane*) You must not leave me, Jane!

Jane: (*Struggling*) No, let me go.

Rochester: Jane, Jane, don't struggle so.

Jane: (*Still struggling*) I'm a free person. I will go and do as I please.

Rochester: (*Holding Jane in his arms tightly*) Yes, yes, yes, you will. You will decide your own destiny. (Jane stops struggling and looks at Rochester.) Jane, I offer you my hand, my heart, and all my possessions.

Jane: You laugh at me.

Rochester: No, no, Jane. I want you to live with me, to pass through life as my second self, my best earthly companion. Jane, have you not faith in me?

Jane: None whatsoever.

Rochester: You doubt me?

Jane: Absolutely.

Rochester: Jane, you know I don't love Blanche. I love you like my own flesh. Jane, say that you will marry me. Say it quickly. Jane, you accept me?

Jane: (*Looking at Rochester with doubts*) Are you in earnest? I can hardly believe you.

Rochester: I swear.

Jane: Then, sir…

Rochester: Call me by my name, call me Edward.

Jane: (*Smiling*) Then, Edward. I will marry you.

They kiss.

Rochester: God forgive me. And let no man meddle with me. I am to keep her.

Jane: There is no one to meddle. I have no family to interfere.

Rochester: No.

They kiss again. Happily and hand in hand, they run into Thornfield.

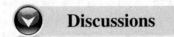

Discussions

1. What kind of a woman is Jane? What does Jane pursue in her whole life?
2. When Jane leaves her aunt for Lowood, she says to her that she will never come back to see her. Yet when she hears that Mrs. Reed is in her deathbed, she comes back to Gateshead again. How do you think of it? Is it good to hate somebody forever?
3. What kind of a man is Mr. Rochester? How does he win Jane's love?
4. When Jane learns that Mr. Rochester has a wife, she leaves him and Mr. Rochester suffers a lot himself. Is Jane cruel to do that? What is your opinion about her leaving him and coming back to him one year later?
5. If Mr. Rochester had not lost his hand and become blind, if Jane had not inherited a sum of money from her uncle, would she also get married with him?

Unit 3　Emily Brontë and *Wuthering Heights*

Emily Brontë (1824—1848) was the fifth of the six children of their parents. She went to school in Brussels with Charlotte in 1842. In 1846 the three sisters published a collection of their poems, in which she contributed 21 poems. In July 1847, the publishers accepted *Wuthering Heights*, which was published in December under the pseudonym Ellis Bell. It was also in that month that Emily died of consumption. A posthumous second edition was edited by Charlotte in 1850. The title of the novel comes from the Yorkshire manor on the moors of the story. The narrative centers on the all-encompassing, passionate, but ultimately doomed love between Catherine Earnshaw and Heathcliff, and how this unresolved passion eventually destroys them and the people around them.

Fig 3.1　Emily Brontë

Fig 3.2　A Book Cover of *Wuthering Heights*

Plot

In 1801, Mr. Lockwood, a rich man from the south of England, rents Thrushcross Grange in the north of England for peace and recuperation. Soon after his arrival, he visits his landlord, Mr. Heathcliff, who lives in the remote moorland farmhouse called "Wuthering Heights". He finds the inhabitants of Wuthering Heights to be a rather strange group: Mr. Heathcliff appears a gentleman but his mannerisms suggest otherwise; the reserved mistress of the house is in her mid-teens; and a young man appears to be one of the family, although he dresses and talks like a servant.

Being snowed in, Mr. Lockwood stays the night and is shown to an unused chamber, where he finds books and graffiti from a former inhabitant of the farmhouse named Catherine. When he falls asleep, he has a nightmare in which he sees Catherine as a ghost trying to enter through the window. Heathcliff rushes to the room after hearing him yelling in fear. He believes Mr. Lockwood is telling the truth, and inspects the window, opening it in a futile attempt to let Catherine's spirit in from the cold. After nothing eventuates, Heathcliff shows Mr. Lockwood to his own bedroom, and returns to keep guard at the window.

As soon as the sun rises, Mr. Lockwood is escorted back to Thrushcross Grange by Heathcliff. There, he asks his housekeeper, Nelly Dean, to tell him the story of the family from the Heights.

Thirty years prior, the Earnshaw family lived at Wuthering Heights. The children of the family are the teenaged Hindley and his younger sister, Catherine. Mr. Earnshaw travels to Liverpool, where he finds a homeless boy—"dark-skinned gypsy in aspect" — whom he decides to adopt, naming him "Heathcliff". Hindley finds himself robbed of his father's affections and becomes bitterly jealous of Heathcliff. However, Catherine grows very attached to him. Soon, the two children spend hours on the moors together and hate every moment apart.

Because of the domestic discord caused by Hindley's and Heathcliff's sibling rivalry, Hindley is eventually sent to college. However, he marries a woman named Frances and returns three years later, after Mr. Earnshaw dies. He becomes master of Wuthering Heights, and forces Heathcliff to become a servant instead of a member of the family.

Several months after Hindley's return, Heathcliff and Catherine travel to Thrushcross Grange to spy on the Linton family. However, they are spotted and try to escape. Catherine, having been caught by a dog, is brought inside the Grange to have injuries tended to while Heathcliff is sent home. Catherine eventually returns to Wuthering Heights as a changed woman, looking and acting as a lady. She laughs at Heathcliff's unkempt appearance. When the Lintons visit the next day, Heathcliff dresses up to impress her. It fails when Edgar, one of the Linton children, argues with him. Heathcliff is locked in the attic, where Catherine later tries to comfort him. He swears vengeance on Hindley.

In the summer of the next year, Frances gives birth to a son, Hareton, but she dies before the year is out. This leads Hindley to descend into a life of drunkenness and waste.

Two years pass and Catherine has become close friends with Edgar, growing more distant from Heathcliff. One day in August, while Hindley is absent, Edgar comes to visit Catherine. She has an argument with Nelly, which then spreads to Edgar who tries to leave. Catherine stops him and, before long, they declare themselves lovers.

Later, Catherine talks with Nelly, explaining that Edgar has asked her to marry him and she has accepted. She says that she does not really love Edgar but Heathcliff. Unfortunately she can never marry Heathcliff because of his lack of status and education. She therefore plans to marry Edgar and use that position to help raise Heathcliff's standing. Unfortunately, Heathcliff overhears the first part about not being able to marry him and runs away, disappearing without a trace. After three years, Edgar and Catherine are married.

Six months after the marriage, Heathcliff returns as a gentleman, having grown stronger and richer during his absence. Catherine is delighted to see him although Edgar is not so keen. Edgar's sister, Isabella, now eighteen, falls in love with Heathcliff, seeing him as a romantic hero. He despises her but encourages the infatuation, seeing it as a chance for revenge on Edgar. When he embraces Isabella one day at the Grange, there is an argument with Edgar which causes Catherine to lock herself in her room and fall ill.

Heathcliff has been staying at the Heights, gambling with Hindley and teaching Hareton bad habits. Hindley is gradually losing his wealth, mortgaging the farmhouse to Heathcliff to repay his debts.

While Catherine is ill, Heathcliff elopes with Isabella. The fugitives marry and return two months later to Wuthering Heights. Heathcliff hears that Catherine is ill and arranges with Nelly to visit her in secret. In the early hours of the day after their meeting, Catherine gives birth to her daughter, Cathy, and then dies.

The day after Catherine's funeral, Isabella flees Heathcliff and escapes to the south of England where she eventually gives birth to Linton, Heathcliff's son. Hindley dies six months after Catherine. Heathcliff finds himself the master of Wuthering Heights and the guardian of Hareton.

Twelve years later, Cathy has grown into a beautiful, high-spirited girl who has rarely passed outside the borders of the Grange. Edgar hears that Isabella is dying and leaves to pick up her son with the intention of adopting him. While he is gone, Cathy meets Hareton on the moors and learns of her cousin's and Wuthering Heights' existence.

Edgar returns with Linton who is a weak and sickly boy. Although Cathy is attracted to him, Heathcliff wants his son with him and insists on having him taken to the Heights. Three years later, Nelly and Cathy are on the moors when they meet Heathcliff who takes them to Wuthering Heights to see Linton and Hareton. He has plans for Linton and Cathy to marry so that he will inherit Thrushcross Grange. Cathy and Linton begin a secret friendship.

In August of the next year, while Edgar is very ill, Nelly and Cathy visit Wuthering Heights and are held captive by Heathcliff who wants to marry his son to Cathy and, at the same time, prevents her from returning to her father before he dies. After five days, Nelly is released and Cathy escapes with Linton's help just in time to see her father before he dies.

With Heathcliff now the master of both Wuthering Heights and Thrushcross Grange, Cathy has no choice but to leave Nelly and to go and live with Heathcliff and Hareton. Linton dies soon afterwards and, although Hareton tries to be kind to her, she retreats into herself. This is the point of the story at which Lockwood arrives.

After being ill with a cold for some time, Lockwood decides that he has had enough of the moors and travels to Wuthering Heights to inform Heathcliff that he is returning to the south.

In September, eight months after leaving, Lockwood finds himself back in the area and decides to stay at Thrushcross Grange (since his tenancy is still valid until October). He finds that Nelly is now living at Wuthering Heights. He makes his way there and she fills in the rest of the story.

Nelly moves to the Heights soon after Lockwood leaves to replace the housekeeper who has departed. In March, Hareton has an accident and is confined to the farmhouse. During this time, a friendship develops between Cathy and Hareton. This continues into April when Heathcliff begins to act very strangely, seeing visions of Catherine. Without eating for four days, he is found dead in Catherine's room. He is buried next to Catherine.

Lockwood departs but, before he leaves, he hears that Hareton and Cathy plan to marry on New Year's Day. Lockwood passes the graves of Catherine, Edgar and Heathcliff, pausing to contemplate the peaceful quiet of the moors.

Select Reading: Chapter 9

"I've no more business to marry Edgar Linton than I have to be in heaven; and if the wicked man in there had not brought Heathcliff so low, I shouldn't have thought of it. It would degrade me to marry Heathcliff now; so he shall never know how I love him: and that, not because he's handsome, Nelly, but because he's more myself than I am. What ever our souls are made of, his and mine are the same; and Linton's is as different as a moonbeam from lightning, or frost from fire."

Ere this speech ended, I became sensible of Heathcliff's presence. Having noticed a slight movement, I turned my head, and saw him rise from the bench, and steal out noiselessly. He had listened till he heard Catherine say it would degrade her to marry him, and then he stayed to hear no further. My companion, sitting on the ground, was prevented by the back of the settle from remarking his presence or departure; but I started, and bade her hush!

"Why?" she asked, gazing nervously round.

"Joseph is here," I answered, catching opportunely the roll of his cart-wheels up the road; "and Heathcliff will come in with him. I'm not sure whether he were not at the door this moment."

"Oh, he couldn't overhear me at the door!" said she. "Give me Hareton, while you get the supper, and when it is ready ask me to sup with you. I want to cheat my uncomfortable conscience, and be convinced that Heathcliff has no notion of these things. He has not, has he? He does not know what being in love is?"

"I see no reason that he should not know, as well as you," I returned; "and if you are his choice, he will be the most unfortunate creature that ever was born! As soon as you become Mrs. Linton, he loses friend, and love, and all! Have you considered how you'll bear the separation, and how he'll bear to be quite deserted in the world? Because, Miss Catherine—"

"He quite deserted! We separated!" she exclaimed, with an accent of indignation. "Who is to separate us, pray? They'll meet the fate of Milo! Not as long as I live, Ellen: for no mortal creature. Every Linton on the face of the earth might melt into nothing, before I could consent to forsake Heathcliff. Oh, that's not what I intend—that's not what I mean! I shouldn't be Mrs. Linton were such a price demanded! He'll be as much to me as he has been all his lifetime. Edgar must shake off his antipathy, and tolerate him, at least. He will, when he learns my true feelings towards him. Nelly, I see now, you think me a selfish wretch; but did it never strike you that if Heathcliff and I married, we should be beggars. Whereas, if I marry Linton, I can aid Heathcliff to rise, and place him out of my brother's power."

"With your husband's money, Miss Catherine?" I asked. "You'll find him not as pliable as you calculate upon; and, though I'm hardly a judge, I think that's the worst motive you've given yet for being the wife of young Linton."

"It is not," retorted she; "it is the best! The others were the satisfaction of my whims: and for Edgar's sake, too, to satisfy him. This is for the sake of one who comprehends in his person my feelings to Edgar and myself. I cannot express it; but surely you and everybody have a notion that there is or should be an existence of yours beyond you. What were the use of my creation, if I were entirely contained here? My great miseries in this world have been Heathcliff's miseries…. Nelly, I am Heathcliff! He's always, always in my mind: not as a pleasure, any more than I am always a pleasure to myself, but as my own being. So don't talk of our separation again: it is impracticable; and…"

She paused, and hid her face in the fold of my gown; but I jerked it forcibly away. I was out of patience with her folly!

译文:"对我来说,嫁给埃德加·林敦,并不比去天堂更热心。要是我家那个恶毒的人不把希思克利夫贬得这么低下,我是绝不会想到这么做的。现在,我要是嫁给希思克利夫的话,那就降低我的身份了。因此他永远也不会知道,我是多么爱他。我这么爱他,并不是因为他长得英俊,内莉,而是因为他比我自己更像我自己。不管我们的灵魂是什么做的,他的和我的完全一样,而林敦的和我们就截然不同了,就像月光跟闪电,冰霜跟火焰。"

她的这番话还没说完,我就已发现希思克利夫原来就在这儿。我发觉有点轻微的响动,就转过头去,正好看到他从长椅上站起身来,悄无声息地走了出去。他一直听到凯瑟琳说嫁给他会降低她的身份,就没有留下来再听下去。我的同伴,因为坐在地上,给高高的椅背挡住了,没有看到他在这儿,也没有看到他离开。可是我吃了一惊,赶快叫她别出声。

"怎么啦?"她问道,紧张不安地朝四周打量着。

"约瑟夫来了,"我回答,这时恰巧听到他的车子一路过来的车轮声。"希思克利夫也会跟他一起进来。这会儿他是不是已经在门口也难说呢。"

"哦,他在门口是听不到我的话的!"她说,"把哈里顿交给我,你去准备晚饭,饭做好叫我一声,我跟你一块儿吃。我要欺骗我自己不安的良心,让自己相信希思克利夫根本没有想到这些事。他没有想到,是吧? 他不懂得什么是爱吧?"

"我可看不出有什么理由说,他不能跟你一样懂得爱。"我回答说,"如果你是他选中的人,那他就要成为天下最不幸的人了。你一旦成为林敦太太,他就失去了朋友,失去了爱,失去了一切! 你可曾想过,你们两人分开后,你怎么受得了? 在这个世界上他也就被完全抛弃,他又怎么能受得了? 因此,凯瑟琳小姐……"

"他被完全抛弃! 我们两人分开!"她带着怒气,大声叫了起来,"请问,是谁要把我们分开? 他们会遭到迈洛的命运! 只要我还活着,艾伦,没人敢这么做。世上所有姓林敦的人全部可以化为乌有,可我绝不会答应抛弃希思克利夫。啊,那不是我原来的打算—那绝不是我的本意! 要付出这样的代价,我就不会去做林敦太太了! 他将和过去一样,一辈子永远在我心中。埃德加必须清除对他的反感,至少也要能容忍他。当他知道了我对他的真实感情,他会这样做的。内莉,现在我明白了,你以为我是一个自私自利的贱女人。可是,难道你从来没有想到,要是希思克利夫跟我结了婚,那我们还不是要去讨饭了吗? 而要是我嫁给林敦,我就可以帮助希思克利夫站起来安排他摆脱我哥哥的逼迫和欺压。"

"用你丈夫的钱吗,凯瑟琳小姐?"我问道,"你会发现他并不像你想的那么顺从。而且,虽说我不便下什么判断,我认为,这是你愿做小伙子林敦妻子的最坏的动机。"

"不,"她反驳说,"这是最好的动机! 其余的全是为了满足我的一时冲动,也是为了埃德加,为了满足他的要求。而这全是为了一个人,在这个人的身上包含了我对埃德加和我对我自己的感情。这事我没法说清楚,可是你,以及每一个人,谅必都有一种想法:除了你之外,还有,或者说应该还有,另一个你的存在。要是我整个全在这儿了,那把我创造出来的用处是什么呢? 在这个世界上,我最大的悲苦就是希思克利夫的悲苦……内莉,我就是希思克利夫! 他永远在我的心中:不是作为一种乐趣,我不把他当作乐趣,如同不把自己当作乐趣,而是作为我自身的存在。所以,别再说什么我们会分开了,这是办不到的。再说……"

她停住了,把脸藏到我裙子的皱褶里,可是我猛地把它推开。对她的傻话,我再也没有耐心听了。

Analysis of Major Characters

Heathcliff: The novel centers around the story of Heathcliff. The first paragraph of the novel provides a vivid physical picture of him, as Lockwood describes how his "black eyes" withdraw suspiciously under his brows at Lockwood's approach. Nelly's story begins with his introduction into the Earnshaw family, his vengeful machinations drive the entire plot, and his death ends the book. The desire to understand him and his motivations has kept countless readers engaged in the novel. Heathcliff defies being understood, and it is difficult for readers to resist seeing what they want or expect to see in him. The novel teases readers with the possibility that Heathcliff is something other than what he seems—that his cruelty is merely an expression of his frustrated love for Catherine, or that his sinister behavior serves to conceal the heart of a romantic hero. Heathcliff's character is expected to contain such a hidden virtue because he resembles a hero in a romance novel. Traditionally, romance novel heroes appear dangerous, brooding, and cold at first, only later to emerge as fiercely devoted and loving. However, Heathcliff does not reform, and his malevolence proves so great and long-lasting that it cannot be adequately explained even as a desire for revenge against Hindley, Catherine, Edgar, etc. As he himself points out, his abuse of Isabella is purely sadistic, as he amuses himself by seeing how much abuse she can take and still come cringing back for more. It is significant that Heathcliff begins his life as a homeless orphan in the streets of Liverpool. When Brontë? composed her book, in the 1840s, the English economy was severely depressed, and the conditions of the factory workers in industrial areas like Liverpool were so appalling that the upper and middle classes feared violent revolt. Thus, many of the more affluent members of society beheld these workers with a mixture of sympathy and fear. In literature, the smoky, threatening, miserable factory-towns were often represented in religious terms, and compared to hell. Heathcliff is frequently compared to a demon by the other characters in the book. Considering this historical context, Heathcliff seems to embody the anxieties that the book's upper and middle-class audience had about the working classes. The reader may easily sympathize with him when he is powerless, as a child tyrannized by Hindley Earnshaw, but he becomes a villain when he acquires power and returns to Wuthering Heights with money and the trappings of a gentleman. This corresponds with the ambivalence the upper classes felt toward the lower classes—the upper classes had charitable impulses toward lower-class citizens when they were miserable, but feared the prospect of the lower classes trying to escape their miserable circumstances by acquiring political, social, cultural, or economic power.

Catherine: The location of Catherine's coffin symbolizes the conflict that tears apart her short life. She is not buried in the chapel with the Lintons. Nor is her coffin placed among the tombs of the Earnshaws. Instead, as Nelly describes in Chapter XVI, Catherine is buried "in a corner of the kirkyard, where the wall is so low that heath and bilberry plants have climbed over it from the moor." Moreover, she is buried with Edgar on one side and Heathcliff on the other, suggesting her conflicted loyalties. Her actions are driven in part by her social ambitions, which initially are awakened during her first stay at the Lintons', and which eventually compel her to marry Edgar. However, she is also motivated by impulses that prompt her to violate social conventions—to love Heathcliff, throw temper tantrums, and run around on the moor. Isabella Linton serves as Catherine's foil. The two women's parallel positions allow us to see their differences with greater clarity. Catherine represents wild nature, in both her high, lively spirits and her occasional cruelty, whereas Isabella represents culture and civilization, both in her refinement and in her weakness.

Edgar: Edgar Linton serves as Heathcliff's foil. Edgar is born and raised a gentleman. He is graceful, well-mannered, and instilled with civilized virtues. These qualities cause Catherine to choose Edgar over Heathcliff and thus to initiate the contention between the men. Nevertheless, Edgar's gentlemanly qualities ultimately prove useless in his ensuing rivalry with Heathcliff. Edgar is particularly humiliated by his confrontation with Heathcliff in Chapter XI, in which he openly shows his fear of fighting Heathcliff. Catherine, having witnessed the scene, taunts him, saying, "Heathcliff would as soon lift a finger at you as the king would march his army against a colony of mice." His refinement is tied to his helplessness and impotence. Edgar's inability to counter Heathcliff's vengeance, and his naive belief on his deathbed in his daughter's safety and happiness make him a weak and sympathetic character.

Themes

Solitude: Many characters seem to enjoy solitude. Heathcliff and Hindley both state their preference for isolation early in the novel, and Lockwood explains that solitude is one of the reasons he chooses to move to the remote Thrushcross Grange. Each of these characters believes that solitude will help them get over romantic disappointments: Heathcliff becomes increasingly withdrawn after Catherine's death. Hindley becomes crueler than ever to others after he loses his wife Frances; and Lockwood's move to the Grange is precipitated by a briefly mentioned romantic disappointment of his own. However, Brontë ultimately casts doubt on solitude's ability to heal psychic wounds. Heathcliff's yearning for Catherine causes him to behave like a monster to people around him. Hindley dies alone as an impoverished alcoholic; and Lockwood quickly gives up on the Grange's restorative potential and moves to London.

Doubles: Catherine Earnshaw notes her own double character when she tries to explain her attraction to both Edgar and Heathcliff. Cathy Linton is a double for her mother. Many parallel pairings suggest that certain characters are doubles of each other: Heathcliff and Catherine, Edgar and Isabella, Hareton and Cathy. Catherine's famous insistence that "I am Heathcliff" reinforces the concept that individuals can share an identity.

Self-knowledge: Brontë frequently dissociates the self from the consciousness. This becomes a major concern when Catherine Earnshaw decides against her better judgment to marry Edgar Linton. She is self-aware enough to acknowledge that she has a double character and that Heathcliff may be a better match for her. But she lacks the confidence to act on this intuition. Self-knowledge also affects how characters get to know others. Isabella knows how violent Heathcliff is, but is unable to acknowledge this because she believes herself capable of controlling him.

Sibling Relationships: Sibling relationships are unusually strong in the Earnshaw and Linton families. The novel's most prominent relationship—the love between Catherine and Heathcliff—begins when the two are raised as siblings at Wuthering Heights. It is never entirely clear whether their love for each other is romantic or the love of extremely close siblings. Although Catherine expresses a desire to marry Heathcliff, they are never shown having sex and their union seems more spiritual than physical. After Catherine's death, Heathcliff gets revenge on Edgar for marrying Catherine by encouraging Isabella to marry him and then mistreating her. Given that Emily Brontë is thought to have had no friends outside of her own family (although she was very close to her brother Branwell and her sisters Anne and Charlotte), it is perhaps unsurprising that close sibling relationships are a driving force in her only novel.

Humanity versus Nature: Emily Brontë is preoccupied with the opposition between human civilization and nature. This is represented figuratively in her descriptions of the moors, but she also ties this conflict to specific characters. For example, Catherine and Heathcliff resolve to grow up as rude as savages in response to Hindley's abuse, and Ellen likens Hindley to a wild-beast. The natural world is frequently associated with evil and reckless passion; when Brontë describes a character as wild, that character is usually cruel and inconsiderate, such as Heathcliff, Catherine Earnshaw and Hindley. However, Brontë also expresses a certain appreciation for the natural world; Linton and Cathy Linton's ideas of heaven both involve peaceful afternoons in the grass and among the trees. Hareton is actually a very noble and gentle spirit, despite his outward lack of civilization and his description as a rustic.

Film Adaptations

Wuthering Heights (1939) is an American black-and-white film directed by William Wyler, starring Merle Oberon, Laurence Oliver, distributed by United Artists. The adaptation is not the whole story of the novel. Heathcliff overhears Cathy's conversation with Nelly and disappears. Two years later, he returns and marries Edgar's naïve sister Isabella. The brokenhearted Cathy soon falls gravely ill. Heathcliff rushes to her side and Cathy dies in Heathcliff's arms. The last thing is the ghosts of Heathcliff and Cathy, walking in the snow, superimposed over a shot of Peniston Crag, which does not exist in the novel. The film omitted any mention of Cathy's daughter and Heathcliff's son, both of whom play a major role in the last portion of the novel. In the film, neither Heathcliff nor Cathy has any children. Isabella does not leave Heathcliff, or die, unlike in the novel where she manages to escape him and later passes away. Instead she remains his troubled but loyal wife even when Mr. Lockwood visits.

Fig 3.3 Young Heathcliff and Catherine

Fig 3.4 Heathcliff and Catherine

Fig 3.5 Catherine and Linton

Fig 3.6 Nelly Dean

Wuthering Heights (1992) is a feature film adaptation directed by Peter Kosminsky, distributed by Paramount Pictures, starring Ralph Fiennes as the tortured Heathcliff and Juliette Binoche as the free spirited Catherine Earnshaw. This particular film is notable for including the oft-omitted second generation story of the children of Cathy, Hindley and Heathcliff.

Fig 3.7 A poster

Fig 3.8 Catherine, Linton and Heathcliff

Fig 3.9 Catherine and Nelly

Fig 3.10 Hareton and Little Cathy

Wuthering Heights (1998) was directed by David Skynner, starring Robert Cavanah as Heathcliff, Orla Brady as Catherine Earnshaw, and Sara Smart as Catherine Linton. It is a full presentation of the whole story. Since it contains the story of two generations, the one hour and fifty minute film seems short.

Fig 3.11　Young Heathcliff and Catherine

Fig 3.12　Heathcliff, Catherine and Nelly Dean

Fig 3.13　Catherine and Edgar Linton

Fig 3.14　Catherine Linton and Hareton Earnshaw

　　Wuthering Heights (2011) is a British romantic drama film directed by Andrea Arnold, starring Kaya Scodelario as Catherine and James Howson as Heathcliff, distributed by Artificial Eye (UK), Oscilloscope and Laboratories (USA). As in most other film adaptations, the novel's second half, about the romance between Catherine Linton and Linton Heathcliff, is omitted. However, in addition, this version omitted the first three chapters of the novel, including the Mr. Lockwood character. Arnold's Heathcliff is not the gypsy of the novel. Here, he's portrayed as black, and the reluctant members of his new family in a farmhouse on a wind-battered Yorkshire moor react to their father's act of charity in adopting him, considering the time and place. Like most screen versions, Arnold's film drops its curtain when Heathcliff's almost-lover Cathy, also his adopted sister, leaves the story, and so ignores the second half. But this spin pays as much attention to weather and animals, plants and insects as it does to the tragedy of unfulfilled love as its core. Nature offers cameos from hawks, dogs, rabbits, sheep and beetles. For Arnold, landscape and wildlife are substitutes for needless dialogue and exposition. Arnold prefers little talk. The film's lack of final tragedy is a difficulty. Still, it looks astounding and there are clever choices in every scene.

Fig 3.15　A Poster

Fig 3.16　Heathcliff and Catherine

Wonderful Dialogues from the 1992 Film

(1) **Cathy and Nelly about Linton's Proposal**

There was storm outside. Cathy goes to Nelly.

Cathy: (*Happily*) Nelly, will you keep a secret for me?

Nelly: Is it worth keeping?

Cathy: Today, Edgar Linton asked me to marry him.

Nelly: Well.

Cathy: How should I answer?

Nelly: Well, really, Miss Cathy. How should I know?

Cathy: I accepted him. (*Laughing heartily*)

Heathcliff is around and overhears her.

Nelly: Do you love Mr. Edgar?

Cathy: Of course, I do. Of course, I can't help it.

Nelly: Why do you love him, Cathy?

Cathy: Because he's handsome and pleasant to be with. (*Laughing*)

Nelly: Bad.

Cathy: Because he's young and cheerful.

Nelly: Bad still.

Cathy: And because he'll be rich and I shall be the greatest woman of the neighborhood.

Nelly: (*Seriously*) Is that what you really want? Well, marry Mr. Edgar, then, where's your obstacle?

Cathy: (*Also seriously, thinking for a while and pointing at her heart with her finger*) Here, in my soul and in my heart, I'm convinced I'm wrong. I shouldn't have thought of it. It would degenerate me to marry Heathcliff. (*A little anxiously Nelly peers towards a direction where Heathcliff hides himself, which Cathy knows not.*) So he'll never know how I love him. My great miseries in this world have been Heathcliff's miseries. And I watched and felt each from the beginning. My love for Linton is like the foliage in the woods. Time will change it, as the winter changes the trees. My love for Heathcliff is like the eternal rocks beneath, a source of little visible delight, but necessary. Nelly, I am Heathcliff. (*Tears runs down from her eye.*)

Nelly: (*Looking behind*) Sh…

Cathy: Why? (*Dog barks.*)

Nelly: It's Joseph, and Heathcliff might be with him. (*Dog continues barking.*) I fact, I'm not sure he wasn't here earlier.

Joseph: (*Coming in from heavy rain*) Young devil of a gypsy gets worse and worse. He's left the gate open and took off across the moors.

Cathy: (*Standing up anxiously and walking towards Joseph*) Go and look for him. Call him back. No, go after him. (*Pushing Joseph out into the rain and turning to Nelly*) Do you think he heard?

Nelly: I think he heard something.

Cathy: What? What did I say?

Nelly: I think he heard up to where you said it would degenerate you to marry him.

Cathy: (*Crying and going out into the rain, running*) Heathcliff.

Nelly: (*Running out and following her, putting a dress on her*) Please come in, Miss Cathy.

Cathy: (*Still crying*) I've lost him! I've lost him. (*Calling*) Heathcliff…

(2) **Heathcliff and Cathy in her Chamber**

Cathy is very ill in bed after giving birth to a baby. Heathcliff knows it and pays her the last visit.

Heathcliff: Cathy (*Coming to her bed*), how can I bear it? (*Kissing her*)

Cathy: You and Edgar have broken my heart. And now you come to me as if you were the one to be pitied. I shall not pity you. You've killed me. (*Heathcliff shakes his head*) You've killed me, well, you'll be happy when I'm in the earth.

Heathcliff: Are you possessed with the devil to talk as to me when you're dying? Can't you see that all those words will be branded in my memory and eating deeper eternally while you are at peace?

Cathy: I shall not be at peace. (*Heathcliff throws her, stands up and walks to and fro in the chamber*) I don't mean to torture you, please, Heathcliff. Do come to me, please.

Heathcliff: Why did you betray your own heart, Cathy? You love me. (*Approaching her*) Then, what right had you to leave me? The poor fancy you felt for Linton? Nothing that God or Satan could inflict would have parted us. You of your own will did it. I've not broken your heart, Cathy. You have broken it. And in breaking it, you've broken mine.

Cathy: If I have done wrong, I'm dying for it. You left me, too. But I forgive you. Forgive me.

Heathcliff: It's hard. It's hard to forgive anyone those lies. Yes, I forgive what you've done to me. I love my murderer. But yours? How can I? How can I? (*Crying and kissing her*)

 Discussions

1. Heathcliff was an orphan in the street. Catherine's father brought him home out of sympathy. If the father had not brought this boy home, there would not have been such tragedies to the family. How do you think of bringing an orphan home and raising him up?
2. Heathcliff's unrequited love turns into hate and revenge. How do you think of his behavior and what can you learn from his tragedy?
3. If Catherine had not loved Edgar Linton, the tragedies would have been avoided. What a lesson can you draw from her naïve decision? Could she really avoid it?
4. Most of the story is narrated by the house keeper Nelly Dean. Why does the author use her to tell the story? What is her role in the novel?
5. Several film adaptations omit the second generation of the story. How do you think of it? Is it good or bad to see those adaptations? How can we make a compensation for that?

Unit 4 Jane Austen and *Pride and Prejudice*

Jane Austen (1775—1817) was an English novelist. She published four novels, namely, *Sense and Sensibility* (1811), *Pride and Prejudice* (1813), *Mansfield Park* (1814), *Emma* (1816) in her life and another two, namely, *Northanger Abbey* and *Persuasion* were published posthumously in 1818. The plots of her novels, set among the landed gentry, highlight the dependence of women on marriage to secure social standing and economic security. Her realism, biting irony and social commentary have gained her historical importance among scholars and critics. *Pride and Prejudice* is the most widely read in English literature, even in world literature.

Fig 4.1 Jane Austen

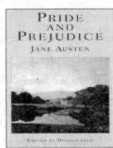

Fig 4.2 A Book Cover of
Pride and Prejudice

Plot

The news that a wealthy young gentleman named Charles Bingley has rented the manor of Netherfield Park causes a great stir in the nearby village of Longbourn, especially in the Bennet household. The Bennets have five unmarried daughters—from oldest to youngest, Jane, Elizabeth, Mary, Kitty, and Lydia—and Mrs. Bennet is desperate to see them all married. After Mr. Bennet pays a social visit to Mr. Bingley, the Bennets attend a ball at which Mr. Bingley is present. He is taken with Jane and spends much of the evening dancing with her. His close friend, Mr. Darcy, is less pleased with the evening and haughtily refuses to dance with Elizabeth, which makes everyone view him as arrogant and obnoxious.

At social functions over subsequent weeks, however, Mr. Darcy finds himself increasingly attracted to Elizabeth's charm and intelligence. Jane's friendship with Mr. Bingley also continues to burgeon, and Jane pays a visit to the Bingley mansion. On her journey to the house she is caught in a downpour and catches ill, forcing her to stay at Netherfield for several days. In order to tend to Jane, Elizabeth hikes through muddy fields and arrives with a spattered dress, much to the disdain of the snobbish Miss Bingley, Charles Bingley's sister. Miss Bingley's spite only increases when she notices that Darcy, whom she is pursuing, pays quite a bit of attention to Elizabeth.

When Elizabeth and Jane return home, they find Mr. Collins visiting their household. Mr. Collins is a young clergyman who stands to inherit Mr. Bennet's property, which has been "entailed", meaning that it can only be passed down to male heirs. Mr. Collins is a pompous fool, though he is quite enthralled by the Bennet girls. Shortly after his arrival, he makes a proposal of marriage to Elizabeth. She turns him down, wounding his pride. Meanwhile, the Bennet girls have become friendly with militia officers stationed in a nearby town. Among them is Wickham, a handsome young soldier who is friendly toward Elizabeth and tells her how Darcy cruelly cheated him out of an inheritance.

At the beginning of winter, the Bingleys and Darcy leave Netherfield and return to London, much to Jane's dismay. A further shock arrives with the news that Mr. Collins has become engaged to Charlotte Lucas, Elizabeth's best friend and the poor daughter of a local knight. Charlotte explains to Elizabeth that she is getting older and needs the match for financial reasons. Charlotte and Mr. Collins get married and Elizabeth promises to visit them at their new home. As winter progresses, Jane visits the city to see friends (hoping also that she might see Mr. Bingley). However, Miss Bingley visits her and behaves rudely, while Mr. Bingley fails to visit her at all. The marriage prospects for the Bennet girls appear bleak.

That spring, Elizabeth visits Charlotte, who now lives near the home of Mr. Collins' patron, Lady Catherine de Bourgh, who is also Darcy's aunt. Darcy calls on Lady Catherine and encounters Elizabeth, whose presence leads him to make a number of visits to the Collins' home, where she is staying. One day, he makes a shocking proposal of marriage, which Elizabeth quickly refuses. She tells Darcy that she considers him arrogant and unpleasant, then scolds him for steering Bingley away from Jane and disinheriting Wickham. Darcy leaves her but shortly thereafter delivers a letter to her. In this letter, he admits that he urged Bingley to distance himself from Jane, but claims he did so only because he thought their romance was not serious. As for Wickham, he informs Elizabeth that the young officer is a liar and that the real cause of their disagreement was Wickham's attempt to elope with his young sister, Georgiana Darcy.

This letter causes Elizabeth to reevaluate her feelings about Darcy. She returns home and acts coldly toward Wickham. The militia is leaving town, which makes the younger, rather man-crazy Bennet girls distraught. Lydia manages to obtain permission from her father to spend the summer with an old colonel in Brighton, where Wickham's regiment will be stationed. With the arrival of June, Elizabeth goes on another journey, this time with the Gardiners, who are relatives of the Bennets. The trip takes her to the North and eventually to the neighborhood of Pemberley, Darcy's estate. She visits Pemberley, after making sure that Darcy is away, and delights in the building and grounds, while hearing from Darcy's servants that he is a wonderful, generous master. Suddenly, Darcy arrives and behaves cordially toward her. Making no mention of his proposal, he entertains the Gardiners and invites Elizabeth to meet his sister.

Shortly thereafter, however, a letter arrives from home, telling Elizabeth that Lydia has eloped with Wickham and that the couple is nowhere to be found, which suggests that they may be living together out of wedlock. Fearful of the disgrace such a situation would bring on her entire family, Elizabeth hastens home. Mr. Gardiner and Mr. Bennet go off to search for Lydia, but Mr. Bennet eventually returns home empty-handed. Just when all hope seems lost, a letter comes from Mr. Gardiner saying that the couple has been found and that Wickham has agreed to marry Lydia in exchange for an annual income. The Bennets are convinced that Mr. Gardiner has paid off Wickham, but Elizabeth learns that the source of the money, and of her family's salvation, was none other than Darcy.

Now married, Wickham and Lydia return to Longbourn briefly, where Mr. Bennet treats them coldly. They then depart for Wickham's new assignment in the North of England. Shortly thereafter, Bingley returns to Netherfield and resumes his courtship of Jane. Darcy goes to stay with him and pays visits to the Bennets but makes no mention of his desire to marry Elizabeth. Bingley, on the other hand, presses his suit and proposes to Jane, to the delight of everyone but Bingley's haughty sister. While the family celebrates, Lady Catherine de Bourgh pays a visit to Longbourn. She corners Elizabeth and says that she has heard that Darcy, her nephew, is planning to marry her. Since she considers a Bennet an unsuitable match for a Darcy, Lady Catherine demands that Elizabeth promise to refuse him. Elizabeth spiritedly refuses, saying she is not engaged to Darcy, but she will not promise anything against her own happiness. A little later, Elizabeth and Darcy go out walking together and he tells her that his feelings have not altered since the spring. She tenderly accepts his proposal, and both Jane and Elizabeth are married.

Select Reading: Chapter X

Mrs. Hurst sang with her sister, and while they were thus employed, Elizabeth could not help observing, as she turned over some music books that lay on the instrument, how frequently Mr. Darcy's eyes were fixed on her. She hardly knew how to suppose that she could be an object of admiration to so great man; and yet that he should look at her because he disliked her was still more strange. She could only imagine however, at last, that she drew his notice because there was a something about her more wrong and reprehensible, according to his ideas of right, than in any other person present. The supposition did not pain her. She liked him too little to care for his approbation.

After playing some Italian songs, Miss Bingley varied the charm by a lively Scotch air; and soon afterwards Mr. Darcy, drawing near Elizabeth, said to her: "Do not you feel a great inclination, Miss Bennet, to seize such an opportunity of dancing a reel?"

She smiled, but made no answer. He repeated the question, with some surprise at her silence.

"Oh!" said she, "I heard you before; but I could not immediately determine what to say in reply. You wanted me, I know, to say 'Yes', that you might have the pleasure of despising my taste; but I always delight in overthrowing those kind of schemes, and cheating a person of their premeditated contempt. I have therefore made up my mind to tell you that I do not want to dance a reel at all—and now despise me if you dare."

"Indeed I do not dare."

Elizabeth, having rather expected to affront him, was amazed at his gallantry; but there was a mixture of sweetness and archness in her manner which made it difficult for her to affront anybody; and Darcy had never been so bewitched by any woman as he was by her. He really believed, that were it not for the inferiority of her connections, he should be in some danger.

译文：赫斯特夫人替妹妹伴唱。就在她俩如此表演的时候，伊丽莎白一面翻阅着钢琴上的几本琴谱，一面情不由己注意到，达西总是不断地拿眼睛盯着她。她简直不敢想象，她居然会收到一个如此了不起的男人的爱慕。然而，假如说达西是因为讨厌她才那么望着她，那就奇怪了。最后，她只能这样想：她所以引起达西的注意，那是因为照他的标准衡量，她比在场的任何人都让人看不顺眼。她做出了这个假想之后，并没有感到痛苦。她压根儿不喜欢达西，因此也不稀罕他的垂青。

宾利小姐弹了几支意大利曲子之后，便想换换情调，弹起了一支欢快的苏格兰小曲。过了不久，达西先生走到伊丽莎白跟前，对她说道："贝内特小姐，你是不是很想抓住这个机会跳一曲里尔舞？"

伊丽莎白笑了笑，却没有回答。达西见她闷声不响，觉得有些奇怪，便又问她一次。

"哦！"伊丽莎白说，"我早就听见了，只是一下子拿不准怎么回答你。我知道，你是想让我说一声'想跳'，然后你就可以洋洋得意地蔑视我的低级趣味。但是，我一向就喜欢戳穿这种把戏，捉弄一下蓄意蔑视我的人。因此，我决定跟你说：我压根不想跳里尔舞，现在，你是好样的就蔑视我吧。"

"实在不敢。"

伊丽莎白本来打算羞辱他一下，眼下见他那么恭敬，不由得愣住了。不过，她天生一副既温柔又调皮的神态，使她很难羞辱任何人。达西真让她给迷住了，他以前还从未对任何女人如此着迷过。他心里正经在想，假若不是因为她有几个低贱的亲戚，他还真有点危险呢。

Analysis of Major Characters

Elizabeth: The second daughter in the Bennet family, and the most intelligent and quick-witted, Elizabeth is the protagonist of the novel and one of the most well-known female characters in English literature. Her admirable qualities are numerous—she is lovely, clever, and converses as brilliantly as anyone. Her honesty, virtue, and lively wit enable her to rise above the nonsense and bad behavior that pervade her class-bound and often spiteful society. Her sharp tongue and tendency to make hasty judgments often lead her astray. The novel is essentially the story of how she (and her true love, Darcy) overcome all obstacles—including their own personal failings—to find romantic happiness. Elizabeth must not only cope with a hopeless mother, a distant father, two badly behaved younger siblings, and several snobbish, antagonizing females, but also overcome her own mistaken impressions of Darcy, which initially lead her to reject his proposals of marriage. Her charms are sufficient to keep him interested. As she gradually comes to recognize the nobility of Darcy's character, she realizes the error of her initial prejudice against him.

Darcy: The son of a wealthy, well-established family and the master of the great estate of Pemberley, Darcy is Elizabeth's male counterpart and her ideal match. Intelligent and forthright, he too has a tendency to judge too hastily and harshly, and his high birth and wealth make him overly proud and overly conscious of his social status. His haughtiness makes him initially bungle his courtship. When he proposes to her, he dwells more on how unsuitable a match she is than on her charms, beauty, or anything else complimentary. Her rejection of his advances builds a kind of humility in him. Darcy demonstrates his continued devotion to Elizabeth, in spite of his distaste for her low connections, when he rescues Lydia and the entire Bennet family from disgrace, and when he goes against the wishes of his haughty aunt, Lady Catherine de Bourgh, by continuing to pursue Elizabeth. Darcy proves himself worthy of Elizabeth, and she ends up repenting her earlier, overly harsh judgment of him.

Jane and Bingley: Elizabeth's beautiful elder sister and Darcy's wealthy best friend, Jane and Bingley engage in a courtship that occupies a central place in the novel. They first meet at the ball in Meryton and enjoy an immediate mutual attraction. They are spoken of as a potential couple throughout the book, long before anyone imagines that Darcy and Elizabeth might marry. They are so similar in nature and behavior that they can be described together: both are cheerful, friendly, and good-natured, always ready to think the best of others; they lack entirely the prickly egotism of Elizabeth and Darcy. Jane's gentle spirit serves as a foil for her sister's fiery, contentious nature, while Bingley's eager friendliness contrasts with Darcy's stiff pride. Their principal characteristics are goodwill and compatibility, and the contrast of their romance with that of Darcy and Elizabeth is remarkable. Jane and Bingley exhibit to the reader true love unhampered by either pride or prejudice, though in their simple goodness, they also demonstrate that such a love is mildly dull.

Mr. Bennet: Mr. Bennet is the patriarch of the Bennet household—the husband of Mrs. Bennet and the father of the five daughters. He is a man driven to exasperation by his ridiculous wife and difficult daughters. He reacts by withdrawing from his family and assuming a detached attitude punctuated by bursts of sarcastic humor. He is closest to Elizabeth because they are the two most intelligent Bennets. Initially, his dry wit and self-possession in the face of his wife's hysteria make him a sympathetic figure. Detached from his family, he is a weak father and, at critical moments, fails his family. In particular, his foolish indulgence of Lydia's immature behavior nearly leads to general disgrace when she elopes with Wickham. Further, upon her disappearance, he proves largely ineffective. It is left to Mr. Gardiner and Darcy to track Lydia down and rectify the situation. Ultimately, Mr. Bennet would rather withdraw from the world than cope with it.

Mrs. Bennet: Mrs. Bennet is a miraculously tiresome character. Noisy and foolish, she is a woman consumed by the desire to see her daughters married and seems to care for nothing else in the world. Ironically, her single-minded pursuit of this goal tends to backfire, as her lack of social graces alienates the very people (Darcy and Bingley) whom she tries desperately to attract. Austen uses her continually to highlight the necessity of marriage for young women. Mrs. Bennet also serves as a middle-class counterpoint to such upper-class snobs as Lady Catherine and Miss Bingley, demonstrating that foolishness can be found at every level of society.

Themes

Pride: Pride prevents the characters from seeing the truth of a situation and from achieving happiness in life. Pride is one of the main barriers that create an obstacle to Elizabeth and Darcy's marriage. Darcy's pride in his position in society leads him initially to scorn anyone outside of his own social circle. Elizabeth's vanity clouds her judgment, making her prone to think ill of Darcy and to think well of Wickham. In the end, Elizabeth's rebukes of Darcy help him realize his fault and change accordingly, as demonstrated in his genuinely friendly treatment of the Gardiners, whom he previously would have scorned because of their low social class. Darcy's letter shows Elizabeth that her judgments were wrong and she realizes that they were based on vanity, not on reason.

Prejudice: Darcy's pride is founded on social prejudice, while Elizabeth's initial prejudice against him is rooted in pride of her own quick perceptions. Darcy has been brought up to scorn all those outside his own social circle. He must overcome his prejudice in order to see that Elizabeth would be a good wife for him and to win Elizabeth's heart. The overcoming of his prejudice is demonstrated when he treats the Gardiners with great civility.

Family: Family is portrayed as primarily responsible for the intellectual and moral education of children. Mr. and Mrs. Bennet's failure to provide this education for their daughters leads to the utter shamelessness, foolishness, frivolity, and immorality of Lydia. Elizabeth and Jane have managed to develop virtue and strong characters in spite of the negligence of their parents, perhaps through the help of their studies and the good influence of Mr. and Mrs. Gardiner, who are the only relatives that take a serious concern in the girls' well-being and provide sound guidance. Elizabeth and Jane are constantly forced to put up with the foolishness and poor judgment of their mother and the sarcastic indifference of their father. Even when Elizabeth advises her father not to allow Lydia to go to Brighton, he ignores the advice because he thinks it too difficult to deal with Lydia's complaining. The result is the scandal of Lydia's elopement with Wickham.

Women and Marriage: Women like Charlotte Lucas have to marry man they are not in love with in order to gain financial security. The entailment of Mr. Bennet's estate leaves his daughters in a poor financial situation which both requires them to marry and makes it more difficult to marry well. Conventionally, though women are as intelligent and capable as men, they are still put in an inferior status in society. That's quite unjust. The novelist herself goes against convention by remaining single and earning a living through her novels. In her personal letters she advises friends only to marry for love. Through the plot of the novel it is clear that Austen wants to show how Elizabeth is able to be happy by refusing to marry for financial purposes and only marrying a man whom she truly loves and esteems.

Class: The novel does not put forth an egalitarian ideology or call for the leveling of all social classes, yet it does criticize an over-emphasis on class. Darcy's inordinate pride is based on his extreme class-consciousness. While those such as Miss Bingley and Mrs. Hurst, who are born into the aristocracy, are idle, mean-spirited and annoying, Mr. and Mrs. Gardiner are not members of the aristocracy in terms of wealth or birth but are natural aristocrats by virtue of their intelligence, good-breeding and virtue. The comic formality of Mr. Collins and his obsequious relationship with Lady Catherine serve as a satire class consciousness and social formalities. In the end, the verdict on class differences is moderate. Elizabeth accepts class relationships as valid. Darcy realizes that institutions are intended to serve the end of human happiness.

Individual and Society: The novel portrays a world in which society takes an interest in the private virtue of its members. When Lydia elopes with Wickham, it is scandal to the whole society and an injury to entire Bennet family. Darcy considers his failure to expose the wickedness of Wickham's character to be a breach of his social duty because if Wickham's true character had been known others would not have been so easily deceived by him. While Austen is critical of society's ability to judge properly, she does believe that society has a crucial role in promoting virtue. Austen has a profound sense that individuals are social beings and that their happiness is found through relationships with others. Apart from society, there is no individual.

Virtue: Austen's novels unite Aristotelian and Christian conceptions of virtue. She sees human life as purposeful and believes that human beings must guide their appetites and desires through their use of reason. Elizabeth's folly in her misjudgments of Darcy and Wickham is that her vanity has prevented her from reasoning objectively. Lydia seems almost completely devoid of virtue because she has never trained herself to discipline her passions or formed her judgment such that she is capable of making sound moral decisions. Human happiness is found by living a life in accordance with human dignity, which is a life in accordance with virtue. Self-knowledge has a central place in the acquisition of virtue, as it is a prerequisite for moral improvement. Darcy and Elizabeth are only freed of their pride and prejudice when their dealings with one another help them to see their faults and spur them to improve.

Film Adaptations

Pride and Prejudice (1940) was directed by Robert Z. Leonard, starring Laurence Oliver, Green Garson, and Maureen O'Sullivan, released by Metro-Goldwyn-Mayer. The film was described as the most deliciously pert comedy of old manners, the most crisp and crackling satire in costume that we in this corner can remember ever having seen on the screen. Green Garson is Elizabeth, stepping right out of the book, or rather out of one's fondest imagination: poised, graceful, self-contained, witty, spasmodically stubborn and as lovely as a woman can be. Laurence Oliver is Darcy, the arrogant, sardonic Darcy whose pride went before a most felicitous fall. Though there are changes to the original novel, the film is still called an unusually successful adaptation of Jane Austen's most famous novel. The satire is slightly reduced and coarsened and the period advanced in order to use more flamboyant costumes, but the spirit is entirely in keeping with Austen's sharp, witty portrait of rural 19th century social *mores*. This film adaptation is notorious for drastically diverging from the novel and being excessively Hollywoodized, and for putting the women in clothes based on the styles of the late 1820s and the styles of the 1830s which were quite different from the Regency styles appropriate to the novel's setting. The timeframe of the film's plot progression is quite noticeably compressed, with certain events being juxtaposed in the film that were separated by days, weeks or even months in the novel. The film eliminates two journeys which are pivotal plot points in the novel. Some characters were eliminated completely from this film adaptation, such as Mr. and Mrs. Gardiner, Georgiana Darcy. The removal of these plot points, as well as the characters associated with them, drastically alters the development of Elizabeth and Darcy's characters and the evolution of the romance between them.

Fig 4.3　The Bennets

Fig 4.4　Five daughters of the Bennets

Fig 4.5　Elizabeth and Darcy

Fig 4.6　Collins

Pride and Prejudice (1995) is a six-episode 1995 British television drama, directed by Simon Langton, starring Jennifer Ehle as Elizabeth and Colin Firth as Mr. Darcy, produced by Sue Birtwistle. The adaptation is said to be probably as good as it can get for a literary classic. Firth is not in the slightest bit soft and fluffy and Jennifer Ehle shows the right brand of spirited intelligence as Elizabeth. Jennifer Ehle makes Elizabeth strikingly intelligent and authoritative without being o-verbearing, and Firth brilliantly captures Mr. Darcy's snobbish pride while conveying, largely through intense stares, that he is falling in love despite himself. It is considered as so dominant, so universally adored, that it has lingered in the public consciousness as a cinematic standard. But the walks across meadows are languorous and ornately choreographed dances of the British production are too slow. The adaptation is a good deal more thorough than necessary and not the best Austen on the suddenly crowded market.

Fig 4.7　The Bennets

Fig 4.8　Five daughters of the Bennets

Fig 4.9　Elizabeth and Darcy

Fig 4.10　Collins

Pride and Prejudice (2005) was directed by Joe Wright, starring Keira Knightley as Elizabeth, Matthew Macfadyen as Mr. Darcy, released by Working Title Films and Staudio Canal. It was regarded as only the second faithful film version after the famed, but oddly flawed, black-and-white 1940 adaptation. It is called a stellar adaptation, bewitching the viewer completely and incandescently with an exquisite blend of emotion and wit. Wright's attention to realism is criticized for being careless with the customs and conventions that were part of the fabric of Austen's world. The film lacks Austen's brilliant sense of irony. The romantic melodrama is played up at the expense of her razor-sharp wit. The film's time constraints did not capture the depth and complexity of the television serial and Wright's adaptation is obviously not as daring or revisionist as the television adaption.

Fig 4.11 Five daughters of the Bennets

Fig 4.12 Elizabeth and Darcy

Wonderful Dialogues from the 1995 Film

(1) **At the Ball**

Bingley: Come, Darcy. I must have you dance! I Must. I hate to see you standing about in this stupid manner. You have must better dance!

Elizabeth is overhearing them.

Darcy: I certainly shall not at an assembly such as this. It would be insupportable. Your sisters are engaged. You know it would punish me to stand up with any other woman.

Bingley: Good God, Darcy! I wouldn't be as fastidious as you are for a kingdom! Upon my honor, I never met so many pleasant girls in my life! Several of them are uncommonly pretty.

Darcy: You have been dancing with the only handsome girl in the room.

Bingley: Darcy, she is the most beautiful creature I ever beheld. Look, look! (*Looking towards Elizabeth who is listening to them more attentively*) There is one of her sisters. She's very pretty, too. I dare say very agreeable.

Darcy: She's tolerable, I suppose, but not handsome enough to tempt me. (*Elizabeth overhears the words and feels displeased.*) I'm in no honor to consider young ladies who are slighted by other men. Go back to your partner. Enjoy her smiles. You're wasting your time on me.

Bingley leaves. Elizabeth peers at Darcy with contempt. She stands up and leaves.

(2) **Proposal**

Darcy: (*Looking at Elizabeth who is sitting. Walking to and fro uneasily. Sitting down at last. Elizabeth is waiting for his words. Then standing up*) In vain I have struggled. It will not do! My feelings will not be repressed. You must allow me to tell you how ardently I admire and love you. In declaring myself thus I'm aware that I will be going expressly against the wishes of my family, my friends, and, I hardly need add, my own better judgment. (*Elizabeth looks at him puzzlingly.*) The relative situation of our families makes any alliance between as a reprehensible connection. As a rational man I cannot but regard it as such myself, but it cannot be helped. (*Elizabeth become serious.*) Almost from the earliest moments, I have come to feel from you a passionate admiration and regard, which, despite my struggles, has overcome every rational objection. I beg you, most fervently, to relieve my suffering and consent to be my wife.

Elizabeth: (*Calmly and decidedly*) In such cases as these, I believe the established mode is to express a sense of obligation. But I cannot. (*Darcy feels surprised at her answer.*) I have never desired your good opinion and you have certainly bestowed it most unwillingly. I'm sorry to cause pain to any one, but it was unconsciously done and I hope will be of short duration.

Darcy: (*Walking to and fro sadly*) And this is all the reply I'm to expect? I might wonder why, with so little effort at civility, I am rejected?

Elizabeth: (*A little emotionally*) I might wonder why, with so evident a desire to offend me, you chose to tell me that you like me against your will, your reason, and even against your character? Was this not some excuse for incivility if I was uncivil? I have every reason in the world to think ill of you. What could tempt me to accept the man who has ruined the happiness of a most beloved sister? Can you deny that you have done it?

Darcy: I have no wish to deny it. I did everything in my power to separate my friend from your sister and I rejoice in my success. Towards him I have been kinder than towards myself.

Elizabeth: It's not merely that on which my dislike of you is founded. Long before my dislike was decided when I heard Mr. Wickham's story of your dealings with him. How can you defend yourself on that subject?

Darcy: Such interest in that gentleman's concerns!

Elizabeth: Who that knows of his misfortunes can help feeling an interest?

Darcy: (*Emotionally*) His misfortunes! Yes, his misfortunes have been great indeed!

Elizabeth: And of your infliction! You have reduced him to his present state of poverty and yet you can treat his misfortunes with contempt and ridicule!

Darcy: And this is your opinion of me? My faults by this calculation are heavy indeed. Perhaps these offences might have been overlooked, had not your pride been hurt by the confession of the scruples which long prevented my forming serious design on you, had I concealed my struggles and flattered you. But disguise of every sort is my abhorrence. Nor am I ashamed of the feelings I related. They were natural. Did you expect me to rejoice in the inferiority of your connections (*Elizabeth stands up with contempt*) to congratulate myself on the hope of relations whose condition in life is so below my own?

Elizabeth: You are mistaken, Mr. Darcy. Your declaration merely spared me any concern for refusing you, had you been more gentleman-like. You could not make me the offer of your hand in any way that would tempt me to accept it. From the beginning, your manners convinced me of your arrogance, your conceit and your selfish disdain for the feelings of others. Within a month, I felt you were the last man who I could ever marry!

Darcy: You've said quite enough, madam!

(3) Second Proposal

Elizabeth and Darcy walking together.

Elizabeth: Mr. Darcy (*Darcy turns back*), I can go no longer without thanking you for your kindness to my poor sister. Ever since I have known of it, I've been most anxious to tell you how grateful I am for my family and for myself. (*Darcy walks on*) You must not blame my aunt for telling me. Lydia betrayed it first and then I couldn't rest till I knew everything. I know what trouble and what mortification it must have cost you. Please let me say this, please allow me to thank you on behalf of all my family, since they don't know to whom they are indebted.

Darcy: (*Still walking on, Elizabeth follows.*) If you will thank me. Let it be for yourself alone. Your family owes me nothing. As much as I respect them, I believe I thought only of you. You're too generous to trifle with me. If your feelings are what you were last April, tell me so. (*They Look at each other.*) My affections and wishes are unchanged. But one word from you will silence me on this subject forever.

Elizabeth: (*Shyly*) Oh, my feelings… my feelings are…I am ashamed to remember what I said then. My feelings are so different. In fact, they are quite the opposite. (*Smiling sweetly at Darcy. Then they walk on together.*)

 Discussions

1. How are Darcy's pride and Elizabeth's prejudice shown in the novel? And what do they do to overcome their pride and prejudice at last?
2. What's your impression on Mr. Bennet and Mrs. Bennet? Are they good parents?
3. What's your impression on Lydia and Wickham? How do you think of their elopement?
4. What's your impression on Jane and Bingley? Why does Elizabeth scold Darcy for steering Bingley away from Jane and how does Darcy answer it?
5. What's your impression on Charlotte and Collins? Do they love each other? What's the reason for Charlotte to accept Collins' proposal of marriage?

Unit 5 Thomas Hardy and *Tess of the D'Urbervilles*

Thomas Hardy (1840—1928) was an English novelist and poet. He was influenced both in his novels and in his poetry by Romanticism. Like Dickens, he was highly critical of much in Victorian society, focusing more on a declining rural society. While Hardy wrote poetry throughout his life and regarded himself primarily as a poet, his first collection was not published until 1898. Initially, he gained fame as the author of novels, including *Far from the Madding Crowd* (1874), *The Mayor of Casterbridge* (1886), *Tess of the D'Urbervilles* (1891), and *Jude the Obscure* (1895). Most of his fictional works were set in the semi-fictional region of Wessex. They explored tragic characters struggling against their passions and social circumstances. His Wessex is based on the medieval Anglo-Saxon kingdom and eventually came to include the counties in southwest and south central England. *Tess of the D'Urbervilles* is about the tragic life of a pure woman called Tess.

Fig 5.1 Thomas Hardy

Fig 5.2 A Book Cover of *Tess of the D'Urbervilles*

Plot

Phase the First: The Maiden (1-11)

The novel is set in impoverished rural Wessex during the Long Depression. Tess is the oldest child of John and Joan Durbeyfield, uneducated rural peasants. One day, Parson Tringham informs John that he has noble blood. Tringham has discovered that "Durbeyfield" is a corruption of "D'Urberville", the surname of a noble Norman family, now extinct. The news immediately goes to John's head.

That same day, Tess participates in the village May Dance, where she meets Angel Clare, youngest son of Reverend James Clare, who is on a walking tour with his two brothers. He stops to join the dance, and finds partners in several other girls. Angel notes Tess's beauty, too late to dance with her, as he is already late for a promised meeting with his brothers. Tess feels slighted. Tess's father, overjoyed with learning of his noble lineage, gets too drunk to drive to market that night, so Tess undertakes the journey herself. However, she falls asleep at the reins, and the family's only horse encounters a speeding wagon and is fatally wounded. The blood spreads over her white dress, a symbol of the forthcoming unpleasant events. Tess feels so guilty over the horse's death that she agrees, against her better judgment, to visit Mrs. D'Urberville, a wealthy widow who lives in the nearby town of Trantridge, and "claim kin". She is unaware that in reality, Mrs. D'Urberville's husband, Simon Stoke, purchased the baronial title and adopted the new surname, and so is not related to the D'Urbervilles.

Tess does not succeed in meeting Mrs. D'Urberville, but her libertine son Alec takes a fancy to Tess and secures her a position as poultry keeper on the D'Urberville estate. He immediately begins making advances. Tess dislikes Alec and repels him verbally but endures his persistent unwanted attention, feeling she has no choice, as she must earn enough to replace her family's only means of support, the dead horse. The threat that Alec presents to Tess's virtue is obscured for Tess by her inexperience and almost daily commonplace interactions with him. He calls her "coz" (cousin), indicating a male protector, not a ravisher. Late one night, walking home from town with some other Trantridge villagers, Tess inadvertently antagonizes Car Darch, Alec's most recently discarded favorite, and finds herself about to come to blows. When Alec rides up and offers to "rescue" her from the situation, she accepts. He does not take her home, but rides through the fog until they reach an ancient grove called "The Chase". Here, Alec informs her that he is lost and leaves on foot to get his bearings. Tess stays behind and falls asleep atop the coat he lent her. After Alec returns he callously seduces her. Alec is later referred to as "the seducer".

Phase the Second: Maiden No More (12-15)

Tess begins to despise Alec. Against his wishes, she goes home to her father's cottage, where she keeps almost entirely to her room. The next summer, she gives birth to a sickly boy, who lives only a few weeks. On his last night alive, Tess baptises him herself, after her father locks the doors to keep the parson away. The child is given the name "Sorrow". Tess buries Sorrow in unconsecrated ground, makes a homemade cross and lays flowers on his grave in an empty marmalade box.

Phase the Third: The Rally (16-24)

More than two years after the Trantridge debacle, Tess, now 20, is ready to make a new start. She seeks employment outside the village, where her past is not known, and secures a job as a milkmaid at Talbothays Dairy, working for Mr. and Mrs. Crick. There, she befriends three of her fellow milkmaids, Izz, Retty, and Marian, and re-encounters Angel Clare, who is now an apprentice farmer and has come to Talbothays to learn dairy management. Although the other milkmaids are sick with love for him, Angel soon singles out Tess, and the two gradually fall in love.

Phase the Fourth: The Consequence (25-34)

Angel spends a few days away from the dairy visiting his family at Emminster. His brothers Felix and Cuthbert, ordained ministers both, note Angel's coarsened manners, while Angel considers his brothers staid and narrow-minded. Following evening prayers, Angel discusses his marriage prospects with his father. The Clares have long hoped that Angel would marry Mercy Chant, a pious schoolmistress, but Angel argues that a wife who knows farm life would be a more practical choice. He tells his parents about Tess, and they agree to meet her. His father, the Reverend James Clare, tells Angel about his efforts to convert the local populace, and mentions his failure to tame a young miscreant named Alec D'Urberville.

Angel returns to Talbothays Dairy and asks Tess to marry him. This puts Tess in a painful dilemma: Angel obviously thinks her a virgin and, although she does not want to deceive him, she shrinks from confessing lest she lose his love and admiration. Such is her passion for him that she finally agrees to the marriage, explaining that she hesitated because she had heard he hated old families and thought he would not approve of her D'Urberville ancestry. However, he is pleased by this news, because he thinks it will make their match more suitable in the eyes of his family.

As the marriage approaches, Tess grows increasingly troubled. She writes to her mother for advice. Joan tells her to keep silent about her past. Her anxiety increases when a man from Trantridge, named Groby, recognizes her while she is out shopping with Angel and crudely alludes to her sexual history. Angel overhears and flies into an uncharacteristic rage. Tess resolves to deceive Angel no more, and writes a letter describing her dealings with D'Urberville and slips it under his door. After Angel greets her with the usual affection the next morning, she discovers the letter under his carpet and realizes that he has not seen it, and she destroys it.

The wedding goes smoothly although a bad omen of a cock crowing in the afternoon is noticed by Tess. Tess and Angel spend their wedding night at an old D'Urberville family mansion, where Angel presents his bride with some beautiful diamonds that belonged to his godmother and confesses that he once had a brief affair with an older woman in London. When she hears this story, Tess feels sure that Angel will forgive her own history, and finally tells him about what Alec did to her.

Phase the Fifth: The Woman Pays (35-44)

Angel is appalled by the revelation, and spends the wedding night on a sofa. Tess, devastated, accepts the sudden estrangement as something she deserves. After a few awkward, awful days, she suggests they separate, saying that she will return to her parents. Angel gives her some money and promises to try to reconcile himself to her past, but warns her not to try to join him until he sends for her. After a quick visit to his parents, Angel takes ship for Brazil to start a new life. Before he leaves, he encounters Izz on the road and impulsively asks her to come to Brazil with him, as his mistress. She accepts, but when he asks her how much she loves him, she admits "Nobody could love 'ee more than Tess did! She would have laid down her life for 'ee. I could do no more!" Hearing this, he abandons the whim, and Izz goes home weeping bitterly.

Tess returns home for a time but, finding this unbearable, decides to join Marian at acre farm called Flintcomb-Ash. They are later joined by Izz. On the road, she is again recognised and insulted by Groby, who proves to be her new employer. At the farm, the three former milkmaids perform very hard physical labor.

One day, Tess attempts to visit Angel's family at the parsonage in Emminster. As she nears her destination, she encounters Angel's priggish older brothers and the woman his parents once hoped he would marry, Mercy Chant. They do not recognize her, but she overhears them discussing Angel's unwise marriage. Shamed, she turns back. On the way, she overhears a wandering preacher and is shocked to discover that he is Alec D'Urberville, who has been converted to Methodism under the Reverend James Clare's influence.

Phase the Sixth: The Convert (45-52)

Alec and Tess are each shaken by their encounter, and Alec begs Tess never to tempt him again as they stand beside an ill-omened stone monument called the Cross-in-Hand. However, Alec soon comes to Flintcomb-Ash to ask Tess to marry him. She tells him she is already married. He returns at Candlemas when Tess is hard at work feeding a threshing machine. He tells her he is no longer a preacher and wants her to be with him. When he insults Angel she slaps him, drawing blood. Tess then learns from her sister, Liza-Lu, that her father, John, is ill and that her mother is dying. Tess rushes home to look after them. Her mother soon recovers, but her father unexpectedly dies.

The family is evicted from their home, as Durbeyfield held only a life lease on their cottage. Alec tells Tess that her husband is never coming back and offers to house the Durbeyfields on his estate. Tess refuses his assistance. She had earlier written Angel a psalm-like letter, full of love, self-abasement, and pleas for mercy. Now she finally admits to herself that Angel has wronged her and scribbles a hasty note saying that she will do all she can to forget him, since he has treated her so unjustly.

The Durbeyfields plan to rent some rooms in the town of Kingsbere, ancestral home of the D'Urbervilles, but they arrive there to find that the rooms have already been rented to another family. All but destitute, they are forced to take shelter in the churchyard, under the D'Urberville window. Tess enters the church and in the D'Urberville Aisle, Alec reappears and importunes Tess again. In despair, she looks at the entrance to the D'Urberville vault and wonders aloud, "Why am I on the wrong side of this door?"

In the meantime, Angel has been very ill in Brazil and, his farming venture having failed, heads home to England. On the way, he confides his troubles to a stranger, who tells him that he was wrong to leave his wife. What she was in the past should matter less than what she might become. Angel begins to repent his treatment of Tess.

Phase the Seventh: Fulfillment (53-59)

Upon his return to his family home, Angel has two letters waiting for him: Tess's angry note and a few cryptic lines from "two well-wishers" (Izz and Marian), warning him to protect his wife from "an enemy in the shape of a friend". He sets out to find Tess and eventually locates Joan, now well-dressed and living in a pleasant cottage. After responding evasively to his enquiries, she finally tells him her daughter has gone to live in Sandbourne, a fashionable seaside resort. There, he finds Tess living in an expensive boarding house under the name "Mrs. D'Urberville". When he asks for her, she appears in startlingly elegant attire and stands aloof. He tenderly asks her forgiveness. But Tess, in anguish, tells him he has come too late. Thinking he would never return, she yielded at last to Alec D'Urberville's persuasion and has become his mistress. She gently asks Angel to leave and never come back. He departs. Tess returns to her bedroom, where she falls to her knees and begins a lamentation. She blames Alec for causing her to lose Angel's love a second time, accusing Alec of having lied when he said that Angel would never return to her.

The landlady tries to listen in at the keyhole, but withdraws hastily when the argument becomes heated. She later sees Tess leave the house, then notices a spreading red spot—a bloodstain—on the ceiling. She summons help, and Alec is found stabbed to death in his bed.

Angel, totally disheartened, has left Sandbourne. Tess hurries after him and tells him that she has killed Alec, saying that she hopes she has won his forgiveness by murdering the man who ruined both their lives. Angel doesn't believe her at first, but grants his forgiveness and tells her that he loves her. Rather than head for the coast, they walk inland, vaguely planning to hide somewhere until the search for Tess is ended and they can escape abroad from a port. They find an empty mansion and stay there for five days in blissful happiness, until their presence is discovered one day by the cleaning woman.

They continue walking and, in the middle of the night, stumble upon Stonehenge where Tess lies down to rest on an ancient altar. Before she falls asleep, she asks Angel to look after her younger sister, Liza-Lu, saying that she hopes Angel will marry her after she is dead. At dawn, Angel sees that they are surrounded by police. He finally realizes that Tess really has committed murder and asks the men in a whisper to let her awaken naturally before they arrest her. When she opens her eyes and sees the police, she tells Angel she is "almost glad" because "now I shall not live for you to despise me." Her parting words are, "I am ready."

Tess is escorted to prison. The novel closes with Angel and Liza-Lu watching from a nearby hill as the black flag signaling Tess's execution is raised over the prison. Angel and Liza-Lu then join hands and go on their way.

Select Reading: Chapter XII

It was a Sunday morning in late October, about four months after Tess Durbeyfield's arrival at Trantridge, and some few weeks subsequent to the night ride in The Chase.

Ascending by the long white road that Tess herself had just labored up, she saw a two-wheeled vehicle, beside which walked a man, who held up his hand to attract her attention.

She obeyed the signal to wait for him with unspeculative repose, and in a few minutes man and horse stopped beside her.

"Why did you slip away by stealth like this?" said D'Urberville, with upbraiding breathlessness; "on a Sunday morning, too, when people were all in bed! I only discovered it by accident, and I have been driving like the deuce to overtake you. Just look at the mare. Why go off like this? You know that nobody wished to hinder your going. And how unnecessary it has been for you to toil along on foot, and encumber yourself with this heavy load! I have followed like a madman, simply to drive you the rest of the distance, if you won't come back."

"I shan't come back," said she.

"I thought you wouldn't—I said so! Well, then, put up your basket, and let me help you on."

She listlessly placed her basket and bundle within the dog-cart, and stepped up, and they sat side by side. She had no fear of him now, and in the cause of her confidence her sorrow lay.

"One would think you were a princess from your manner, in addition to a true and original D'Urberville—ha! ha! Well, Tess, dear, I can say no more. I suppose I am a bad fellow—a damn bad fellow. I was born bad, and I have lived bad, and I shall die bad in all probability. But, upon my lost soul, I won't be bad towards you again, Tess. And if certain circumstances should arise—you understand—in which you are in the least need, the least difficulty, send me one line, and you shall have by return whatever you require. I may not be at Trantridge—I am going to London for a time—I can't stand the old woman. But all letters will be forwarded."

She said that she did not wish him to drive her further, and they stopped just under the clump of trees.

"Tess, will you come back to me! Upon my soul I don't like to let you go like this!"

"Never, never! I made up my mind as soon as I saw—what I ought to have seen sooner; and I won't come."

"Then good morning, my four months' cousin—goodbye!"

He leapt up lightly, arranged the reins, and was gone between the tall red-berried hedges.

Tess did not look after him, but slowly wound along the crooked lane. It was still early, and though the sun's lower limb was just free of the hill, his rays, ungenial and peering, addressed the eye rather than the touch as yet. There was not a human soul near. Sad October and her sadder self seemed the only two existences haunting that lane.

译文：那是十月末的一个礼拜天早晨，大约在苔丝·德伯菲尔德来到川特里奇一个月之后，也就是那次在猎苑的骑马夜行的几个礼拜之后。

她看到一辆双轮马车沿着自己刚才艰难走过的长长的白色的路走了上来，车旁走着一个人，正扬起手招引她的注意。

她接收了信号，不加思索地平静地等着。几分钟之后那人和马就来到了她的面前。

"你为什么像这样偷偷地溜走呢？"德伯维尔气喘吁吁地责备她，"何况是在星期天早上，大家都还在睡觉！我也是偶然才发现的。我不要命地奔跑才赶上了你，你看看我这马！你为什么就这样不告而别呢？你知道谁也不会阻拦你的。你有什么必要这么吃力地走路，还带上这么累赘的行李？我像一个疯子一样追赶你，不过是想用车送你走完这最后一段路。你还是回去吧！"

"我不会回去的，"她说。

"我估计你不会，我早说过！好吧，把篮子放上去，我来帮你。"

她把篮子和行李卷没精打采地放上轻便马车，自己也踏了上去。两人并排坐在一起。她现在不再怕他了。而她的悲哀也正在于不再怕他。

"你看你那神气，人家也许会以为你不但是个货真价实的嫡系德伯维尔，而且就是个公主哩。哈！哈！好了，苔丝，宝贝，我不能再说什么了。我看呀，我就是个坏蛋——一个大坏蛋。天生就坏，一辈子都坏，保准不得好死。不过，我以我堕落的灵魂向你保证，我以后再也不会对你坏了，苔丝。如果以后出现了什么问题，你明白我的意思，只要你有一点点需要我，只要有一点点困难，都不妨给我写个条子，你立即就可以得到你需要的一切。即使我不在川特里奇，我要到伦敦去一段时间，那老太婆叫我受不了，所有的信都会转过去的。"

她说她不想再要他用车送下去了，马车就在树丛边停了下来。

"苔丝，你愿意回到我身边来吗？以我的灵魂起誓，我是不愿意就像这样让你走的。"

"决不,决不!我已经下定了决心,我一明白过来,我早就应该明白过来了;我不会再来了。"

"那就再见了,我四个月的堂妹,再见!"

他轻轻一跳,上了马车,理好缰绳,便在高大的结着红色莓子的树篱之间消失了。

苔丝没有望他,只顾慢慢地沿着曲折的篱巷走回家去。天色还早,虽然太阳的下部刚摆脱山峦的羁绊,它那尚觉暗淡的初露的光芒照在身上已有了暖意,尽管落在眼里还不耀眼。附近一个人影也没有,在那篱径之间出现的似乎只有忧伤的十月和她那更忧伤的自己。

Analysis of Major Characters

Tess Durbeyfield: She is intelligent, strikingly attractive, and distinguished by her deep moral sensitivity and passionate intensity. In part, Tess represents the changing role of the agricultural workers in England in the late nineteenth century. Possessing an education that her unschooled parents lack, since she has passed the Sixth Standard of the National Schools, Tess does not quite fit into the folk culture of her predecessors, but financial constraints keep her from rising to a higher station in life. She belongs in that higher world. The Durbeyfields are the surviving members of the noble and ancient family of the D'Urbervilles. There is aristocracy in Tess's blood, visible in her graceful beauty—yet she is forced to work as a farmhand and milkmaid. When she tries to express her joy by singing lower-class folk ballads at the beginning of the third part of the novel, they do not satisfy her—she seems not quite comfortable with those popular songs. But, on the other hand, her diction, while more polished than her mother's, is not quite up to the level of Alec's or Angel's. She is in between, both socially and culturally. Thus, Tess is a symbol of unclear and unstable notions of class in nineteenth-century Britain, where old family lines retained their earlier glamour, but where cold economic realities made sheer wealth more important than inner nobility. Beyond her social symbolism, Tess represents fallen humanity in a religious sense. Tess's clan was once glorious and powerful but is now sadly diminished. Tess thus represents what is known in Christian theology as original sin, the degraded state in which all humans live, even when she is not wholly or directly responsible for the sins for which she is punished. This torment represents the most universal side of Tess: she is the myth of the human who suffers for crimes that are not her own and lives a life more degraded than she deserves.

Alec D'Urberville: An indifferent twenty-four-year-old man, heir to a fortune, and bearer of a name that his father purchased, Alec is the nemesis and downfall of Tess's life. His first name, Alexander, suggests the conqueror—as in Alexander the Great—who seizes what he wants regardless of moral propriety. Yet he is more slippery than a grand conqueror. His full last name, Stoke-D'Urberville, symbolizes the split character of his family, whose origins are simpler than their pretensions to grandeur. After all, Stokes is a blunt and inelegant name. The divided and duplicitous character of Alec is evident to the very end of the novel, when he quickly abandons his newfound Christian faith upon remeeting Tess. It is hard to believe that Alec holds his religion or anything else sincerely. His supposed conversion may only be a new role he is playing. This duplicity of character is so intense in Alec, and its consequences for Tess so severe, that he becomes diabolical. The first part of his surname conjures associations with fiery energies, as in the stoking of a furnace or the flames of hell. His devilish associations are evident when he wields a pitchfork while addressing Tess early in the novel, and when he seduces her as the serpent in Genesis seduced Eve. Additionally, like the famous depiction of Satan in Milton's *Paradise Lost*, Alec does not try to hide his bad qualities. In fact, like Satan, he revels in them. There is frank acceptance in this admission and no shame. Like Tess herself, he represents a larger moral principle rather than a real individual man. Like Satan, Alec symbolizes the base forces of life that drive a person away from moral perfection and greatness.

Angel Clare: A free thinking son born into the family of a provincial parson and determined to set himself up as a farmer instead of going to Cambridge like his conformist brothers, Angel represents a rebellious strife toward a personal vision of goodness. He is a secularist who yearns to work for the "honor and glory of man", rather than for the honor and glory of God in a more distant world. A typical young nineteenth-century progressive, Angel sees human society as a thing to be remolded and improved, and he fervently believes in the nobility of man. He rejects the values handed to him, and sets off in search of his own. His love for Tess, a mere milkmaid and his social inferior, is one expression of his disdain for tradition. This independent spirit contributes to his aura of charisma and general attractiveness that makes him the love object of all the milkmaids with whom he works at Talbothays. As his name suggests, Angel is not quite of this world, but floats above it in a transcendent sphere of his own. He shines rather than burns. His love for Tess may be abstract when he calls her "Daughter of Nature" or "Demeter". Tess may be more an archetype or ideal to him than a flesh and blood woman with a complicated life. Angel's ideals of human purity are too elevated to be applied to actual people. He awakens to the actual complexities of real-world morality after his failure in Brazil, and only then he realizes he has been unfair to Tess. His moral system is readjusted as he is brought down to Earth. Ironically, it is not the angel who guides the human in this novel, but the human who instructs the angel, although at the cost of her own life.

Themes

A Fate and Chance: The characters in Hardy's novel of seduction, abandonment, and murder appear to be under the control of a force greater than they are. Marlott is Tess's home and, as the name of the town implies, her lot in life appears to be marred or damaged. As the novel opens, Tess's father, John Durbeyfield, learns that he is the last remaining member of the once illustrious D'Urberville family. The parson who tells him admits he had previously "resolved not to disturb Durbeyfield with such a useless piece of information", but he is unable to control his "impulses". This event, which starts Tess's tragedy, seems unavoidable, as do many others in the novel. In scene after scene something goes wrong. The most obvious scene in which fate intervenes occurs when Tess writes Angel a letter telling him of her past, but upon pushing it under his door, she unwittingly pushes it under the rug on the floor in the room. If only he could have found it and read it before they were married. If only Angel could have danced with Tess that spring day when they first met. But for Hardy, like Tess, the Earth is a "blighted star" without hope. At the end of the novel, after Tess dies, Hardy writes, "'Justice' was done, and the President of the Immortals, in Aeschylean phrase, had ended his sport with Tess". Tess was powerless to change her fate, because she had been the plaything of a malevolent universe.

Culture Clash: During Tess's time, the industrialization of the cities was diminishing the quality of life of the inhabitants of rural areas. The contrast between what is rural (and therefore good) and what is urban (and therefore bad) is apparent in Tess's last names. When Tess is unquestioningly innocent she is "of the field", as the name Durbeyfield implies. D'Urberville invokes both "urban" and "village," and because it belongs to a diminished ancient family, the name is further associated with decrepitude and decay. It is significant that Angel's "fall" happens when he was "nearly entrapped by a woman much older than himself" in London. When Angel and Tess leave Talbothays to take the milk to the train, Hardy writes, "Modern life stretched out its steam feeler to this point three or four times a day, touched the native existences, and quickly withdrew its feeler again, as if what it touched had been uncongenial." He uses the word "feeler" as if the train were a type of insect, indicating his disgust with the intrusion. Later, he calls the thresher at Flintcomb-Ash "the red tyrant" and says "that the women had come to serve" it. As the old ways fade away, people serve machines but not each other.

Knowledge and Ignorance: Knowledge, whether from formal education or innate sensibility, causes conflict between those who see the truth of a situation, and those who are ignorant. Tess and Angel feel isolated from their parents, who appear set in their ways, unable to grasp new ideas. The intellectual gap between Tess, who has gone to school, and her mother is enormous, but Tess's strong sense of right and wrong widens the gap even more. With Angel, in particular, Hardy recognizes that true knowledge is not just a product of schooling. He contrasts Angel, who alone in his family is not a college graduate, with his brother Cuthbert Clare, a classical scholar who marries the "priggish" Mercy Chant. Although Angel has less formal education, he alone recognizes Tess' worth and wisely chooses her over Mercy's religiosity. When he rejects Tess after their marriage, he does so because her confession "surprised him back into his early teachings", the strict moralistic beliefs of his father. True knowledge, therefore, is understanding one another and one's self, and is an essential ingredient for happiness. The village parson refuses to preside at a Christian burial for Tess's infant because he "was a newcomer, and did not know her." When Angel leaves Tess, "he··· hardly knew that he loved her still."

God and Religion: The religious characters are pious hypocrites, except for Angel's father, who appears to have a good heart. The local parson's hypocritical attitude forces Tess to bury her child in the section of the cemetery reserved for drunkards and suicides. Alec's appearance as a preacher is a thinly disguised criticism of religious convictions that are held for appearances only. After seeing Tess again, Alec's true nature is again revealed. The stifled atmosphere of the Emminster parsonage where Rev. Clare and his wife live is contrasted with the lively warmth of the Talbothays dairy. In one of the novel's few humorous incidents, Angel sits down to eat with his parents and brothers, expecting to feast on the black puddings (a sausage made of blood and suet) and mead Dairyman Crick's wife had given to him when he left the dairy. On the contrary, he is told that the food has been given to the poor and the drink would be saved for its medicinal properties and used as needed. His disappointment is obvious.

Sex: Sex is presented as a natural part of life. The scene of Tess's seduction by Alec takes place in The Chase, an ancient stand of woods that dates from before the time of established societal morality. The valley of the Froom, where Talbothays is located, is described as so lush and fertile that "it was impossible that the most fanciful love should not grow passionate." Tess and Angel fall in love there. Tess's three milkmaid friends toss and turn in their beds, tortured by sexual desire. Later, when Tess forgives Angel his "eight-and-forty hours dissipation with a stranger", Angel cannot forgive her similar fault. Hardy condemns such unequal treatment.

Ache of Modernism: Hardy describes modern farm machinery with infernal imagery. Angel's middle-class fastidiousness makes him reject Tess, a woman in harmony with the natural world. When he parts from her and goes to Brazil, the handsome young man gets so ill that he is reduced to a mere yellow skeleton. All these instances are typically interpreted as indications of the negative consequences of man's separation from nature, both in the creation of destructive machinery and in the inability to rejoice in pure nature.

Film Adaptations

Tess of the D'Urbervilles (1979) is a romance film directed by Roman Polanski, starring Nastassja Kinski, Peter Firth and Leigh Lawson, distributed by Columbia Pictures. The film is set in England, but was actually photographed in France. It is a beautifully visualized period piece that surrounds Tess with the attitudes of her time—attitudes that explain how restricted her behavior must be, and how society views her genuine human emotions as inappropriate. The exploration of doomed young sexuality makes audience agree that the lovers should never grow old. The film is a masterpiece, capturing in amazing detail the scenery and atmosphere of the England of yore. It is a resonant and visually stunning period piece about a beautiful but unfortunate young woman born in an ungrateful time and divided between two men who are bound to abuse her. Even if the film may feel too long, the cinematography and art direction are a marvel to behold. The film's chief drawback, however, is its lack of vitality. The fans of the novel may claim that the film's screenplay deviated from the spirit of the book and that German actress Nastassia Kinski was miscast in the lead. Both Leigh Lawson as Tess' rich cousin and Peter Firth as Tess's husband acquit themselves more honorably.

Fig 5.3 Tess and Alec

Fig 5.4 Tess and Angel

Fig 5.5 Milking the cow   Fig 5.6 Working on a farm

Tess of the D'Urbervilles (2008) is a 4-hour BBC television adaptation, directed by David Blair, starring Gemma Arterton as Tess, Hans Matheson as Alec, and Eddie Redmayne as Angel Clare, produced by David Snodin. The director was thought to be able to make full and gorgeous use of Hardy's depiction of Tess as Earth Goddess. The visceral visual beauty is elicited from the landscape. Arterton is a marvelous Tess, she is wide-eyed and lovely, conveying the pitiful plight of her simple character trapped in an unforgiving society. The adaptation is a reminder of Hardy's timeless appeal until something better comes along. But it soon becomes an arduous trek. The impoverished Durbeyfields and other villagers look a bit too well scrubbed and freshly laundered and that Wessex itself is a bit too pretty.

Fig 5.7 May dance   Fig 5.8 Tess and Alec

Fig 5.9 Tess and Angel   Fig 5.10 Tess and the Stonehenge

A Wonderful Dialogue from the 1979 Film

At the table of an old mansion after the wedding ceremony, Angel gives Tess the family jewel. Tess puts it on and looks very beautiful. Angel pulls her in front of the mirror and embraces her.

Angel: I have a confession to make, my love.

Tess: (*Puzzled*) You have something to confess?

Angel: Why not? You think far too highly of me. Listen. I want you to forgive me and not be angry with me for failing to tell you earlier. I said nothing for fear of losing you. I shall be brief, darling. (*Walking away from her*) Not long before we met, I lived in London for a time. There, I met a woman older than myself. Ours was a false relationship, a sad one. It was all over in a few weeks. (*Looking at Tess*) That's all there is to tell. Do you forgive me?

Tess: (*Walking towards Angel*), Oh, Angel. (*Embracing him*)

Angel: You're so utterly good and gentle. I was mad to fear your resentment.

Tess: (*Releasing the embrace*) I have a confession too. Angel. Something of the same kind.

Angel: What confession?

Tess: I'll be just as brief. (*Sitting down*) His name is D'Urberville, like mine, Alexander D'Urberville. His family bought the title. Their real name is Stoke. (*Angle sitting down*) It was fate that drove me to work for false relations as a way of helping my own folk to live. Alec, Alexander, took advantage of me, relying on his strength and my fear. I became his mistress in despair without love. Like yours, my sad union ended after a few weeks. I bore a child, which died very young. My life was in ruins till the day I met you.

Angel: (*Standing up and stirring the fire*) I'm going out. (*Walking out*)

Angel is walking on a path in a low spirit. Tess runs out of the mansion and approaches him.

Tess: You don't forgive me? I forgive you, Angel.

Angel: Yes. I know.

Tess: But you··· you don't forgive me?

Angel: You were one person. Now you are another. Have mercy (*Laughing bitterly and walking on*).

Tess: Angel?

Angel: Have mercy. (*Still laughing bitterly*)

Tess: Angel. What do you mean by that laugh? How can you speak to me like this? It frightens me. How can you?

Angel: You are not the woman I loved.

Tess: Well, who am I, then?

Angel: Another woman in her shape (*still walking on*).

Tess: (*Stopping and speaking to herself*) He says···he says I'm not the woman he loved but another woman in her shape. (*Running towards Angel*) Angel, please, I was a child, a child when it happened. I knew nothing of men.

Angel: (*Seriously*) You were sinned against, that I grant you.

Tess: So you don't forgive me.

Angel: I forgive you. But forgiveness isn't all.

Tess: Nor love me?

Angel: I cannot help associating your lack of firmness with the decline of your family. Decrepit families imply deficient willpower and decadent conduct. I thought you were a child of nature. But you were the last in a line of degenerate aristocrats.

Angel walks on. Tess stands there silently for a while, then walks back alone.

 Discussions

1. Alec takes Tess's advantage by her fear and his strength. Since Angel has been away for a long time without a message to her, Alec wins her back. But after Angel comes back and finds her, Tess kills Alec and tries to escape. What's your opinion about Alec?
2. On Tess's child's last night alive, why does Tess's father lock the door to keep the parson away? And then why does the parson refuse to give the child a Christian burial?
3. After Angel tells Tess about his dissipation with a woman in London, Tess forgives him immediately. But after Tess tells him about her past, he leaves her. What's your opinion about Angel?
4. Several years after he leaves Tess, Angel comes back to find her, which leads to her killing Alec. Do you think that the tragedy can be avoided? If there is such a case in life, what should the people involved do to avoid making the situation worse?
5. The 1979 film omits some details of the original work and even makes some changes. Please name some of them and try to explain why the director does so.

Unit 6　Charles Dickens and *A Tale of Two Cities*

Charles Dickens didn't write much about historical events. *A Tale of Two Cities* (1859) is an exception. It is set in London and Paris before and during the French Revolution. It depicts the plight of the French peasantry demoralised by the French aristocracy in the years leading up to the revolution, the corresponding brutality demonstrated by the revolutionaries toward the former aristocrats in the early years of the revolution, and many unflattering social parallels with life in London during the same time period. It follows the lives of several protagonists through these events. The most notable are Charles Darnay and Sydney Carton. Darnay is a former French aristocrat who falls victim to the indiscriminate wrath of the revolution despite his virtuous nature, and Carton is a dissipated English barrister who endeavours to redeem his ill-spent life out of his unrequited love for Darnay's wife.

Fig 6.1　Charles Dickens

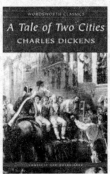

Fig 6.2　A Book Cover of *A Tale of Two Cities*

Plot

The year is 1775, and social ills plague both France and England. Jerry Cruncher, an odd-job man who works for Tellson's Bank, stops the Dover mail-coach with an urgent message for Jarvis Lorry. The message instructs Lorry to wait at Dover for a young woman, and Lorry responds with the cryptic words, "Recalled to Life." At Dover, Lorry is met by Lucie Manette, a young orphan whose father, a once-eminent doctor whom she supposed dead, has been discovered in France. Lorry escorts Lucie to Paris, where they meet Defarge, a former servant of Doctor Manette, who has kept Manette safe in a garret. Driven mad by eighteen years in the Bastille, Manette spends all of his time making shoes, a hobby he learned while in prison. Lorry assures Lucie that her love and devotion can recall her father to life, and indeed they do.

The year is now 1780. Charles Darnay stands accused of treason against the English crown. A bombastic lawyer named Stryver pleads Darnay's case, but it is not until his drunk, good-for-nothing colleague, Sydney Carton, assists him that the court acquits Darnay. Carton clinches his argument by pointing out that he himself bears an uncanny resemblance to the defendant, which undermines the prosecution's case for unmistakably identifying Darnay as the spy the authorities spotted. Lucie and Doctor Manette watched the court proceedings, and that night, Carton escorts Darnay to a tavern and asks how it feels to receive the sympathy of a woman like Lucie. Carton despises and resents Darnay because he reminds him of all that he himself has given up and might have been.

In France, the cruel Marquis Evrémonde runs down a plebian child with his carriage. Manifesting an attitude typical of the aristocracy in regard to the poor at that time, the Marquis shows no regret, but instead curses the peasantry and hurries home to his chateau, where he awaits the arrival of his nephew, Darnay, from England. Arriving later that night, Darnay curses his uncle and the French aristocracy for its abominable treatment of the people. He renounces his identity as an Evrémonde and announces his intention to return to England. That night, the Marquis is murdered; the murderer has left a note signed with the nickname adopted by French revolutionaries: "Jacques."

A year passes, and Darnay asks Manette for permission to marry Lucie. He says that, if Lucie accepts, he will reveal his true identity to Manette. Carton, meanwhile, also pledges his love to Lucie, admitting that, though his life is worthless, she has helped him dream of a better, more valuable existence. On the streets of London, Jerry Cruncher gets swept up in the funeral procession for a spy named Roger Cly. Later that night, he demonstrates his talents as a "Resurrection-Man", sneaking into the cemetery to steal and sell Cly's body. In Paris, meanwhile, another English spy known as John Barsad drops into Defarge's wine shop. Barsad hopes to turn up evidence concerning the mounting revolution, which is still in its covert stages. Madame Defarge sits in the shop knitting a secret registry of those whom the revolution seeks to execute. Back in London, Darnay, on the morning of his wedding, keeps his promise to Manette; he reveals his true identity and, that night, Manette relapses into his old prison habit of making shoes. After nine days, Manette regains his presence of mind, and soon joins the newlyweds on their honeymoon. Upon Darnay's return, Carton pays him a visit and asks for his friendship. Darnay assures Carton that he is always welcome in their home.

The year is now 1789. The peasants in Paris storm the Bastille and the French Revolution begins. The revolutionaries murder aristocrats in the streets, and Gabelle, a man charged with the maintenance of the Evrémonde estate, is imprisoned. Three years later, he writes to Darnay, asking to be rescued. Despite the threat of great danger to his person, Darnay departs immediately for France.

As soon as Darnay arrives in Paris, the French revolutionaries arrest him as an emigrant. Lucie and Manette make their way to Paris in hopes of saving him. Darnay remains in prison for a year and three months before receiving a trial. In order to help free him, Manette uses his considerable influence with the revolutionaries, who sympathize with him for having served time in the Bastille. Darnay receives an acquittal, but that same night he is arrested again. The charges, this time, come from Defarge and his vengeful wife. Carton arrives in Paris with a plan to rescue Darnay and obtains the help of John Barsad, who turns out to be Solomon Pross, the long-lost brother of Miss Pross, Lucie's loyal servant.

At Darnay's trial, Defarge produces a letter that he discovered in Manette's old jail cell in the Bastille. The letter explains the cause of Manette's imprisonment. Years ago, the brothers Evrémonde (Darnay's father and uncle) enlisted Manette's medical assistance. They asked him to tend to a woman, whom one of the brothers had raped, and her brother, whom the same brother had stabbed fatally. Fearing that Manette might report their misdeeds, the Evrémondes had him arrested. Upon hearing this story, the jury condemns Darnay for the crimes of his ancestors and sentences him to die within twenty-four hours. That night, at the Defarge's wine shop, Carton overhears Madame Defarge plotting to have Lucie and her daughter (also Darnay's daughter) executed as well; Madame Defarge, it turns out, is the surviving sibling of the man and woman killed by the Evrémondes. Carton arranges for the Manettes' immediate departure from France. He then visits Darnay in prison, tricks him into changing clothes with him, and, after dictating a letter of explanation, drugs his friend unconscious. Barsad carries Darnay, now disguised as Carton, to an awaiting coach, while Carton, disguised as Darnay, awaits execution. As Darnay, Lucie, their child, and Dr. Manette speed away from Paris, Madame Defarge arrives at Lucie's apartment, hoping to arrest her. There she finds the supremely protective Miss Pross. A scuffle ensues, and Madame Defarge dies by the bullet of her own gun. Sydney Carton meets his death at the guillotine, and the narrator confidently asserts that Carton dies with the knowledge that he has finally imbued his life with meaning.

Select Reading: Chapter 52

The key was put in the lock, and turned. Before the door was opened, or as it opened, a man said in a low voice, in English: "He has never seen me here; I have kept out of his way. Go you in alone; I wait near. Lose no time!"

The door was quickly opened and closed, and there stood before him face to face, quiet, intent upon him, with the light of a smile on his features, and a cautionary finger on his lip, Sydney Carton.

There was something so bright and remarkable in his look, that, for the first moment, the prisoner misdoubted him to be an apparition of his own imagining. But, he spoke, and it was his voice; he took the prisoner's hand, and it was his real grasp.

"Of all the people upon earth, you least expected to see me?" he said.

"I could not believe it to be you. I can scarcely believe it now. You are not"—the apprehension came suddenly into his mind—"a prisoner?"

"No, I am accidentally possessed of a power over once of the keepers here, and in virtue of it I stand before you. I come from her—your wife, dear Darnay."

The prisoner wrung his hand.

"I bring you a request from her."

"What is it?"

"A most earnest, pressing, and emphatic entreaty, addressed to you in the most pathetic tones of the voices so dear to you, that you well remember."

The prisoner turned his face partly aside.

"You have no time to ask me why I bring it, or what it means; I have no time to tell you. You must comply with it—take off those boots you wear, and draw on these of mine."

There was a chair against the wall of the cell, behind the prisoner. Carton, pressing forward, had already, with the speed of lightning, got him done into it, and stood over him, barefoot.

"Draw on these boots of mine. Put your hands to them; put your will to them. Quick!"

"Carton, there is no escaping from this place; it never can be done. You will only die with me. It is madness."

"It would be madness if I asked you to escape; but do I? When I ask you to pass out at that door, tell me it is madness and remain here. Change that cravat for this one of mine, that coat for this of mine. While you do it, let me take this ribbon from your hair, and shake out your hair like this of mine!"

With wonderful quickness, and with a strength both of will and action, that appeared quite supernatural, he forced all these changes upon him. The prisoner was like a young child in his hands.

"Carton! Dear carton! It is madness. It cannot be accomplished, it never can be done, it has been attempted, and has always failed. I implore you not to add your death to the bitterness of mine."

"Do I ask you, my dear Darnay, to pass the door? When I ask that, refuse. There are pen and ink and paper on this table. Is your hand steady enough to write?"

"It was when you came in."

"Steady it again, and write what I shall dictate. Quick, friend, quick!"

Pressing his hand to his bewildered head, Darnay sat down at the table, Carton, with his right hand in his breast, stood close beside him.

译文：钥匙插进锁孔，一拧，门还没开，或正要开，他听见有人在低声说话，说的是英语："他从没有在这儿见过我，我是避开他的。你一个人进去吧，我就在附近等候，抓紧时间。"

门匆匆打开又关上了。面对面站在他眼前，脸上挂着笑意，一声不响，凝望着他，一根手指警告地放在嘴唇前的是西德尼·卡尔顿。

他的形象是那样光辉，那样出众，囚犯刚见到他时几乎误以为是产生于自己想象中的幽灵。但是他却说话了，声音也是他的声音。他抓住囚犯的手，那手也确实是他的手。

"在全世界的人里你最想不到会跟你见面的恐怕就是我吧？"他说。

"我简直不能相信是你。现在也还难以相信。你不会是也坐牢了吧？"他突然担心起来。

"没有。我只偶然控制了这儿一个管牢的，借此机会来看看你。我是从她——你的妻子，哪儿来的，亲爱的达尔内。"

囚犯绞着自己的手。

"我给你带来了她的一个请求。"

"什么请求？"

"一个最真诚、最迫切、最重要的请求。是你最难忘的亲爱的声音用最动人的口气提出的请求。"

囚犯把脸微微地扭到了一边。

"你没有时间了，别问我为什么带来这个愿望，也别问它是什么意思，我没有时间告诉你。

你得照办,脱掉脚上的靴子,穿上我的。"

牢房里靠墙有一把椅子,正在囚徒身后。卡尔顿往前一挤,像闪电一样把他推进椅子,自己光着脚,俯看着他。

"穿上我的靴子。用手拉,使劲,快!"

"卡尔顿,从这个地方是逃不掉的。根本办不到。你会跟我一起死去的。这是发疯。"

"我要是叫你逃倒真是发疯。可我叫你逃了没有?到我叫你逃出那道门的时候再说是发疯吧,你还可以不走呢!把你的蝴蝶结跟我的交换,上衣也跟我交换。你换衣服,我取下你这条发带,把你的头发抖散,弄得跟我的一样。"

卡尔顿动作神速。他们靠仿佛超自然的意志力和行动力强迫他迅速换了装,囚犯在他手下完全像个儿童。

"卡尔顿,亲爱的卡尔顿!这是发疯。这是办不到的,根本不行。有人干过,全都失败了。我请求你别在我的痛苦之上再赔上你的这条命了。"

"我要你走出那道门没有?到我要你走的时候再拒绝吧。桌子上有笔,有墨水,有纸。你的手还能写字而不发抖么?"

"你刚进来的时候,我的手倒是不发抖的。"

"那就别再发抖,照我所说的写吧!快,朋友,快!"

达内尔一手摸着感到困惑的头,在桌旁坐了下来。卡尔顿右手放在前襟里,逼近他站着。

Analysis of Major Characters

Sydney Carton: Sydney Carton proves the most dynamic character. He first appears as a lazy, alcoholic attorney who cannot muster even the smallest amount of interest in his own life. He describes his existence as a supreme waste of life and takes every opportunity to declare that he cares for nothing and no one. But Carton in fact feels something that he perhaps cannot articulate. In his conversation with the recently acquitted Charles Darnay, Carton's comments about Lucie Manette, while bitter and sardonic, betray his interest in and bud feelings for the gentle girl. Eventually, Carton reaches a point where he can admit his feelings to Lucie herself. Before Lucie weds Darnay, Carton professes his love to her, though he still persists in seeing himself as essentially worthless. This marks a vital transition for Carton and lays the foundation for the supreme sacrifice that he makes at the novel's end. On the one hand, Carton is regarded as a Christ-like figure, a selfless martyr whose death enables the happiness of his beloved and ensures his own immortality. On the other hand, Carton's death is considered to be redemptive. As Carton goes to the guillotine, the narrator tells readers that he envisions a beautiful, idyllic Paris "rising from the abyss" and sees "the evil of this time and of the previous time of which this is the natural birth, gradually making expiation for itself and wearing out." Just as the apocalyptic violence of the revolution precedes a new society's birth, perhaps it is only in the sacrifice of his life that Carton can establish his life's great worth.

Madame Defarge: Possessing a remorseless bloodlust, Madame Defarge embodies the chaos of the French Revolution. The initial chapters of the novel find her sitting quietly and knitting in the wine shop. However, her apparent passivity belies her relentless thirst for vengeance. With her stitches, she secretly knits a register of the names of the revolution's intended victims. As the revolution breaks into full force, Madame Defarge reveals her true viciousness. She turns on Lucie in particular, and, as violence sweeps Paris, she invades Lucie's physical and psychological space. She bursts into the young woman's apartment in an attempt to catch Lucie mourning Darnay's imminent execution. Dickens notes that Madame Defarge's hatefulness does not reflect any inherent flaw, but rather results from the oppression and personal tragedy that she has suffered at the hands of the aristocracy, specifically the Evrémondes, to whom Darnay is related by blood, and Lucie by marriage. Madame Defarge's death by a bullet from her own gun—she dies in a scuffle with Miss Pross—symbolizes Dickens's belief that the sort of vengeful attitude embodied by Madame Defarge ultimately proves a self-damning one.

Doctor Manette: Dickens uses Doctor Manette to illustrate one of the dominant motifs of the novel: the essential mystery that surrounds every human being. As Jarvis Lorry makes his way toward France to recover Manette, the narrator reflects that "every human creature is constituted to be that profound secret and mystery to every other." For much of the novel, the cause of Manette's incarceration remains a mystery both to the other characters and to the reader. Even when the story concerning the evil Marquis Evrémonde comes to light, the conditions of Manette's imprisonment remain hidden. Though the reader never learns exactly how Manette suffered, his relapses into trembling sessions of shoemaking evidence the depth of his misery. Like Carton, Manette undergoes a drastic change over the course of the novel. He is transformed from an insensate prisoner who mindlessly cobbles shoes into a man of distinction. The contemporary reader tends to understand human individuals not as fixed entities but rather as impressionable and reactive beings, affected and influenced by their surroundings and by the people with whom they interact. In Dickens's age, however, this notion was rather revolutionary. Manette's transformation testifies to the tremendous impact of relationships and experience on life. The strength that he displays while dedicating himself to rescuing Darnay seems to confirm the lesson that Carton learns by the end of the novel—that not only does one's treatment of others play an important role in others' personal development, but also that the very worth of one's life is determined by its impact on the lives of others.

Charles Darnay and Lucie Manette: E. M. Forster famously criticized Dickens's characters as flat, lamenting that they seem to lack the depth and complexity that make literary characters realistic and believable. Charles Darnay and Lucie Manette certainly fit this description. A man of honor, respect and courage, Darnay conforms to the archetype of the hero but never exhibits the kind of inner struggle that Carton and Doctor Manette undergo. His opposition to the Marquis' snobbish and cruel aristocratic values is admirable, but, ultimately, his virtue proves too uniform, and he fails to exert any compelling force on the imagination. Along similar lines, Lucie likely seems to modern readers as uninteresting and two-dimensional as Darnay. In every detail of her being, she embodies compassion, love and virtue. She manifests her purity of devotion to Darnay in her unquestioning willingness to wait at a street corner for two hours each day, on the off chance that he will catch sight of her from his prison window. While Darnay and Lucie may not act as windows into the gritty essence of humanity, in combination with other characters they contribute to a more detailed picture of human nature. First, they provide the light that counters the vengeful Madame Defarge's darkness, revealing the moral aspects of the human soul so noticeably absent from Madame Defarge. Secondly, throughout the novel they manifest a virtuousness that Carton strives to attain and that inspires his very real and believable struggles to become a better person.

Themes

Resurrection: Book I, named "Recalled to Life", concerns the rediscovery of Doctor Manette, who has been jailed in the Bastille for eighteen years. Code for the secret mission to rescue him from Paris is the simple phrase "recalled to life", which starts Mr. Lorry thinking about the fact that the prisoner has been out of society long enough to have been considered dead. This theme is treated more humorously through Jerry Cruncher's profession as a Resurrection-Man. Although his trade of digging up dead bodies and selling their parts seems gruesome, it provides him with the crucial knowledge that a spy named Roger Cly has been literally resurrected—in that he was never buried at all. The most important resurrections in the novel are those of Charles Darnay. First, Sydney Carton's resemblance to him saves him from being convicted and executed in England, and then, the same resemblance allows the latter to switch places with him in the Conciergerie. These resurrections are surrounded with heavily religious language that compares Carton's sacrifice of his own life for others' sins to Christ's sacrifice on the cross.

Class Struggle: Dickens chooses a side, ultimately showing opposition to the revolution due to the ruthless and uncontrolled force of its aroused mobs. Even so, the story of the Marquis's rape of the peasant along with other details of aristocratic mistreatment of the lower classes provides some justification for the goals of the French mob. In the end, he portrays the mob as having moved beyond the pale to a degree beyond what happened in England. The French mob acts with such force that it resembles a natural element like fire or water.

Fate: This historical novel carefully marks the passage of time, and the introductory sentences of chapters often contain specific references to years or months. Keeping track of time is important because time carries out fate, which is an extremely important presence. From the first chapter, which describes trees waiting to be formed into guillotines in France, Dickens describes the revolution as something inevitable. Individual characters also feel the pull of fate. For example, Darnay feels himself drawn back to France as if under the influence of a magnet. Lucie's presentiment that the noise of feet echoing in her home portends some future intrusion correctly predicts what is bound to happen—Darnay's past does catch up with him, and he must pay for the wrongs of his ancestors. Fate operates ominously rather than optimistically among the characters, especially given Madame Defarge's representation as one of the mythical fates connecting the future to darkness.

Doubles: From the very title of the novel, Dickens signals that this is a novel about duality. Things, from the settings (London, Paris) to the people, come in pairs. The pairs are occasionally related together. A crucial incidence of related doubling involves the resemblance between Charles Darnay and Sydney Carton, a similarity that drives the plot. The pairs are more often oppositional, just as in the dichotomous opening: "It was the best of times, it was the worst of times." Lucie's physical and moral brightness is played off against the dark Madame Defarge.

Reversals and Inversions: One of the primary effects of the upheaval caused by the French Revolution was due to its literally revolutionary influence. It turned society upside down and banged it on its head. When Darnay returns to France, he observes that the noblemen are in prison, while criminals are their jailors. The replacement of Darnay with Carton at the end of the novel is another reversal, illustrating that a bad man can replace a good man in such a revolutionary society.

Family: The novel focuses attention on the preservation of family groups. The first manifestation of this theme occurs in Lucie's trip to meet her father in Paris. Although she worries that he will seem like a ghost rather than her father, the possibility of a reunion is enough to make her undertake the long trip. After Lucie marries Charles Darnay, the novel tends to be concerned with their struggle to keep their family together. When Darnay laments his own death sentence, it is for the sake of his family, not for his own sake. The final triumph is the sacrifice of Carton, a man who is unattached to any sort of family, who thus preserves the group consisting of the Doctor, Lucie, her husband and her children.

Social Injustice: This theme is related to the theme of class struggle, because those who feel the negative effects of injustice begin to struggle against it. Dickens maintains a complex perspective on the French Revolution because although he did not particularly sympathize with the gruesome and often irrational results, he certainly sympathized with the unrest of the lower orders of society. Dickens vividly paints the aristocratic maltreatment of the lower classes, such as when Monseigneur only briefly stops to toss a coin toward the father of a child whom he has just run over. Because the situation in France was so dire, Dickens portrays the plight of the working class in England as rather difficult, though slightly less difficult than in other works such as *Hard Times* or *Oliver Twist*, which also emphasize social injustice.

Film Adaptations

A Tale of Two Cities (1935) was directed by Jack Conway, starring Ronald Colman as Sydney Carton. It achieves a crisis of extraordinary effectiveness at the guillotine, leaving the audience quivering under its emotional sledge-hammer blows. Ronald Colman gives his ablest performance in years as Sydney Carton.

Fig 6.3 A Poster of the 1935 Film

Fig 6.4 Lucie and her father

Fig 6.5　Lucie and Darnay

Fig 6.6　Lucie and Carton

  A Tale of Two Cities (1958) was directed by Ralph Thomas, starring Dirk Bogarde and Dorothy Tutin. The director insisted on the film being shot in black and white. It was shot in the Loire Valley in France with several thousand American soldiers posted nearby in Orléans used as extras.

Fig 6.7　A Poster of the 1958 Film

Fig 6.8　Lucie, Miss Pross

Fig 6.9　Carton and the Seamstress

Fig 6.10　Carton being guillotined

  A Tale of Two Cities (1980) was directed by Jim Goddard and released on December 2 by Hallmark Hall of Fame Productions. It showed the true love between Carton and the seamstress, Carton and Lucie, and Darnay and Lucie.

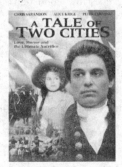
Fig 6.11　A Poster of the 1980 Film

Fig 6.12　Marquis Evrémonde

A Tale of Two Cities (1996), directed by Michael E. Briant, released by BBC Worldwide Limited.

Fig 6.13　A DVD Cover of the 1996 Film

Fig 6.14　Dr. Manette and His Daughter Lucie

Fig 6.15　Lucie and Darnay

Fig 6.16　Lucie and Carton

A Wonderful Dialogue from the 1996 Film

Miss Manette is looking after her father, Dr. Manette, who is lying in bed at home. The servant knocks at the door.

Servant: There is a gentleman?

Dr. Manette: What gentleman? Who is he?

Servant: A Carton, who has been here before, who used not to be presentable.

Miss Manette: (*To father*) I'll see him.

Servant: It is you that he wants. But I told him he is not in the season.

Miss Manette: (*To servant*) Would you serve my father please and take the tray when he finishes it? (*Coming downstairs and seeing Carton standing there*) How good of you to call, Mr. Carton.

Carton: (*Turning back*) Miss Manette.

Miss Manette: I feel you are not well, Mr. Carton.

Carton: I lead a life which is not conducive to good health.

Miss Manette: It is not. Oh, forgive me, Mr. Carton, a pity to live no better life.

Carton: God knows it is.

Miss Manette: Then why not change it?

Carton: It is too late for that. I shall never be better than I am. I should sink lower and be worse (*Sobbing. Miss Manette is a little shocked and goes to close the door.*) I pray you to forgive me, Miss Manette. I broke down before the knowledge of what I did want to say to you. Will you hear me?

Miss Manette: If it will do anything good, Mr. Carton, if it will make you any happier, then, it will make me very glad.

Carton: God bless you for your sweet compassion, Miss Manette. I'm like one who died young. All my life might have been.

Miss Manette: Mr. Carton, I'm sure that the best part of it might still be. I'm sure that you might be much, much worthier of yourself.

Carton: Say of yourself, Miss Manette. I'll know better and never forget it. I distress you. Therefore, I shall be brief, Miss Manette. If it had been possible that you could have returned the love of a man you see before you, a poor creature of misuse as you know him to be, he would have been conscious that in spite of his happiness, he would have brought you to misery and sorrow and pulled you down with him. I know you have no tendency for me, and I ask not. I am even thankful that it can not be.

Miss Manette: Without it, can I not save you? Can I not recall you to forgive me again to a better course?

Carton: No, Miss Manette. All you can ever do for me is done. I will show you to know that you've given the last dream of my soul. Since I know you, Miss Manette, I have had formed an idea of striving afresh, beginning anew all I dream. But I wish you to know that it is you who inspired it.

Miss Manette: It's unfortunate to have made you more unhappy than you were before you knew me.

Carton: Don't say so, Miss Manette, for you would have claimed anything good, but you are not the cause of my becoming worse.

Miss Manette: Then have I no power for good with a tool?

Carton: The uttermost good that I am capable of I have come here to realize. Let me carry to the rest of my life to remembrance, that I open my heart to you the last of all the world.

Miss Manette: What I entreat you to believe again and again is capable of better feel…

Carton: I entreat you to know more, Miss Manette. I have proved myself no better. I only ask you never to share my secret with any one.

Miss Manette: Mr. Carton, the secret is yours, not mine. And I promise to respect you.

Servant: (*Coming*) There's another gentleman.

Darnay: I think I am referred to. Oh, Mr. Carton.

Carton: Ah, Mr. Darney. I am about to leave. Goodbye, Miss Manette. (*Kissing her in the hand*) and thank you, Miss B (*Leaving and Miss Manette follows him out.*) My last supplication of all is: for you and for any one dear to you I'll do anything. Please always remember that I am in this world a man who would give his life to keep a life you love beside you. Thanks again. God bless you.

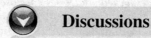

Discussions

1. One of the novel's most important motifs is the figure of the double. What is the effect of Dickens's doubling technique? Does he use doubles to draw contrasts, comparisons, or both?
2. Some critics charge that Dickens, in much of his work, failed to create meaningful characters because he exaggerated them to parodic extremes. Do you find this a fair assessment of his characterization in the novel? Does the author's use of caricature detract from his novel's ability to speak to human nature?
3. Dickens relies heavily on coincidence to fuel the plot of *A Tale of Two Cities*: letters are found bearing crucial information, for example, and long-lost brothers are discovered in crowded public places. Do such incidents strengthen or weaken the plot and overall themes of the novel?
4. Discuss Dickens's attitude toward the French Revolution. Does he sympathize with the revolutionaries?
5. Based on Dickens's portrayals of the villainous characters in his novel (particularly Madame Defarge), what conclusions might the reader draw about the author's notions of human evil? Does he seem to think that people are born evil? If so, do they lack the ability to change? Or does he suggest that circumstances drive human beings to their acts of cruelty?

Unit 7 Charles Dickens and *David Copperfield*

Charles Dickens (1812—1870) was an English writer and social critic. He created some of the world's most memorable fictional characters and is generally regarded as the greatest novelist of the Victorian period. His notable works include *The Pickwick Papers* (1836—1837), *Oliver Twist* (1837—1839), *David Copperfield* (1849—1850), *Bleak House* (1852—1853), *Hard Times* (1854), *A Tale of Two Cities* (1859), *Great Expectations* (1861) and so on. During his life, his works enjoyed unprecedented fame, and by the twentieth century his literary genius was broadly acknowledged by critics and scholars. Authors often draw their portraits of characters from people they have known in real life. *David Copperfield* is regarded as strongly autobiographical.

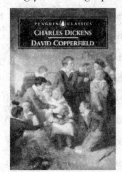

Fig 7.1　Charles Dickens　　　　Fig 7.2　A Book Cover of *David Copperfield*

Plot

Now a grown man, David Copperfield tells the story of his youth. As a young boy, he lives happily with his mother and his nurse, Peggotty. His father died before he was born. During David's early childhood, his mother marries the violent Mr. Murdstone, who brings his strict sister, Miss Murdstone, into the house. The Murdstones treat David cruelly, and David bites Mr. Murdstone's hand during one beating. The Murdstones send David away to school.

Peggotty takes David to visit her family in Yarmouth, where David meets Peggotty's brother, Mr. Peggotty, and his two adopted children, Ham and Little Em'ly. Mr. Peggotty's family lives in a boat turned upside down—a space they share with Mrs. Gummidge, the widowed wife of Mr. Peggotty's former partner. After this visit, David attends school at Salem House, which is run by a man named Mr. Creakle. David befriends and idolizes an egotistical young man named James Steerforth. David also befriends Tommy Traddles, an unfortunate, fat young boy who is bullied more than the others.

David's mother dies, and David returns home, where the Murdstones neglect him. He works at

Mr. Murdstone's wine-bottling business and moves in with Mr. Micawber, who mismanages his finances. When Mr. Micawber leaves London to escape his creditors, David decides to search for his father's aunt, Miss Betsey Trotwood—his only living relative. He walks a long distance to Miss Betsey's home, and she takes him in on the advice of her mentally unstable friend, Mr. Dick. Miss Betsey sends David to a school run by a man named Doctor Strong. David moves in with Mr. Wickfield and his daughter, Agnes, while he attends school. Agnes and David become best friends. Among Wickfield's boarders is Uriah Heep, a snakelike young man who often involves himself in matters that are none of his business. David graduates and goes to Yarmouth to visit Peggotty, who is now married to Mr. Barkis, the carrier. David reflects on what profession he should pursue.

On his way to Yarmouth, David encounters James Steerforth, and they take a detour to visit Steerforth's mother. They arrive in Yarmouth, where Steerforth and the Peggottys become fond of one another. When they return from Yarmouth, Miss Betsey persuades David to pursue a career as a proctor, a kind of lawyer. David apprentices himself at the London firm of Spenlow and Jorkins and takes up lodgings with a woman named Mrs. Crupp. Mr. Spenlow invites David to his house for a weekend. There, David meets Spenlow's daughter, Dora, and quickly falls in love with her.

In London, David is reunited with Tommy Traddles and Mr. Micawber. Word reaches David, through Steerforth, that Mr. Barkis is terminally ill. David journeys to Yarmouth to visit Peggotty in her hour of need. Little Em'ly and Ham, now engaged, are to be married upon Mr. Barkis's death. David, however, finds Little Em'ly upset over her impending marriage. When Mr. Barkis dies, Little Em'ly runs off with Steerforth, who she believes will make her a lady. Mr. Peggotty is devastated but vows to find Little Em'ly and bring her home.

Miss Betsey visits London to inform David that her financial security has been ruined because Mr. Wickfield has joined into a partnership with Uriah Heep. David, who has become increasingly infatuated with Dora, vows to work as hard as he can to make their life together possible. Mr. Spenlow, however, forbids Dora from marrying David. Mr. Spenlow dies in a carriage accident that night, and Dora goes to live with her two aunts. Meanwhile, Uriah Heep informs Doctor Strong that he suspects Doctor Strong's wife, Annie, of having an affair with her young cousin, Jack Maldon.

Dora and David marry, and Dora proves a terrible housewife, incompetent in her chores. David loves her anyway and is generally happy. Mr. Dick facilitates a reconciliation between Doctor Strong and Annie, who was not, in fact, cheating on her husband. Miss Dartle, Mrs. Steerforth's ward, summons David and informs him that Steerforth has left Little Em'ly. Miss Dartle adds that Steerforth's servant, Littimer, has proposed to her and that Little Em'ly has run away. David and Mr. Peggotty enlist the help of Little Em'ly's childhood friend Martha, who locates Little Em'ly and brings Mr. Peggotty to her. Little Em'ly and Mr. Peggotty decide to move to Australia, as do the Micawbers, who first save the day for Agnes and Miss Betsey by exposing Uriah Heep's fraud against Mr. Wickfield.

A powerful storm hits Yarmouth and kills Ham while he attempts to rescue a shipwrecked sailor. The sailor turns out to be Steerforth. Meanwhile, Dora falls ill and dies. David leaves the country to travel abroad. His love for Agnes grows. When David returns, he and Agnes, who has long harbored a secret love for him, get married and have several children. David pursues his writing career with increasing commercial success.

Select Reading: Chapter IV

I come into the second-best parlour after breakfast, with my books, and an exercise-book, and a slate. My mother is ready for me at her writing-desk, but not half so ready as Mr. Murdstone in his easy-chair by the window (though he pretends to be reading a book), or as Miss Murdstone, sitting near my mother stringing steel beads. The very sight of these two has such an influence over me, that I begin to feel the words I have been at infinite pains to get into my head, all sliding away, and going I don't know where. I wonder where they do go?

I hand the first book to my mother. Perhaps it is a grammar, perhaps a history or geography. I take a last drowning look at the page as I give it into her hand, and start off aloud at a racing pace while I have got it fresh. I trip over a word. Mr. Murdstone looks up. I redden, tumbling over half-a-dozen words, and stop. I think my mother would show me the book if she dared, but she does not dare, and she says softly:

"Oh, Davy, Davy!"

"Now, Clara," says Mr. Murdstone, "be firm with the boy. Don't say, 'oh, Davy, Davy!' That's childish. He knows his lesson, or he does not know it."

"He does not know it," Miss Murdstone interposes awfully.

"I am really afraid he does not," says my mother.

"Then, you see, Clara," returns Miss Murdstone, "you should just give him the book back, and make him know it."

"Yes, certainly," says my mother, "that is what I intend to do, my dear Jane. Now Davy, try once more, and don't be stupid."

I obey the first clause of the injunction by trying once more, but am not so successful with the second, for I am very stupid. I tumble down before I get to the old place, at a point where I was all right before, and stop to think. But I can't think about the lesson. I think of the number of yards of net in Miss Murdstone's cap, or of the price of Mr. Murdstone's dressing-gown, or any such ridiculous problem that I have no business with, and don't want to have anything at all to do with. Mr. Murdstone makes a movement of impatience which I have been expecting for a long time. Miss Murdstone does the same. My mother glances submissively at them, shuts the book, and lays it by as an arrear to be worked out when my other tasks are done.

There is a pile of these arrears very soon, and it swells like a rolling snowball. The bigger it gets, the more stupid I get. The case is so hopeless, and I feel that I am wallowing in such a bog of nonsense, that I give up all idea of getting out, and abandon myself to my fate. The despairing way in which my mother and I look at each other, as I blunder on, is truly melancholy. But the greatest effect in these miserable lessons is when my mother (thinking nobody is observing her) tries to give me the cue by the motion of her lips. At that instant, Miss Murdstone, who has been lying in wait for nothing else all along, says in a deep warning voice:

"Clara!"

My mother starts, colours, and smiles faintly. Mr. Murdstone comes out of his chair, takes the book, throws it at me or boxes my ears with it, and turns me out of the room by the shoulders.

译文：早饭后,我带着书、一本练习簿和一块石板来到那第二号的客厅。母亲已在她的书桌边等着我了,但更着急地等着我的是坐在靠窗安乐椅上的默德斯通先生(虽说他假装在看一本书),或是坐在母亲身边串钢珠的默德斯通小姐。一看到这两人使我受了如此大的影响,我竟开始感到我花了那么大力气记下的单词都溜掉了,都溜到一个我不知道的地方去了。

真的,我不知道它们溜到什么地方去了呢。

我把第一本书交给我母亲。或许是本语法,或许是本历史,或许是本地理。把书交到她手上时,我拼命朝几页书上看了最后一眼,并趁我还记得时就用赛跑的速度一个劲地背。我背错了一个词,默德斯通先生便抬起眼皮看着我。我又背错了一个词,默德斯通小姐便抬起眼皮看着我。我脸红了,结结巴巴,背错了半打单词,终于停下。我想,我母亲准会把书给我看看,如果她敢的话,可她不敢。她只是柔声柔气地说:"哦,卫卫,卫卫!"

"啊,克拉拉,"默德斯通先生说,"对这个孩子必须坚定些。不要说'哦,卫卫,卫卫,'那是很孩子气的。他要么就知道他的功课,要么就是不知道。"

"他不知道,"默德斯通小姐恶声恶气地插言道。

"我真担心他不知道,"母亲说。

"那么,你知道,克拉拉,"默德斯通小姐答道,"你应该把书还给他,教他知道。"

"是啊,当然是啊,"我母亲说,"我正是想那样做,我亲爱的珍。好了,卫卫,再努力一次,不要糊涂哦。"

我遵照这教诲的头半部分,又努力了一次,但执行那下半部分时却不怎么成功,因为我糊涂得不得了。还没背到先前背不下的地方,我就开始出错了,而上次我还能正确地背出来呢。我只好停下去想。可我不是想我的功课。我做不到这点。我想的是默德斯通小姐帽里的兜网有多少码,或默德斯通先生的晨袍值多少钱,或一切与我无关而我也不想与其有关的可笑问题。默德斯通先生不耐烦地动了一下,我早就等着他这么做了。默德斯通小姐也同样动作了一下。我母亲很服从地看了他们一眼便把书合上并把它放到一边,准备等我把别的功课完成后再来补这笔欠账。

很快,这笔欠账就像滚雪球一样积了好大一堆。欠账越多,我越糊涂。情形就是这样令人失望,以至我觉得我已陷入一个荒谬的泥淖而我又已打消了一切脱身的念头,听任命运左右了。我结结巴巴尽出错时,我母亲和我无比沮丧地对看的样子真是令人伤心。但是,这令人痛苦的功课中最令人痛苦的仍是当母亲想努努嘴给我暗示时(她以为没人会注意她)。就在那时,一直在专心致志等着这事发生的默德斯通小姐用很低沉的声音警告道:"克拉拉!"母亲一惊,脸色都变了,充满畏意地笑笑。默德斯通先生从椅子上起身,拿起书朝我扔过来或用书扇我的耳光,然后揪住我肩膀把我揉出了房间。

Analysis of Major Characters

David Copperfield: Although David narrates his story as an adult, he relays the impressions he had from a youthful point of view. His perception of the world deepens as he comes of age. Readers see David's initial innocence in the contrast between his interpretation of events and readers' own understanding of them. Although David is ignorant of Steerforth's treachery, readers are aware from the moment they meet Steerforth that he doesn't deserve the adulation David feels toward him. David doesn't understand why he hates Uriah or why he trusts a boy with a donkey cart who steals his money and leaves him in the road, but we can sense Uriah's devious nature and the boy's treacherous intentions. In David's first-person narration, Dickens conveys the wisdom of the older man implicitly, through the eyes of a child. David's complex character allows for contradiction and development over the course of the novel. Though David is trusting and kind, he also has moments of cruelty, like the scene in which he intentionally distresses Mr. Dick by explaining Miss Betsey's dire situation to him. David also displays great tenderness, as in the moment when he realizes his love for Agnes for the first time. David, especially as a young man in love, can be foolish and romantic. As he grows up, he develops a more mature point of view and searches for a lover who will challenge him and help him grow. David fully matures as an adult when he expresses the sentiment that he values Agnes's calm tranquility over all else in his life.

Betsey Trotwood: David's eccentric and temperamental yet kind-hearted great-aunt, she becomes his guardian after he runs away from a factory in London. She is present on the night of David's birth but leaves after hearing that Clara Copperfield's child is a boy instead of a girl, and is not seen until David is older and flees to her house in Dover from London. She is portrayed as affectionate towards David, and defends him and his late mother when Mr. Murdstone arrives to take custody of David, confronting the man and rebuking him for his abuse of David and his mother, before threatening Mr. Murdstone and driving him off the premises. Universally believed to be a widow, she conceals the existence of her never-do-well husband who constantly bleeds her for money.

Edward Murdstone: The main antagonist of the first half of the novel, he is Young David's cruel stepfather who beats him for falling behind in his studies. David reacts by biting Mr. Murdstone, who then sends him to Salem House, the private school owned by his friend Mr. Creakle. After David's mother dies, Mr Murdstone sends him to work in his factory in London, where he has to clean wine bottles. He appears at Betsey Trotwood's house after David runs away to show signs of repentance when confronted by Copperfield's great-aunt about his treatment of Clara and David, but later in the book readers hear he has married another young woman and applied his old principles of firmness.

Daniel Peggotty: Peggotty's brother, a humble but generous Yarmouth fisherman who takes his nephew Ham and niece Em'ly into his custody after each of them has been orphaned, and welcomes David as a child when he holidays to Yarmouth with Peggotty. When Em'ly is older and runs away with David's friend Steerforth, he travels around the world in search of her. He eventually finds her in London, and after that they emigrate to Australia.

Little Em'ly: A niece of Mr. Peggotty, she is a childhood friend of David Copperfield, who loved her in his childhood days. On the eve of her wedding to her cousin and fiancé, Ham, she abandons him for Steerforth with whom she disappears abroad for several years. After Steerforth deserts her, she doesn't go back home, because she has disgraced herself and her family. Her uncle, Mr. Peggotty, who has been searching for her since she left home, finds her in London (the text implies that she was on the brink of being forced into prostitution). To have a fresh start away from her now degraded reputation, she and her uncle emigrate to Australia.

Uriah Heep: Uriah serves a foil to David and contrasts David's qualities of innocence and compassion with his own corruption. Though Uriah is raised in a cruel environment similar to David's, his upbringing causes him to become bitter and vengeful rather than honest and hopeful. Dickens's physical description of Uriah marks him as a demonic character. He refers to Uriah's movements as snakelike and gives him red hair and red eyes. Uriah and David not only have opposing characteristics but also operate at cross-purposes. For example, whereas Uriah wishes to marry Agnes only to hurt David, David's marriages are both motivated by love. The frequent contrast between Uriah's and David's sentiments emphasizes David's kindness and moral integrity. While David's character development is a process of increased self-understanding, Uriah grows in his desire to exercise control over himself and other characters. As Uriah gains more power over Mr. Wickfield, his sense of entitlement grows and he becomes more and more power-hungry. The final scenes of the novel, in which Uriah praises his jail cell because it helps him know what he should do, show Uriah's need to exert control even when he is a helpless prisoner. But imprisonment does not redeem his evil. It compounds his flaws. To the end, Uriah plots strategies to increase his control. Because he deploys his strategies to selfish purposes that bring harm to others, he stands out as the novel's greatest villain.

James Steerforth: Steerforth is a slick, egotistical, wealthy young man whose sense of self-importance overwhelms all his opinions. Steerforth underscores the difference between what readers understand and what David sees and fails to see in his youthful naïveté. David takes Steerforth's kindness for granted without analyzing his motives or detecting his duplicity. When Steerforth befriends David at Salem House, David doesn't suspect that Steerforth is simply trying to use David to make friends and gain status. Though Steerforth belittles David from the moment they meet, David is incapable of conceiving that his new friend might be taking advantage of him. Because Steerforth's duplicity is so clear to us, David's lack of insight into Steerforth's true intentions emphasizes his youthful innocence. Steerforth likes David only because David worships him, and his final betrayal comes as a surprise to David but not to readers.

Clara Peggotty: She is the housekeeper of the family home and plays a big part in David's upbringing. She is the sister of Yarmouth fisherman Daniel Peggotty, and the aunt of Ham Peggotty and Little Em'ly. She is described as having cheeks like a red apple. She is gentle and caring, opening herself and her family to David whenever he is in need. She remains faithful to David Copperfield all her life, being like a second mother to him, never abandoning him, his mother, or his great-aunt Miss Betsey Trotwood. In her kind motherliness, Peggotty contrasts markedly with the harsh and unloving Miss Murdstone, the sister of David's cruel stepfather Mr. Murdstone. She marries the carrier Mr. Barkis and is afterwards sometimes referred to as Mrs. Barkis, a name Aunt Betsey Trotwood regards as much more suitable. On her husband's death Peggotty inherits £ 3,000, a large sum in present day terms.

Themes

Social Class: The novel can be viewed in large measure as a commentary on social status and class-based wealth. Favoritism and undeserved respect are shown constantly for those of a higher class. In the case of Steerforth, it is obvious that he is treated much better than David and the other students at Salem House. He is highly regarded by David and even by Mr. Peggotty and Ham, both of whom are of a lower class, when in fact Steerforth is the one who should be respecting them for their moral character. He constantly puts down those below him in status, such as Mr. Mell and Ham once he gets engaged to Little Em'ly. The strife for social status can also be seen through David's and Dora's courtship and marriage. David's first thought after hearing of Miss Betsey's financial downfall is shame at being poor, and Dora cries at the thought of David being poor and of having to do her own housework. David is constantly striving to make money so that he can live and provide Dora with a life of wealth. Little Em'ly also expresses unhappiness at her low social status and longs to be a "lady", which is why she runs off with Steerforth in the first place.

True Happiness: The narrator notes in particular the innocent joy David had as a child before his mother married Mr. Murdstone. The plot in general focuses on David's search for true happiness. All of the characters find or try to find their own routes to happiness. Some, such as David and the Peggottys, find true happiness through their families and spouses. Others, such as the Micawbers and Uriah, believe that money will bring them great happiness, although the Micawbers are also happy just remaining with one another. Still others, such as Dora, find happiness in simple, frivolous pleasures.

Good vs. Evil: This theme is prevalent especially as a symbolic battle for David's soul between Agnes Wickfield and Steerforth. Agnes represents David's good angel. She is his voice of reason and is the person who is able to calm him and give him the advice that he needs. Steerforth, in contrast, is his bad angel. He is the one who feeds David's desire for upper-class. Uriah also is very commonly a symbol of evil. He is eventually defeated by Agnes, Miss Betsey, Mr. Micawber and Traddles, all of whom are symbols of good. Yet, there are times when the evil wins out, namely in the case of David's mother Clara and the Murdstones. The evil overpowers her and contributes to her death.

The Undisciplined Heart: David's undisciplined heart is his tendency to fall victim to passion. He falls very quickly and very strongly for girls. This is especially the case regarding Dora, with whom he falls in love even before he has had the chance to say one word to her. He learns that she does not like to work around the house and is unwilling to learn about keeping a house, but he still decides to marry her. Minor examples of David's undisciplined heart include his feelings for Miss Shepherd, a brief crush on a person he barely knew, and his impractical crush on another woman much older than him. It is not until the very end of the novel that he learns to control or understand his undisciplined heart, and it is then that he finally realizes that Agnes is the person whom he truly loves maturely.

Children and Their Treatment: Dickens is fascinated with children, and this novel examines in detail how children are treated. The narrator mentions near the beginning of the novel how impressive it is that children can remember so many details so clearly, and he claims that he is proud to have such a childlike memory himself. Furthermore, the simpler, more childlike characters are among the sweetest in the novel. For example, Tommy Traddles is very simple and sweet in demeanor, and he goes on to be a successful lawyer, engaged to a beautiful, generous woman. Dora Spenlow may not know how to do household chores, but her devotion to David is extremely touching and admirable, and it wins David's heart. Finally, Mr. Dick, very simple-minded, is perhaps the best-liked character. Childlike simplicity and innocence thus are valued in the moral world of the novel. When Dickens writes scenes that show cruelty to children, he most likely is demonstrating an evil to raise readers' passions against such cruelty.

Female Empowerment: The novel explores feminine power to some degree, seeming to favor strong, powerful women, such as Peggotty and Miss Betsey. In contrast, women who do not hold much power or who simply exist in their marriages, such as Clara Copperfield, do not fare very well. Miss Betsey, an admired character throughout the novel, fights against her husband and manages to acquire a divorce, a feat that was not simple for women at the time (although he continues to bother her for money some time afterward). Mr. and Mrs. Micawber are a good example of a married couple in which each spouse holds almost an equal amount of power, and they are a very happy couple, even though they are broke. Thus, Dickens seems to be a proponent of feminine power in the sense of basic equality in institutions such as marriage.

The Role of the Father: The role of the father figure is one of the first issues that come up in the novel, for David is born six months after his father dies. Dickens is apparently suggesting that a father figure is essential for happiness and developing a good character. Still, not all fathers or father figures fit the norm or are even beneficial. Peggotty seems to be David's father figure growing up, for he describes her as large and "hard". Thus, he has a disciplinary figure along with his warm, loving mother to give him a balanced childhood. Little Em'ly and Ham have Mr. Peggotty, and both turn out to be very good people, especially Ham. Little Em'ly is simply seduced by Steerforth, who never has a father figure and even admits that he regrets that and wishes that he could have had a father figure so that he could be a better person. Uriah has no father mentioned either, and he is one of the most evil characters.

Film Adaptations

David Copperfield (1935) was directed by George Cukor, starring W. C. Fields, Lionel Barrymore, Freddie Bartholomew, released by Metro-Goldwyn-Mayer. The film was well-received on its release. It was then called the most profoundly satisfying screen manipulation of a great novel the camera has ever given us. There were several notable differences in the film from the book. For instance, in the film David never attends Salem House boarding school, and so the characters he met there do not appear, with the exception of Steerforth, who instead made his appearance as head boy of David's school he attended after going to live with Betsey Trotwood. It is an effective and indelible film, marred only by having to leave so much out and by the horrendously inappropriate casting of W. C. Fields as Micawber. His laboring to get the words out is painful to watch.

Fig 7.3　A Poster of *David Copperfield*

Fig 7.4　David, his mother, the Murdstones

Fig 7.5　Working at a factory

Fig 7.6　David, Betsy Trotwood and Dick

　　David Copperfield (1969) was directed by Delbert Mann, starring Richard Attenborough, Cyril Cusack, Edith Evans and produced by 20th Century Fox Television. The director emptied out the Hollywood British colony and a great deal of the United Kingdom itself of name players to bring this production of film into being. The constellation of stars swirls around young Robin Phillips who is a most winning adult David Copperfield. Laurence Olivier was nominated for playing the cruel schoolmaster Mr. Creakle. The whole novel is a flashback, but Mann adopted the technique of bringing the older Copperfield back to writing his memoirs as a way of cutting a lot of extra materials away and getting to the main events in the protagonist's life.

Fig 7.7　A Poster

Fig 7.8　A DVD Cover

Fig 7.9　Mr. Creakle

Fig 7.10　David and Agnes

David Copperfield (1999) is a two-part BBC television drama adaptation, directed by Simon Curtis, starring Daniel Radcliffe, Ciarán McMenamin, Maggie Smith, Pauline Quirke, Alun Armstrong etc. The quality of this production is seamless. One criticism is that it lacks originality, remaining too faithful to the novel. At three hours, it seems too short. Well-known personalities, such as Uriah Heep, flash past in a trice and even Mr. Micawber feels underused. The good people have no faults. Peggotty oozes love, compassion and common sense, an idealized nanny from a simple, generous-hearted family. Mr. Micawber and Mrs. Micawber are nothing but kindness. David's great aunt is the exception to the rule. She starts off a dragon and ends up a dove. The omission of Traddles is a loss. The most serious problems are the introduction of a narrator who is constantly narrating and keeping the audience at one remove from the events, and the actor who played the grown-up David, who constantly smiled and smirked, sometimes even in the tragic scenes. He seemed to have no other facial expression.

Fig 7.11　A DVD Cover

Fig 7.12　David, the Murdstones

Fig 7.13　David and Agnes

Fig 7.14　David, Betsey Trotwood and Dick

Wonderful Dialogues from the 1999 Film

(1) **David and Little Em'ly upon the Beach**

David: My father is dead, too.

Em'ly: I know. Do you mind?

David: I never met him. Mr. Peggotty must be a good man.

Em'ly: Better than good. If I was a lady, I'd give him a waistcoat with diamond buttons, a large gold watch and a bagful of money (*Running towards the wooden causeway*).

David: Emily! Emily! Take care.

Em'ly: (*Standing at the far end of the causeway*) I'm only frightened when the wind blows.

I lie awake, thinking I hear Uncle Dan and Ham out at sea crying for help. That's why I want to be a lady. I could keep them safe on land.

Voice-over: Her words echo to me down the years. They haunt me still.

(2) David and His New Father Murdstone

Murdstone comes to David's bedroom. He asks David's mother Clara and the servant Pegotty out and closes the door.

Murdstone: David, if I have an obstinate dog or horse to deal with. What do you think I do? (*David shakes his head.*) I beat him. I make him wince and smart. I say to myself, "I'll conquer that fellow." And even if it costs him every drop of blood he has. I'll do it. (*Holding David's arm and speaking viciously*) Do we understand each other? (*David nods his head.*) Good. Now, wash your face and come downstairs directly.

He opens the door and leaves.

(3) David and Peggotty

After David bites Murdstone, he is left alone in his bedroom for seven days and nights. He finds freedom from pages of books left by his father. The night before he is sent to Salem, Peggotty quietly comes to his door.

Peggotty: (*Speaking in a low voice*) Davy? Davy?

David: Peggotty? Oh, Peggotty! (*Running to the door from the bed*)

Peggotty: Hush, dear. Be as quiet as a mouse or the cats'll hear us.

David: What is to become of me, Peggotty?

Peggotty: School, near London.

David: When?

Peggotty: Tomorrow. Listen to me, my darlin' boy. Don't lose heart and never forget how much your Peggotty loves you!

David: Is mama very angry with me, Peggotty?

Peggotty: No, no, not very.

David: Shan't I see her?

Peggotty: Tomorrow. I'll take care of your Mama. Davy dear, I promise. I won't leave her, not ever. As long as Clara Peggotty draws breath, you and your Mama will always have a friend.

David: Don't cry, Peggotty!

Peggotty: I ain't cryin'. (*Throwing some coins inside through the under part of the door*) Your Mama gave me these for you, Davy. (*David picks up the coins from inside. Peggotty kisses the door and so does David.*) Goodbye, my darlin' boy. Goodbye (*Leaving the door with tears in her eyes*).

(4) David and Mr. Micawber

Mr. Micawber just comes out of prison. He speaks to David.

Micawber: You have···no close family of your own, Copperfield? Beyond Mr. Murdstone, I mean.

David: He hates me. I have no one else. An aunt in Dover hasn't seen me since I was a baby and I don't think she wants to meet me now.

Micawber: My advice is seek her out. She may be overjoyed to reacquaint herself with you.

Mrs. Micawber: (*Running towards Mr. Micawber happily with a baby in her arms*) Wilkins! Our debts are settled! You're a free man again! (*Mr. Micawber kisses her.*)

Micawber: The Lord Chancellor's acknowledged a miscarriage of justice. I wrote to him personally.

Mrs. Micawber: My family's remembered their obligations.

Micawber: Not, in short, before time.

Mrs. Micawber: They think Micawber should exert his talents in our hometown of Plymouth.

Micawber: (*To David*) I shall never think of our period of difficulty without remembering you.

Mrs. Micaber: (*Coming to David*) God bless you. (*Kissing him*) I never will forget you.

Micawber: (*Shaking hands with David*) Farewell, my young friend. Farewell. (*Going into the carriage and putting his head out*) Remember, Copperfield. Annual income-£ 20. Annual expenditure-£ 20.00.06. result-misery.

The carriage moves away quickly and David waves his hand towards it.

 Discussions

1. How does Dickens challenge the accepted views of women during his time to promote the idea of the empowered female?
2. Does Dickens equate high social class with low moral character and vice versa? Does he equate low social class with unhappiness? Explain with examples from the text.
3. Although David is narrating his story as an adult, his memories, as he says, are similar to those of a child. Why does Dickens choose to narrate the story in this way, and how does it affect the way in which it is told?
4. The novel was written by Dickens as something of an autobiography. What elements of the novel coincide with Dickens' own life? Why do you think Dickens made the story deviate from his own life at certain points?
5. What role does Uriah Heep play in the novel? Why does Dickens characterize him in the way that he does?

Unit 8　James Fenimore Cooper and *The Last of the Mohicans*

James Fenimore Cooper (1789—1851) was a prolific and popular American writer of the early 19th century. His historical romances of frontier and Indian life in the early American days created a unique form of American literature. He lived most of his life in Cooperstown, New York, which was established by his father William. He attended Yale University for three years but was expelled for misbehavior. Before embarking on his career as a writer he served in the U.S. Navy as a Midshipman, which greatly influenced many of his novels and other writings. He is best remembered as a novelist who wrote numerous sea-stories and the historical novels known as the *Leatherstocking Tales*. Among naval historians his works on the early U.S. Navy have been well received, but they were sometimes criticized by his contemporaries. Among his most famous works is the Romantic novel *The Last of the Mohicans*, often regarded as his masterpiece. It is a historical novel first published in February 1826. The story takes place in 1757, during the French and Indian War (the Seven Years' War)❶, when France and Great Britain battled for control of the North American colonies. During this war, the French called on allied Native American tribes to fight against the more numerous British colonists in this region⋯

 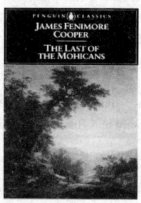

　Fig 8.1　James Fenimore Cooper　　Fig 8.2　A Book Cover of *The Last of the Mohicans*

---

❶The French and Indian War (1754—1763) was fought primarily between the colonies of British America and New France, with both sides supported by military units from their parent countries of Great Britain and France. In 1756, the war escalated from a regional affair into a world-wide conflict. The war was fought primarily along the frontiers separating New France from the British colonies from Virginia to Nova Scotia in Canada. It began with a dispute over control of the confluence of the Allegheny and Monongahela rivers, called the Forks of the Ohio, and the site of the French Fort Duquesne and present-day Pittsburgh, Pennsylvania. The dispute erupted into violence in May 1754, during which Virginia militiamen under the command of George Washington ambushed a French patrol. The outcome was that France ceded French Louisiana west of the Mississippi River to its ally Spain in compensation for Spain's loss to Britain of Florida (which Spain had ceded to Britain in exchange for the return of Havana, Cuba). France's colonial presence north of the Caribbean was reduced to the islands of Saint Pierre and Miquelon, confirming Britain's position as the dominant colonial power in the eastern half of North America.

Plot

Cora and Alice Munro, daughters of Lieutenant Colonel Munro, are traveling with a column of reinforcements from Fort Edward to Fort William Henry, where Munro is commanding an army. In the party are David Gamut, the singing teacher, and Major Duncan Heyward, the group's military leader.

Magua, a Huron scout allied with the French, leads them into an ambush. Natty Bumppo (also known as Hawkeye) and his two Mohican friends, Chingachgook and his son Uncas, rescue the party just in time. Knowing that Magua (also known the cunning fox) will soon return with reinforcements, Hawkeye and the Mohicans lead their new companions to a nearby cave. A group of Hurons sent by Magua chase them into the cave. After a fierce struggle, Hawkeye and his friends decide to split up the group for safety. Hawkeye and the Mohicans hide in a nearby stream, while Heyward, Gamut, and the Munro sisters retreat into the cavern.

Magua returns with more Hurons and captures the four in the cave. The Hurons take their captives to a stream, where they rest briefly. The Hurons interrogate Heyward, who tells them that Hawkeye and the Mohicans have escaped. He learns from them that Uncas' nickname is the Bounding Elk and that Hawkeye is referred to as the Long Rifle.

When Cora demands why the Hurons were so eager to capture them, Magua says that Colonel Munro and the Canada fathers introduced him to firewater, causing him to get drunk and be expelled from his tribe. He allied with the Mohawks, but continued to drink. After Munro had him whipped after some drunken disorder, Magua returned to the Hurons and is leading them in revenge against the British. He offers to spare the party if Cora will go with him as his wife to the Huron village, but she refuses.

Hawkeye, Uncas, and Chingachgook return and ambush the Hurons, killing most of them. Magua escapes. Heyward and Hawkeye lead the Munro women to Fort William Henry, now surrounded by the French.

Munro sends Hawkeye to Fort Edward for reinforcements. While bearing General Webb's reply, he is captured by the French, who deliver him to Fort William Henry without the letter. Heyward tries to parley with the French, but learns nothing. He returns to Colonel Munro and announces his love for Alice. Munro reveals that Cora's mother was of mixed race of African ancestry from the West Indies, and gives his permission for Heyward's courtship.

The French general, Montcalm, invites Munro to a parley. He shows him Webb's letter: the British general has refused to send reinforcements. Realizing that his cause is lost, Munro agrees to Montcalm's terms. The British soldiers, together with their wounded, and women and children, are allowed to leave the fort and withdraw. Outside the fort, the column is set upon by 2000 Indian warriors. In the chaos of the massacre, Magua finds Cora and Alice, and leads them away toward the Huron village. David Gamut follows them.

Three days later, Hawkeye and the Mohicans, Heyward, and Colonel Munro enter the ruins of

Fort William Henry. The next morning they follow Magua's trail, evading a party of native warriors chasing them by canoe. Outside the Huron village, they come across Gamut. The Hurons consider him mad for all his singing and won't kill him. Gamut says that Alice is being held in this village, Cora in one belonging to the Lenape (Delaware) tribe, and Magua is hunting. Disguised as a French medicine man, Heyward enters the Huron village with Gamut, intending to rescue Alice. Hawkeye and Uncas set out to rescue Cora. Chingachgook remains with Colonel Munro, who has become somewhat deranged as a result of events.

Before Heyward can find Alice, Uncas is led into the village, having been captured by the Hurons. Magua returns, and demands that Uncas be put to death, but does not recognise Heyward. Hawkeye steals a bearskin and disguises himself while following Heyward. They rescue Alice, wrapping her in cloth and convincing the Hurons that she is someone the French medicine man has to heal. As Heyward carries Alice toward the Lenape village, Gamut and the disguised Hawkeye return to the village to rescue Uncas.

His guards recognize the bear suit and allow the two to pass. Uncas dons the bear skin while Hawkeye dresses as Gamut and begins to sing. Gamut stays behind. Uncas and Hawkeye flee to the Delaware village.

Discovering Gamut, the Hurons realize that Uncas has escaped. They find Magua, bound and gagged in the cave. Magua tells the Hurons about how Heyward and Hawkeye tricked them to rescue Alice and then Uncas. Learning of how they were deceived, the warriors become enraged. The Hurons vow revenge and reaffirm Magua as their chief.

Magua goes to the Lenape village, where he demands the return of his prisoners, and warns the Lenape of the Long Rifle's reputation. A chief asks the prisoners who is the Long Rifle. Heyward, mistaking Hawkeye's wishes, claims he is the man. Hawkeye also claims the title, and Tamenund makes them do a shooting match, which Hawkeye wins.

Tamenund at first grants Magua's wish to keep his prisoners, but Cora begs him to reconsider. She eventually begs him to hear from a Delaware warrior, referring to Uncas.

When first taken there, Uncas had offended the Delaware. They tear off his clothing and see a turtle tattoo on his chest, the symbol of his clan. Tamenund accedes to all Uncas asks and frees the prisoners, except for Cora, as she belongs to Magua. Magua reluctantly agrees to Uncas's demands but says he will keep Cora. Hawkeye at one point offers himself as a prisoner in place of Cora, but Magua refuses. Uncas and Heyward both vow to hunt down and kill Magua and rescue Cora as the Huron chief leaves with his captive.

According to custom, Tamenund has agreed to give Magua a three-hour head start before permitting the Delaware to try to rescue Cora. As the Delaware use the extra time to prepare for battle, Gamut arrives. He said he saw Magua and Cora at the Huron village, and she was hidden in the cave where they earlier found Alice. The Delaware go off to confront the Huron.

The Delaware are in three parties: one led by Hawkeye and Heyward, one by Uncas, and one by Chingachgook and Munro. They force the Huron back to their village with heavy losses and finally take the village. Magua escapes with Cora and two of his warriors. Uncas, Hawkeye, and Heyward pursue them through the mountains. Cora stops on a rocky ledge, refusing to continue. When Uncas attacks the Huron, both he and Cora are killed. Hawkeye arrives and shoots Magua.

The novel concludes with a lengthy account of the funerals of Uncas and Cora. People sing that Uncas and Cora will marry in the afterlife. Hawkeye renews his friendship with Chingachgook. Tamenund prophesies, "The pale-faces are masters of the earth, and the time of the red-men has not yet come again…"

Select Reading: Chapter 1

It was a feature peculiar to the colonial wars of North America that the toils and dangers of the wilderness were to be encountered before the adverse hosts could meet. A wide and apparently an impervious boundary of forests severed the possessions of the hostile provinces of France and England. The hardy colonist and the trained European who fought at his side, frequently expended months in struggling against the rapids of the streams, or in effecting the rugged passes of the mountains, in quest of an opportunity to exhibit their courage in a more martial conflict. But, emulating the patience and self-denial of the practiced native warriors, they learned to overcome every difficulty; and it would seem that, in time, there was no recess of the woods so dark, nor any secret place so lovely, that it might claim exemption from the inroads of those who had pledged their blood to satiate their vengeance, or to uphold the cold and selfish policy of the distant monarchs of Europe.

Perhaps no district throughout the wide extent of the intermediate frontiers can furnish a livelier picture of the cruelty and fierceness of the savage warfare of those periods than the country which lies between the head waters of the Hudson and the adjacent lakes.

The facilities which nature had there offered to the march of the combatants were too obvious to be neglected. The lengthened sheet of the Champlain stretched from the frontiers of Canada, deep within the borders of the neighboring province of New York, forming a natural passage across half the distance that the French were compelled to master in order to strike their enemies. Near its southern termination, it received the contributions of another lake, whose waters were so limpid as to have been exclusively selected by the Jesuit missionaries to perform the typical purification of baptism, and to obtain for it the title of lake "du Saint Sacrement". The less zealous English thought they conferred a sufficient honor on its unsullied fountains, when they bestowed the name of their reigning prince, the second of the house of Hanover. The two united to rob the untutored possessors of its wooded scenery of their native right to perpetuate its original appellation of "Horican".

It was in this scene of strife and bloodshed that the incidents we shall attempt to relate occurred, during the third year of the war which England and France last waged for the possession of a country that neither was destined to retain.

The imbecility of her military leaders abroad, and the fatal want of energy in her councils at home, had lowered the character of Great Britain from the proud elevation on which it had been placed by the talents and enterprise of her former warriors and statesmen. No longer dreaded by her enemies, her servants were fast losing the confidence of self-respect. In this mortifying abasement, the colonists, though innocent of her imbecility, and too humble to be the agents of her blunders, were but the natural participators. They had recently seen a chosen army from that country, which, reverencing as a mother, they had blindly believed invincible—an army led by a chief who had been selected from a crowd of trained warriors, for his rare military endowments, disgracefully routed by a handful of French and Indians.

译文：北美的殖民战争有一个独特之处,那就是,敌对双方在遇见对手之前,先要面对险恶的原野荒山。法国和英国两军对垒的地区就隔着一望无际、密不透风的森林。那些顽强的殖民者和从欧洲派来与他们并肩作战的军队,常常要花几个月的时间与山间急流搏斗,在羊肠小道上跋涉奔波,然后才能找到一个机会在真正的军事冲突中一显身手。但是,久经考验的土著战士那种耐心和自我克制的精神使他们也学会了克服每一种困难。因此,对那些矢志复仇,或一心推行欧洲君主们冷酷自私的政策的殖民者来说,目前似乎已经没有什么地方,无论是黑暗的森林,还是幽僻的秘密地点,可以阻止他们的侵入了。

在这广袤的中间地带,也许除了哈得孙河源头和毗邻湖泊之间的地区,再没有哪个地方能如此栩栩如生地展示那个时代激烈残酷的战争画面了。

这儿,大自然为战士们的行军提供了诸多便利,非常明显,不容忽视。狭长的尚普兰湖从加拿大边境一直延伸到邻近的纽约省腹地,形成了一个自然的通道,通过法国人为打击敌人必须控制的土地上的一半地盘。湖的南端与另一个湖汇合在一起。此湖湖水清澈,被耶稣会的传教士们专门选作洗礼之地,故得名"圣礼湖"。英国人热情稍逊,将此湖以当朝君主汉诺威王室二王子之名命名,一位这已是那些清泉莫大的荣耀。这两个名称联合在一起,便使得那些质朴的土著,这葱郁林地的真正主人失去原有的权利,不能再按原来的名字称它为"哈丽肯"湖了。

我们要讲述的事就发生在这片流血冲突的土地上。其时英法两国为占有一个谁都注定不能拥有的国家而发动的最后一场战争已进行到第三个年头。

由于在国外的将领懦弱无能,国内当局定计决策又没有魄力,大不列颠先前由杰出的文臣武将为其赢得的崇高地位已经大大降低。她不再让敌人害怕,她的臣仆们也迅速失去了自尊的信心。这些殖民者虽说对当局的懦弱无能一无所知,他们人微言轻,也不可能给国家造成什么错误,但对祖国地位的衰落,他们自然也十分痛心。不久前,他们刚刚见过从祖国开来的一支军队,他们盲目地认为,祖国的军队战无不胜、所向披靡。这支军队的统帅是特选出来的优秀军人,具有出众的军事才能,但它却可耻地被一小撮法国人和印第安人打得落花流水。

Analysis of Major Characters

Hawkeye: Hawkeye goes by several names: Natty Bumppo, La Longue Carabine (The Long Rifle), the scout, and Hawkeye. Hawkeye stars in several of Cooper's novels, which are known collectively as the Leatherstocking Tales. Hawkeye's chief strength is adaptability. He adapts to the difficulties of the frontier and bridges the divide between white and Indian cultures. A hybrid, Hawkeye identifies himself by his white race and his Indian social world, in which his closest friends are the Mohicans Chingachgook and Uncas. Hawkeye's hybrid background breeds both productive alliances and disturbingly racist convictions. On one hand, Hawkeye cherishes individuality and makes judgments without regard to race. He cherishes Chingachgook for his value as an individual, not for a superficial multiculturalism fashionably ahead of its time. On the other hand, Hawkeye demonstrates an almost obsessive investment in his own genuine whiteness. While he supports interracial friendship between men, he objects to interracial sexual desire between men and women. Because of his contradictory opinions, he embodies nineteenth-century America's ambivalence about race and nature. His most racist views predict the cultural warfare around the issue of race that continues to haunt the United States.

Magua: Magua, an Indian of the Huron tribe, plays the crafty villain to Hawkeye's rugged hero. Because of his exile by Colonel Munro, Magua seeks revenge. He does not want to do bodily harm to Munro but wants to bruise the colonel's psyche. Magua has a keen understanding of whites' prejudices, and he knows that threatening to marry the colonel's daughter will terrify Colonel Munro. Magua's threat to marry a white woman plays on white men's fears of interracial marriage. When Magua kidnaps Cora, the threat of physical violence or rape hangs in the air, although no one ever speaks of it. Whereas the interracial attraction between Uncas and Cora strikes us as sweet and promising for happier race relations in the future, the violent unwanted advances of Magua to Cora show an exaggerated fulfillment of white men's fears. However, while anger originally motivates Magua, affection eventually characterizes his feelings for Cora. He refuses to harm her, even when in one instance his actions put himself in danger. Magua's psychology becomes slightly more complicated by the end of the novel, when sympathy tempers his evil.

Major Duncan Heyward: Heyward plays a well-meaning but slightly foolish white man, the conventional counterpart to the ingenious, diverse Hawkeye. While Hawkeye moves effortlessly throughout the wild frontier, Heyward never feels secure. He wants to maintain the swagger and confidence he likely felt in all-white England, but the unfamiliar and unpredictable landscape does him in. Some of Heyward's difficulties stem from his inability to understand the Indians. Still, despite Heyward's failings, Cooper does not satirize Heyward or make him into a buffoon. Heyward does demonstrate constant integrity and a well-meaning nature, both of which mitigate his lack of social understanding. Cooper also treats Heyward gently because Heyward plays the most typical romantic hero in the novel, and so he must appear strong and handsome, not ridiculous and inept. Heyward and Alice, although presented as a bland couple, make up the swooning, cooing pair necessary to a sentimental novel.

Cora Munro: The raven-haired daughter of Colonel Munro, Cora literally embodies the novel's ambivalent opinion about mixed race. She is part Negro, a racial heritage portrayed as both unobjectionable and a cause for vitriolic defensiveness in her father. She becomes entangled with the Indian Uncas, a romantic complication portrayed both as passionate and natural and as doomed to failure. Dark and stoic in comparison to her sister Alice's blonde girlishness, Cora is not the stereotypical nineteenth-century sentimental heroine. Though she carries the weight of the sentimental novel, she also provides the impetus for the adventure narrative, since her capture by Magua necessitates rescue missions. Cora brings together the adventure story's warfare and intrigue and the sentimental novel's romance and loss. With Cora, Cooper makes two genres intersect, creating the frontier romance.

Uncas: Uncas changes more than any other character over the course of the novel. He pushes the limits of interracial relationships, moving beyond Hawkeye's same-sex interracial friendships and falling in love with Cora, a white woman. Whereas Cooper values interracial friendship between men, he presents interracial sexuality as difficult and perhaps always doomed. In the end, Uncas is punished for his taboo desires, perhaps because Cooper thinks he should be punished, or perhaps because Cooper wants to show that Uncas' close-minded society will punish racial mixing. Hawkeye becomes a father figure for Uncas, and Uncas eventually becomes a natural leader of men by combining the skill of Hawkeye with the spirituality of a revered Indian leader.

Themes

Interracial Love and Friendship: The story is about race and the difficulty of overcoming racial divides. Cooper suggests that interracial mingling is both desirable and dangerous. Cooper praises the genuine and longtime friendship between Hawkeye, a white man, and Chingachgook, a Mohican Indian. Hawkeye and Chingachgook's shared communion with nature transcends race, enabling them to team up against Huron enemies and to save white military leaders like Heyward. On the other hand, Cooper shows his conviction that interracial romances are doomed and undesirable. The interracial love of Uncas and Cora ends in tragedy, and the forced interracial relationship between Cora and Magua is portrayed as unnatural. Through Cora, Cooper suggests that interracial desire can be inherited. Cora desires Indian men because her mother was part black.

Literal and Metaphorical Nature: Nature functions both literally and metaphorically. In its literal form, nature is the physical frontier that surrounds the characters and complicates their battles and their chances for survival. In the opening paragraphs of Chapter I, Cooper describes the unpredictability of the colonial terrain, pointing out that the cleared, flat battlefields of Europe are no longer the setting for war. The New World has a new set of natural difficulties, and the men at war must contend not just with each other but with the unfriendly land. The forbidding landscape seems even more daunting to the English because their adversaries, the Indians loyal to France, know the land so well. The skills of the English have no place in the forests of America. David Gamut's religious Calvinism, a European religion, becomes ridiculous in the wilderness.

Metaphorically, the land serves as a blank canvas on which the characters paint themselves. Cooper defines characters by their relationships to nature. Hawkeye establishes his claim to heroism by respecting the landscape. The English Major Heyward establishes his incompetence by misunderstanding the landscape. While he means well, his unfamiliarity with the wilderness thwarts him. Magua uses the landscape to carry out his villainy, hiding women in caves, jumping wildly over abysses, and hiding behind rocks.

Role of Religion in the Wilderness: The character David Gamut allows Cooper to explore the relevance of religion in the wilderness. In theory at least, the American frontier is untouched by human culture. It is a fresh start, a piece of land not ruled by the conventions of European high culture, a place without a firm government or social code. Gamut's aggressive Calvinism symbolizes the entrance of religion, a European model that enters the blank slate of the New World. We know Gamut is a Calvinist because he talks about predestination, the idea that God has a plan for each person and no amount of human effort can change that plan. Hawkeye's frequent mockery of Gamut's psalmody provides the novel's comic relief. The mockery, which comes from the mouth of the hero, also suggests that institutional religion should not attempt to penetrate the wilderness and convert its inhabitants. Because Cooper makes Gamut ridiculous and Hawkeye heroic, it seems that, like Hawkeye, Cooper scoffs at Calvinism's tenets. Gamut's fatalism contrasts with Hawkeye's pragmatism. Hawkeye adapts to his surroundings and helps the other characters to achieve improbable survivals, all of which suggests that Cooper believes humans do have the ability to determine their own fates. By the end of the novel the Calvinist Gamut learns to move beyond the rigidity of his religion and becomes a helpful and committed ally. He succeeds when he finds the ability to leave behind his fatalistic passivity and adapt to the demands of the forest. Cooper's exploration of Calvinism sets the stage for many American writers of subsequent generations. For example, Herman Melville's tragic hero Ahab subscribes to the rigid belief in fate that Calvinism endorses. It is a pity that this theme is completely omitted in the film.

Changing Idea of Family: Cooper uses the frontier setting to explore the changing status of the family unit. Cooper posits that the wilderness demands new definitions of family. Uncas and Hawkeye form a makeshift family structure. When Uncas's real father, Chingachgook, disappears without explanation in the middle portion of the novel, Hawkeye becomes a symbolic father for Uncas. As Uncas develops his leadership qualities and emerges as a hero at the Delaware council of Tamenund, he takes on some of the charisma and skill of Hawkeye, just as a son would inherit behavior from his father. Not only do Uncas and Hawkeye form a family not related by blood, they form a family that transcends race. Despite this redefinition, however, the novel does not allow new family formations that mix race, for Uncas and Cora do not get to act on their interracial attraction. The tragedy of this sentimental novel is that Cora and Uncas cannot redefine the notion of family according to their desires.

Hybridity: The concept of hybridity is central to the novel's thematic explorations of race and family. Hybridity is the mixing of separate elements into one whole, and in the novel it usually occurs when nature and culture intersect, or when two races intersect. For example, Cora is a hybrid because her mother was black and her father white. Hawkeye is a hybrid because he is white by blood and Indian by habit. Part of Hawkeye's success comes from his ability to combine elements of the European and Indian worlds. With Hawkeye, Cooper challenges the idea that essential differences separate the two cultures. Cooper's depictions of hybridity predate the nineteenth century's extensive debate on the term's cultural and scientific meanings. The term "hybridity" became popular at the end of the nineteenth century, when rapid developments in genetics occurred.

Film Adaptations

A number of films have been based on the lengthy book, making various cuts, compressions, and changes. The American adaptations mainly include:

The Last of the Mohicans (1920), starring Wallace Beery, has been deemed culturally significant by the Library of Congress and selected for preservation in the United States National Film Registry;

Fig 8.3　The Title of the 1920 Film　　　　Fig 8.4　Colonel Munro's Daughter

The Last of the Mohicans(1932), a serial version starring Harrey Carey;

The Last of the Mohicans (1936), starring Randolf Scot and Binnie Barnes;

Fig 8.5　1932 Poster　　　　Fig 8.6　1936 Poster

The Last of the Mohicans (1947), starring Jon Hall and Michael O'Shea;

The Last of the Mohicans (1963), starring Jack Taylor, Jose Marco, Luis Induni and Daniel Martin;

The Last of the Mohicans (1992), based indirectly on Cooper's novel, starring Daniel Day-Lewis and directed by Michael Mann. Many of the scenes from the film did not follow the book, in particular, some characters who survive the events of the novel die in the film, and vice versa.

Fig 8.7　Hawkeye, Chingachgook and Uncas　　　　Fig 8.8　Magua

Fig 8.9　Colonel Munro and General Montcalm　　　　Fig 8.10　Cora and Alice Munro

Wonderful Dialogues from the 1992 Film

(1) In a Huron Village

Magua takes their prisoners, Cora, Alice and Heyward to a Huron village to see the Sachem.

Magua: Many of the English are dead, great Sachem. And Magua has become a great leader and seeks your acknowledgement. (*Hawkeye, Chingachgook and Uncas are approaching the village.*) And so, I have brought three of my prisoners to honor you. Magua will see the English officer to the French. And the reward is my gift to you, wise one. The women are the children of the white war chief, Munro. They will burn in our fires. Then all can share in these trophies of honor.

Hawkeye walks towards Sachem in the whoops of the villagers. A Huron attacks him to the ground. He stands up and walks on. He is again attacked to the ground. He stands up and walks on again. He comes to Heyward and asks him to translate every word of him into French.

Hawkeye: (*To Sachem*) I come to you unarmed and in peace to unstuff your ears, Sachem. Let the children of the dead Colonel Munro go free. Take fire out of the English anger over the murder of their helpless ones.

Magua: (*Speaking French. Heyward translating into English*) Montcalm and our friends the French are stronger than the English. We do not fear English anger.

Heyward: (*To Sachem*) Sachem, the French fathers made peace.

Hawkeye: Magua broke it. It is false that the French will be friends still to the Huron.

Magua: It made our French father happy to know that he would never have to fight the same English again. Now, the French also fear Huron. That is good. When the Huron is stronger from their fear, we will make the new terms of trade with the French. We will become traders as the whites. Take land from the Abenaki, furs from the Osage, Sank and Fox. Trade for gold. No less than the whites, as strong as the whites.

Hawkeye: (*To Magua*) Would Magua use the ways of *Le Francais* and the Yengeese would you?

Magua: Yes.

Hawkeye: Would the Huron make his Algonguin brothers foolish with brandy and steal his lands to sell them for gold to the whites? Would Huron have greed for more land than a man can use? Would Huron fool Seneca into talking all the furs of all the animals of the forest for beads and strong whiskey? Would the Huron kill every man, woman and child of their enemy? Those are the ways of the Yengeese and the Francais traders and their masters in Europe infected with the sickness of greed. Magua's heart is twisted. He would make himself into what twisted him. I am Nathaniel of the Yengeese, Hawkeye, adopted son of Chingachgook of the Mohican people. Let the children of the dead Munro and the Yengeese officer go free. This belt, which is a record of the days of my father's people, speaks for my truth.

Magua: You speak poison with two tongues.

Sachem: (*Speaking French, Heyward translating into English*) The white man came and night entered our future with him. Our council has asked the question since I was a boy: what are the Huron to do? Magua is a great war captain but his path has never been the Huron one. Magua take younger daughter of Munro so that Munro's seed doesn't die and Magua's heart is healed. English officer will go back to English so their hatred burns less bright. Dark child of Munro will burn in fire for Magua's dead children. Long Rifle, go in peace.

(2) **Hawkeye and Chingachgook**

At the end of the film Chingachgook, Hawkeye and Cora are standing on the rocks of a mountain top, overlooking the surroundings.

Chingachgook: Great spirit and master of all life, a warrior goes to You swift and straight as an arrow shot into the sun. Welcome him and let him take his place at the council fire of my people. He is Uncas—my son. Tell him to be patient and ask death for speed. For they are all there but one, I, Chingachgook, the last of the Mohicans. (*Staring Hawkeye. Cora walks to Hawkeye. They kiss and embrace.*) The frontier moves with the sun and pushes the Red Man of these wilderness forests in front of it, until one day there will be no where left. Then our race will be no more or be not us.

Hawkeye: That is my father's sadness talking.

Chingachgook: No, it is true. The frontier place is for people like my white son and his woman and their children. And one day there will be no more frontier. And men like you will go too, like the Mohicans. And now people will come, work, struggle. Some will make their life. But once we were here.

Discussions

1. How does the novel bring together elements of the sentimental novel and the frontier adventure story?
2. The Native Americans in Cooper's novel seem either entirely good (Uncas and Chingachgook) or entirely evil (Magua and most of the Hurons). Are there any believable Indian characters in the novel? Is Cooper guilty of invoking racial stereotypes in his portrayal of Indians?
3. Compare and contrast the father-son relationship of Chingachgook and Uncas with the father-daughter relationship of Munro and his daughters.
4. Discuss three examples of the clash between races or cultures. What do the three examples show about Cooper's views on racism?
5. The 1992 film adaptation makes some changes of the novel. Please name some of the changes and try to explain why the director did so.

Unit 9   Mark Twain and *The Adventures of Huckleberry Finn*

Samuel Langhorne Clemens (1835—1910), better known by his pen name Mark Twain, was an American author and humorist. He wrote *The Adventures of Tom Sawyer* (1876) and its sequel *The Adventures of Huckleberyy Finn* (1885), the latter often called the Great American Novel. He grew up in Hannibal, Missouri, which provided the setting for the two novels. After an apprenticeship with a printer, he worked as a typesetter and contributed articles to the newspaper of his older brother Orion. He later became a riverboat pilot on the Mississippi River before heading west to join Orion in Nevada. In 1865, his humorous story, "The Celebrated Jumping Frog of Calaveras County", was published. His wit and satire in prose and in speech earned praise from critics and peers. After his death, he was lauded as the greatest American humorist of his age. William Faulkner called him the father of American literature. *The Adventures of Huckleberry Finn* is among the first in major American literature to be written throughout in vernacular English, characterized by local color regionalism.

Fig 9.1   Mark Twain   Fig 9.2   A Book Cover of *The Adventures of Huckleberry Finn*

Plot

The story begins in fictional St. Petersburg, Missouri, on the shore of the Mississippi River, sometime between 1835 (when the first steamboat sailed down the Mississippi) and 1845. Huckleberry (Huck) Finn and his friend, Thomas (Tom) Sawyer, have each come into a considerable sum of money as a result of their earlier adventures. Huck explains how he is placed under the guardianship of the Widow Douglas, who, together with her stringent sister, Miss Watson, is attempting to civilize him and teach him religion. Finding civilized life confining, his spirits are raised when Tom Sawyer helps him to escape one night to meet up with Tom's gang of self-proclaimed "robbers". Just as the gang's activities begin to bore Huck, he is suddenly interrupted by the reappearance of his shiftless father, "Pap", an abusive alcoholic. Although Huck is successful in preventing Pap from acquiring his fortune, knowing that Pap would only spend the money on alcohol, Pap still gains custody of Huck and leaves town with him.

Pap forcibly moves Huck to his isolated cabin in the woods on the Illinois shoreline. Due to Pap's drunken violence and habit of keeping Huck locked inside the cabin, Huck, during one of his father's absences, saws a hole in the cabin wall, elaborately fakes his own murder, and sets off down river, settling, quite comfortably, on Jackson's Island, in the Mississippi. Here, Huck reunites with Jim, Miss Watson's slave. Jim has also run away after he overheard Miss Watson planning to sell him "down the river" to one of the states further South where the treatment of slaves is far more brutal. Jim plans to make his way to the town of Cairo in Illinois, a free state, so that he can later buy the rest of his enslaved family's freedom. At first, Huck is conflicted about the sin of supporting a runaway slave, but as the two talk in depth and bond over their mutually held superstitions, Huck emotionally connects with Jim, who increasingly becomes Huck's close friend and guardian. After heavy flooding on the river, the two find a raft as well as an entire house floating on the river. Entering the house to seek loot, Jim finds the naked body of a dead man lying on the floor, shot in the back. He quietly prevents Huck from seeing the corpse.

To find out the latest news, Huck dresses as a girl and goes into town. He enters the house of Judith Loftus, a woman new to the area, thinking she will not recognize him as a boy. Huck learns from her about the news of his own supposed murder. Pap was initially blamed, but since Jim ran away he is also a suspect. A reward for Jim's capture has initiated a manhunt; Mrs. Loftus herself has a feeling about Jackson's Island. She is actually very shrewd and becomes increasingly suspicious that Huck is a boy, finally proving it by tests, such as seeing how he catches something in his lap, and how he throws a chunk of lead at a rat. Once he is exposed, she nevertheless allows him to leave her home without commotion, not realizing that he is the allegedly murdered boy they have just been discussing. Huck returns to Jim to tell him the news—they are obviously no longer safe from discovery on the island, so the two hastily load up the raft and depart.

After a while they come across a grounded steamship. Searching it, Huck and Jim stumble upon two thieves discussing murdering a third, and they flee before being noticed. They are later separated in a fog, making Jim intensely anxious, and when they reunite, Huck tricks Jim into thinking he dreamed the entire incident. Jim is not deceived for long, and is deeply hurt that his friend should have teased him so mercilessly. Huck becomes remorseful and apologizes to Jim, though his conscience troubles him about humbling himself before a black man.

Travelling onward, Huck and Jim's raft is struck by a passing steamship, separating the two. Huck is given shelter on the Kentucky side of the river by the Grangerfords, an aristocratic family. He befriends Buck Grangerford, a boy about his age, and learns that the Grangerfords are engaged in a 30-year blood feud against another family, the Shepherdsons. The Grangerfords and Shepherdsons go to the same church and act peaceably inside, though both families bring guns, despite the church's preachings on brotherly love. The vendetta finally comes to a head when Buck's older sister elopes with a member of the Shepherdson clan. In the resulting conflict, all the Grangerford males from this branch of the family are shot and killed, including Buck. Huck is particularly devastated by the brutality of Buck's murder, which he witnesses, but declines to describe. He is immensely relieved to be reunited with Jim, who has rescued and repaired the raft.

Near the Arkansas-Missouri-Tennessee border, Jim and Huck take two on-the-run grifters aboard the raft. The younger man, who is about thirty, introduces himself as the long-lost son of an English duke. The older one, about seventy, then trumps this outrageous claim by alleging that he himself is the Lost Dauphin, the son of Louis XVI and rightful King of France. The duke and king then become permanent passengers on Jim and Huck's raft, committing a series of confidence schemes upon unsuspecting locals all along their journey. To allow for Jim's presence, they first print fake bills for an escaped slave, but later paint him up entirely blue and call him the Sick Arab so that he can move about the raft without being tied up.

On one occasion, they advertise a three-night engagement of a play called "The Royal Nonesuch". The play turns out to be only a couple of minutes' worth of an absurd, bawdy sham. On the afternoon of the first performance, a drunk called Boggs is shot dead by a gentleman named Colonel Sherburn. A lynch mob forms to retaliate against Sherburn, surrounded at his home, disperses the mob by making a defiant speech describing how true lynching should be done. By the third night of "The Royal Nonesuch", the townspeople prepare for their revenge on the duke and king for their money-making scam, but the two cleverly skip town together with Huck and Jim just before the performance begins.

In the next town, the two swindlers then impersonate two brothers of Peter Wilks, a recently deceased man of property. To match accounts of Wilks' brothers, the king attempts an English accent and the duke pretends to be a deaf-mute, while starting to collect Wilks' inheritance. Huck decides that Wilks' three orphaned nieces, who treat Huck with kindness, do not deserve to be cheated and so he tries to retrieve the nieces' stolen inheritance. In a desperate moment, Huck is forced to hide the money in Wilks' coffin, which is buried the next morning. The arrival of two new men who seem to be the real brothers throws everything into confusion, so the townspeople decide to dig up the coffin in order to determine who are the true brothers, but Huck leaves for the raft in the ensuing commotion. Just as Huck and Jim believe they have escaped, the two villains turn up and take charge, to Huck's despair. When Huck is finally able to get away and return to his raft to flee with Jim, he finds to his horror that Jim has been sold to a family that intends to return the slave to his proper owner for the reward. Defying his conscience and accepting the negative religious consequences, he expects for his actions—"All right, then, I'll go to hell!"—Huck resolves to free Jim once and for all.

Huck learns that Jim is being held at the plantation of Silas and Sally Phelps. The family's nephew, Tom, is expected for a visit at the same time of Huck's arrival, so Huck is luckily mistaken for Tom and welcomed into their home. He plays along, hoping to find Jim's location and free him. In a surprising plot twist, it is revealed that the expected nephew is in fact Tom Sawyer. When Huck intercepts Tom on the road and tells him everything, Tom decides to join Huck's scheme, pretending to be his own younger half-brother Sid, while Huck continues to pretend that he is himself Tom Sawyer. In the meantime, Jim has told the family about the two grifters and the new plan for "The Royal Nonesuch", and so the people of town capture the duke and king, who are then tarred and feathered and ridden out of town on a trial.

Rather than simply sneaking Jim out of the shed where he is being held, Tom develops an elaborate plan to free him, involving secret messages, a hidden tunnel, a rope ladder sent in Jim's food, and other elements from adventure books he has read, including an anonymous note to the Phelpses warning them of the whole scheme. During the resulting pursuit, Tom is shot in the leg and Jim remains by his side, risking recapture rather than completing his escape alone. Although a local doctor admires Jim's decency, he has Jim captured while asleep and returned to the Phelpses. After this event, events quickly resolve themselves. Tom's Aunt Polly arrives and reveals Huck and Tom's true identities to the Phelps family. Jim is revealed to be a free man. Miss Watson died two months earlier and freed Jim in her will, but Tom chose not to reveal this information so that he could come up with an elaborate plan to rescue Jim. Jim tells Huck that Huck's father has been dead for some time (he was the dead man they found in the floating house; Jim sensitively hid his identity from Huck until now) so that Huck may return safely to St. Petersburg. Despite Sally's plans to adopt and civilize him, Huck intends to flee west to Indian Territory.

Select Reading: Chapter 31

Once I said to myself it would be a thousand times better for Jim to be a slave at home where his family was, as long as he'd got you to be a slave, and so I'd better write a letter to Tom Sawyer and tell him to tell Miss Watson where he was. But I soon give up that notion, for two things: she'd be mad and disgusted at his rascality and ungratefulness for leaving her, and so she'd sell him straight down the river again; and if she didn't, everybody naturally despises an ungrateful nigger, and they'd make Jim feel it all the time, and so he'd feel ornery and disgraced. And then think of me! It would get all around, that Huck Finn helped a nigger to get his freedom; and if I was to ever see anybody from that town again, I'd be ready to get down and lick his boots for shame. That's just the way: a person does a low-down thing, and then he don't want to take no consequences of it. Think as long as he can hide it, it ain't no disgrace. That was my fix exactly. The more I studied about this, the more my conscience went to grinding me, and the more wicked and low-down and ornery I got to feeling. And at last, when it hit me all of a sudden that here was the plain hand of Providence slapping me in the face and letting me know my wickedness was being watched all time from up there in heaven, whilst I was stealing a poor old woman's nigger that hadn't ever done me no harm, and now was showing me the One that's always on the lookout, and ain't agoing to allow no such miserable doings to go only just so fur and no further. I most dropped in my tracks I was so scared. Well, I tried the best I could to kind of soften it up somehow for myself, by saying I was brung up wicked, and so I warn't so much to blame, but something inside of me kept saying, "There was the Sunday school, you could'a' goen to it; and if you'd a' done it they'd 'a' learned you there that people that acts as I'd been acting about that nigger goes to everlasting fire."

译文:我曾经心里想,杰姆要是注定做奴隶的话,在家乡做要比在外地强一千倍。在家乡,他有家啊。为此,我曾经想,不妨由我写封信给汤姆·莎耶,要他把杰姆目前的情况告诉华珍小姐。不过我很快就放弃了这个念头。原因有两个。她准定会发火,又气又恨,认为他不该如此忘恩负义,竟然从她那儿逃跑。这样,她会干脆把他卖掉,再一次把他卖到下游去。如果她不是这么干,大伙儿自然会一个个都瞧不起忘恩负义的黑奴,他们势必会叫杰姆时时刻刻意识到这一点,搞得他狼狈不堪、无地自容。并且再想想我自己吧!很快便会传开这么一个说法,说赫克·芬出力帮助一个黑奴重获自由。这样,要是我再见到这个镇子上的随便哪一个人,我肯定会羞愧得无地自容,愿意趴在地下求饶。一般的情况往往是这样的嘛。一个人一旦做了什么下流的勾当,可是又不想承担什么责任,自以为只要把事情遮盖起来,这多么丢人现眼啊。这恰恰正是我的情况。我越是想到这件事,我的良心越是受到折磨,我也就越是觉得自己邪恶、下流、没出息。到后来,我突然之间猛然醒悟了,认识到这明明是上帝的手在打我的耳光,让我明白,我的种种邪恶,始终逃不开在上天的眼睛。一个可怜的老妇人平生从没有损害过我一根毫毛,我却把她的黑奴拐跑,为了这个,上帝正指引着我,让我明白什么都逃不过"他"那高悬的明镜。"他"决不允许这类不幸的事再发展下去,只能到此为止。一想到这一些,我差点就立刻跌倒在地,我委实吓得不得了啦。于是我就想方设法,试图为自己开脱。我对自个儿说:我从小就是在邪恶的环境中长大的,因此不能过于怪罪我啊。不过,在我的心里,还有另一个声音子在不停地说,"还有主日学校,你本该到那儿去啊。要是你早去的话,他们会在那儿教导你的嘛,教导你说,谁要像我那样为了黑奴所干的这一切,是要下地狱受到永恒的烈火的煎熬的。"

Analysis of Major Characters

Huckleberry Finn: Huck is a boy who comes from the lowest levels of white society. His father is a drunk and a ruffian who disappears for months. Huck himself is dirty and frequently homeless. Although the Widow Douglas attempts to reform him, he resists her attempts and maintains his independent ways. The community has failed to protect him from his father, and though the Widow finally gives Huck some of the schooling and religious training that he had missed, he has not been indoctrinated with social values in the same way a middle-class boy like Tom Sawyer has been. Huck's distance from mainstream society makes him skeptical of the world around him and the ideas it passes on to him. His instinctual distrust and his experiences as he travels down the river force him to question the things society has taught him. According to the law, Jim is Miss Watson's property, but according to Huck's sense of logic and fairness, it seems right to help Jim. Huck's natural intelligence and his willingness to think through a situation on its own merits lead him to some conclusions that are correct in their context but that would shock white society. For example, Huck discovers, when he and Jim meet a group of slave-hunters, that telling a lie is sometimes the right course of action. Because Huck is a child, the world seems new to him. Everything he encounters is an occasion for thought. Because of his background, he does more than just apply the rules that he has been taught—he creates his own rules. Yet Huck is not some kind of independent moral genius. He must still struggle with some of the preconceptions about blacks that society has ingrained in him. And at the end of the novel, he shows himself all too willing to follow Tom Sawyer's lead. But even these failures are part of what makes Huck appealing and sympathetic. He is only a boy, after all, and therefore fallible. Imperfect as he is, Huck represents what anyone is capable of becoming: a thinking, feeling human being rather than a mere cog in the machine of society.

Jim: Jim is a man of remarkable intelligence and compassion. At first glance, Jim seems to be superstitious to the point of idiocy, but a careful reading of the time that Huck and Jim spend on Jackson's Island reveals that Jim's superstitions conceal a deep knowledge of the natural world and represent an alternate form of truth or intelligence. Moreover, Jim has one of the few healthy, functioning families in the novel. Although he has been separated from his wife and children, he misses them terribly. And it is only the thought of a permanent separation from them that motivates his criminal act of running away from Miss Watson. On the river, Jim becomes a surrogate father, as well as a friend, to Huck, taking care of him without being intrusive or smothering. He cooks for the boy and shelters him from some of the worst horrors that they encounter, including the sight of Pap's corpse, and, for a time, the news of his father's passing. Like Huck, Jim is realistic about his situation and must find ways of accomplishing his goals without incurring the wrath of those who could turn him in. In this position, he is seldom able to act boldly or speak his mind. Nonetheless, despite these restrictions and constant fear, Jim consistently acts as a noble human being and a loyal friend. In fact, Jim could be described as the only real adult in the novel, and the only one who provides a positive, respectable example for Huck to follow.

Tom Sawyer: Whereas Huck's birth and upbringing have left him in poverty and on the margins of society, Tom has been raised in relative comfort. As a result, his beliefs are an unfortunate combination of what he has learned from the adults around him and the fanciful notions he has gleaned from reading romance and adventure novels. Tom believes in sticking strictly to rules, most of which have more to do with style than with morality or anyone's welfare. Tom is thus the perfect foil for Huck: his rigid adherence to rules and precepts contrasts with Huck's tendency to question authority and think for himself. Although Tom's escapades are often funny, they also show just how disturbingly and unthinkingly cruel society can be. Tom knows all along that Miss Watson has died and that Jim is now a free man, yet he is willing to allow Jim to remain a captive while he entertains himself with fantastic escape plans. Tom's plotting tortures not only Jim, but Aunt Sally and Uncle Silas as well. In the end, although he is just a boy like Huck and is appealing in his zest for adventure and his unconscious wittiness, Tom embodies what a young, well-to-do white man is raised to become in the society of his time: self-centered with dominion over all.

The Widow Douglas: She is the wife of the late Justice of the Peace of St. Petersburg—the village that provides the story's setting. Huck likes her because she's kind to him and feeds him when he's hungry. Her attempts to civilize him fail when Huck prefers to live in the woods with his father. He doesn't like to wear the shoes she buys him, and he doesn't like his food cooked the way hers is.

Miss Watson: The Widow's maiden sister. Her favorite subject is the Bible. She owns Jim and considers selling him down river. This causes Jim to run away. Filled with sorrow for driving Jim to this extreme, Miss Watson sets him free in her will.

The King and the Duke: They are two river tramps and con-men who pass themselves off to Huck and Jim as the lost Dauphin of France and the unfortunate Duke of Bridgewater. They make their living off suckers they find in the small, dirty, ignorant Southern villages. Of the two men, the duke is less cruel and more imaginative than the king, neither has any moral sensitivity worth mentioning. These men represent the starkly materialistic ideals of "the man who can sell himself" in their most logical extreme.

Themes

Slavery: The story provides an allegory to explain how and why slavery is wrong. The writer uses Jim, a main character and a slave, to demonstrate the humanity of slaves. Jim expresses the complicated human emotions and struggles with the path of his life. To prevent being sold and forced to separate from his family, Jim runs away from his owner, and works towards obtaining freedom so he can buy his family's freedom. All along their journey downriver, Jim cares for and protects Huck, not as a servant, but as a friend. Thus, the author encourages the reader to feel sympathy and empathy for Jim and outrage at the society that has enslaved him and threatened his life. Only in the final section of the novel does the author develop the central conflict concerning slavery: should Huck free Jim and then be condemned to hell? This decision is life-altering for Huck, as it forces him to reject everything that "civilization" has taught him. Huck chooses to free Jim, based on his personal experiences rather than social norms, thus choosing the morality of the "natural life" over that of civilization.

Conflict between Civilization and Natural Life: Huck represents natural life through his freedom of spirit, uncivilized ways, and desire to escape from civilization. He was raised without any rules or discipline and has a strong resistance to anything that might civilize him. This conflict is introduced in the first chapter through the efforts of the Widow Douglas: she tries to force Huck to wear new clothes, give up smoking, and learn the Bible. The novel seems to suggest that the uncivilized way of life is more desirable and morally superior.

Honor: Though Tom Sawyer does not appear in the 1960 film, in the novel he expresses his belief that there is a great deal of honor associated with thieving. Robbery appears throughout the novel, specifically when Huck and Jim encounter robbers on the shipwrecked boat and are forced to put up with the King and Dauphin, both of whom "rob" everyone they meet. Tom's original robber band is paralleled later in the novel when Tom and Huck become true thieves, but honorable ones, at the end of the novel. They resolve to steal Jim, freeing him from the bonds of slavery, which is an honorable act.

Mockery of Religion: In the first chapter, Huck indicates that hell sounds far more fun than heaven. Later on, in a very prominent scene, the "King", a liar and cheat, convinces a religious community to give him money so he can "convert" his pirate friends. The religious people are easily led astray, which mocks their beliefs and devotion to God.

Superstition: Generally, both Huck and Jim are very rational characters, yet when they encounter anything slightly superstitious, irrationality takes over. The power superstition holds over the two demonstrates that Huck and Jim are child-like despite their apparent maturity. In addition, superstition foreshadows the plot at several key junctions. For instance, when Huck spills salt, Pap returns, and when Huck touches a snakeskin with his bare hands, a rattlesnake bites Jim.

Money: The novel begins by pointing out that Huck has over six thousand dollars to his name. Huck demonstrates a relaxed attitude towards wealth. And because he has so much of it, he does not view money as a necessity, but rather as a luxury. Huck's views regarding wealth clearly contrast with Jim's. For Jim, who is on a quest to buy his family out of slavery, money is equivalent to freedom. In addition, wealth would allow him to raise his status in society. Thus, Jim is on a constant quest for wealth, whereas Huck remains apathetic.

Mississippi River: The majority of the plot takes place on the river or its banks. For Huck and Jim, the river represents freedom. On the raft, they are completely independent and determine their own courses of action. Jim looks forward to reaching the free states, and Huck is eager to escape his abusive, drunkard father and the "civilization" of Miss Watson. However, the towns along the river banks begin to exert influence upon them, and eventually Huck and Jim meet criminals, shipwrecks, dishonesty, and great danger. Finally, a fog forces them to miss the town of Cairo, at which point they were planning to head up the Ohio River, towards the free states, in a steamboat. Originally, the river is a safe place for the two travelers, but it becomes increasingly dangerous as the realities of their runaway life set in on them. Once reflective of absolute freedom, the river soon becomes only a short-term escape.

Film Adaptations

The Adventures of Huckleberry Finn (1960) was directed by Michael Curtiz, starring Tony Randall, Eddie Hodges, and Archie Moore. The novel was a story around the independent-minded Huckleberry, about a journey far from home and a friendship developing between two unlikely traveling companions. Below the surface, it was an examination and satire of the pre-Civil War South. Huck and the escaped slave Jim ride a raft down the Mississippi, encountering the sordidness and chicanery of the adult world and the hypocrisy of a moralistic society that tolerates slavery. Few film adaptations tried to deal with the book's double level. Usually all the attention was thrown on Huck and Jim's adventures, their encounter with the two rascally conmen, the King and the Duke, and a teenage love interest. This film is also accused of the same simplification: Actually, this is not true. Archie Moore, light heavyweight champion of the world, took a break from racking up his 141 knockouts to make his acting debut as Jim. Unfortunately he is unable to connect to the role here and seems amateurish and unsteady for most of the film although he does manage a touch of pathos by the end. Eddie Hodges stars as Huckleberry Finn. His acting style probably worked well at the forty feet distance between the stage and a theater seat, but on screen Hodges plays the role too broadly. He also gives off a well-scrubbed wholesomeness that ill-suits the barefoot Huck Finn. There are several pluses in the film. Tony Randall gives a marvelous performance as the "King", adding subtle touches of craftiness and menace beneath his flamboyant character. There are also a number of great character actors in cameos. The exteriors feature beautifully photographed scenes of rural Southern life.

Fig 9.3　Huck and Pap

Fig 9.4　Huck and Jim

Fig 9.5　The King and the Duke

Fig 9.6　The Sheriff and Huck in Girl's Dress

　　The Adventures of Huckleberry Finn(1993) is a Disney adventure film directed by Stephen Sommers, starring Elijah Wood, Courtney B. Vance, Jason Robards and Robbie Coltrane, distributed by Buena Vista Pictures. It focuses almost exclusively on the first half of the book. The story of Huck and Jim has been told in six or seven earlier films, this is a graceful and entertaining version by a young director, who doesn't dwell on the film's humane message, but doesn't avoid it, either. The transformation of Huck is there on the screen, although much more time is devoted to the story's picaresque adventures, as Huck and Jim meet a series of colorful characters, including some desperate criminals, some feuding neighbors, and the immortal con men the King and the Duke. Huck is played by Elijah Wood, who mercifully seems free of cuteness and other affectations of child stars, and makes a resolute, convincing Huck. The real Huck was probably much tougher and had rougher edges, but Huck has been sanitized for years in the films. Jim, the crucial character in the story, is played by Courtney B. Vance, a New York stage actor who is able to embody the enormous tact with which Jim guides Huck out of the thickets of prejudice and sets him on the road to tolerance and decency. Huck and Jim drift onto the subjects of race and slavery, and Huck is bound to admit, after Jim explains it to him, that black people have the same feelings as everyone else, and are deserving of his respect. This process of Huck's conversion is one of the crucial events in American literature. Some cannot admire it and think it should not be taught in schools because Huck, like every boy of his time, used the word nigger. They are very short-sighted. It doesn't use the word, nor does it really venture very far into the heart of Huck's transformation. It wants to entertain and fears to offend. But it is a good film with strong performances. Nothing in it is wrong, although some depths are lacking.

Fig 9.7　A DVD Cover of the 1993 Film

Fig 9.8　Huck and Jim

A Wonderful Dialogue from the 1960 Film

Huck sees Jim and walks towards him.
Huck: Hello, Jim.
Jim: (*Horrified*) Glory be. You's a ghost.
Huck: I ain't a ghost.
Jim: But you's dead. Your Pap come running into town, yelling that robbers killed you.
Huck: Well. I tricked it up so Pap would think I was dead. But I ain't. (*Walking towards Jim and reaching out*) Here, touch me. Go ahead, touch me. (*Jim touches Huck's head and smiles.*) It sure was a good trick, eh Jim?
Jim: Oh, Huck, that was smart. You smart, all right.
Huck: Thank you, Jim.
Jim: What is you gonna to now?
Huck: I'm going some place where they ain't ringing a bell to get up by or eat by and another one to go to bed by. New Orleans, probably. Have to go there first to get to South America. Got a canoe hid over there in a cove. I'm gonna take her and float down the Mississippi past St. Louis, Cairo.
Jim: Cairo? Illinois?
Huck: (*Smoking*) Then to the big river and right south to New Orleans.
Jim: This raft can float you there better than a canoe. I catched her off the river.
Huck: (*Walking to the raft and standing on it*) She sure is a beaut, Jim. She'd better for sleeping and keeping out of rain if she had a wigwam.
Jim: Yep, a nice dirt floor and she'd be high and dry. Huck, I got skillets, cups, pans and knives and everything. All we need is just a little luck.
Huck: Where was you going, Jim?
Jim: I run away from Widow Dauglas.
Huck: Jim.

Jim: Well, she was gonna sell me so she could pay your Pap.

Huck: You go back to her, Jim. She owns you and what's right's right. Besides, you'll get caught for sure, a slave alone on a raft.

Jim: I'd be safe. I was with a white man or a white boy, even.

Huck: I couldn't help a runaway slave, Jim. Why folks would say I was no better than a low-down abolitionist.

Jim: I know, Huck. I know.

Four people in a boat are looking for Huck's body. Huck and Jim see them and hear their talk. The people think that Jim killed Huck and is now probably on the island.

Huck: They think you killed me. Of course you didn't, because I ain't dead.

Jim: You better go. Take the raft.

Huck: What about you?

Jim: I could go with you, Huck. I was going down to Cairo, Illinois to step across into free territory.

Huck: What do you take me for, Jim, helping a runaway slave? That just wouldn't be right. (*Trying to leave with the raft. Tom follows.*) I'm sorry, Jim. You know I can't take you and all that.

Jim: You just wanna to what's right. I admire you for that.

Huck: Thanks, Jim.

Jim: And when they get here, don't you worry about them finding out you ain't dead. They can whup me or beat me or whatever they want to do. I won't tell them you's alive. I promise.

Huck: Jumping Jehoshaphat! You's the only one that knows, ain't you?

Jim: Especially you Pap, Huck. I won't tell him, especially.

Huck: Pap.

Jim: As for me talking in my sleep, I'll go off somewhere by myself so nobody will hear me.

Huck: You talk in your sleep?

Jim: That's a bad thing I do, but not too much.

Huck: I gotta take you with me, Jim.

Jim: That wouldn't be right.

Huck: (*Pulling Jim*) Don't matter when you got no choice. Leaving you behind just wouldn't be smart. Now, come on, Jim. (*Sounds of gun shots from the river*) Please Jim, come with me.

Jim: If you think that's a smart thing to do, whatever you say is smart. All right, let's go. You got an uncommon level head for a white boy.

Huck: Thank you, Jim.

Jim: (*Taking the pole from Huck's hand*) Here, give me the pole, Huck. You just leave this to old Jim. You take the sweep and let's go. (*The raft moves.*) All we got to do now is keep from getting caught.

Discussions

1. What is Huck's attitude toward people he disagrees with? What does this tell us about Huck?

2. Does Huck change at all during the course of the novel? In what way?
3. What use does Mark Twain make of concrete details of description and character portrayal?
4. In what way can Jim be said to be a father to Huck?
5. The 1960 film made some changes of the original work. Name some of the changes and try to explain why the director did so.

Unit 10　Harriet Beecher Stowe and *Uncle Tom's Cabin*

　　Harriet Beecher Stowe (1811—1896) was an American abolitionist and author. She wrote more than 20 books, including novels, three travel memoirs, and collections of articles and letters. She was influential both for her writings and her public stands on social issues of the day. *Uncle Tom's Cabin* (1852) was a depiction of life for African Americans under slavery. Its emotional portrayal of the impact of slavery captured the nation's attention. It added to the debate about abolition and slavery, and aroused opposition in the South. After the start of the Civil War, Stowe traveled to Washington, D. C. and there met President Abraham Lincoln on November 25, 1862. Lincoln greeted her by saying, "So you are the little woman who wrote the book that started this great war."

 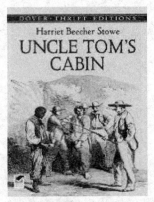

Fig 10.1　Harriet Beecher Stowe　　　　Fig 10.2　A book Cover of *Uncle Tom's Cabin*

Plot

　　Having run up large debts, a Kentucky farmer named Arthur Shelby faces the prospect of losing everything he owns. Though he and his wife, Emily Shelby, have a kindhearted and affectionate relationship with their slaves, Shelby decides to raise money by selling two of his slaves to Mr. Haley, a coarse slave trader. The slaves in question are Uncle Tom, a middle-aged man with a wife and children on the farm, and Harry, the young son of Mrs. Shelby's maid Eliza. When Shelby tells his wife about his agreement with Haley, she is appalled because she has promised Eliza that Shelby would not sell her son.

　　However, Eliza overhears the conversation between Shelby and his wife and, after warning Uncle Tom and his wife, Aunt Chloe, she takes Harry and flees to the North, hoping to find freedom with her husband George in Canada. Haley pursues her, but two other Shelby slaves alert Eliza to the danger. She miraculously evades capture by crossing the half-frozen Ohio River, the boundary separating Kentucky from the North. Haley hires a slave hunter named Loker and his gang to bring Eliza and Harry back to Kentucky. Eliza and Harry make their way to a Quaker settlement, where the Quakers agree to help transport them to safety. They are joined at the settlement by George, who reunites joyously with his family for the trip to Canada.

Meanwhile, Uncle Tom sadly leaves his family and Mas'r George, Shelby's young son and Tom's friend, as Haley takes him to a boat on the Mississippi to be transported to a slave market. On the boat, Tom meets an angelic little white girl named Eva, who quickly befriends him. When Eva falls into the river, Tom dives in to save her, and her father, Augustine St. Clare, gratefully agrees to buy Tom from Haley. Tom travels with the St. Clares to their home in New Orleans, where he grows increasingly invaluable to the St. Clare household and increasingly close to Eva, with whom he shares a devout Christianity.

Up North, George and Eliza remain in flight from Loker and his men. When Loker attempts to capture them, George shoots him in the side, and the other slave hunters retreat. Eliza convinces George and the Quakers to bring Loker to the next settlement, where he can be healed. Meanwhile, in New Orleans, St. Clare discusses slavery with his cousin Ophelia, who opposes slavery as an institution but harbors deep prejudices against blacks. St. Clare, by contrast, feels no hostility against blacks but tolerates slavery because he feels powerless to change it. To help Ophelia overcome her bigotry, he buys Topsy, a young black girl who was abused by her past master and arranges for Ophelia to begin educating her.

After Tom has lived with the St. Clares for two years, Eva grows very ill. She slowly weakens, then dies, with a vision of heaven before her. Her death has a profound effect on everyone who knew her: Ophelia resolves to love the slaves, Topsy learns to trust and feel attached to others, and St. Clare decides to set Tom free. However, before he can act on his decision, St. Clare is stabbed to death while trying to settle a brawl. As he dies, he at last finds God and goes to be reunited with his mother in heaven.

St. Clare's cruel wife, Marie, sells Tom to a vicious plantation owner named Simon Legree. Tom is taken to rural Louisiana with a group of new slaves, including Emmeline, whom the demonic Legree has purchased to use as a sex slave, replacing his previous sex slave Cassy. Legree takes a strong dislike to Tom when Tom refuses to whip a fellow slave as ordered. Tom receives a severe beating, and Legree resolves to crush his faith in God. Tom meets Cassy, and hears her story. Separated from her daughter by slavery, she became pregnant again but killed the child because she could not stand to have another child taken from her.

Around this time, with the help of Tom Loker—now a changed man after being healed by the Quakers—George, Eliza, and Harry at last cross over into Canada from Lake Erie and obtain their freedom. In Louisiana, Tom's faith is sorely tested by his hardships, and he nearly ceases to believe. He has two visions, however—one of Christ and one of Eva—which renew his spiritual strength and give him the courage to withstand Legree's torments. He encourages Cassy to escape. She does so, taking Emmeline with her, after she devises a ruse in which she and Emmeline pretend to be ghosts. When Tom refuses to tell Legree where Cassy and Emmeline have gone, Legree orders his overseers to beat him. When Tom is near death, he forgives Legree and the overseers. George

Shelby arrives with money in hand to buy Tom's freedom, but he is too late. He can only watch as Tom dies a martyr's death.

Taking a boat toward freedom, Cassy and Emmeline meet George Harris's sister and travel with her to Canada, where Cassy realizes that Eliza is her long-lost daughter. The newly reunited family travels to France and decides to move to Liberia, the African nation created for former American slaves. George Shelby returns to the Kentucky farm, where, after his father's death, he sets all the slaves free in honor of Tom's memory. He urges them to think on Tom's sacrifice every time they look at his cabin and to lead a pious Christian life, just as Tom did.

Select Reading: Chapter 14

Among the passengers on the boat was a young gentleman of fortune and family, resident in New Orleans, who bore the name of St. Clare. He had with him a daughter between five and six years of age, together with a lady who seemed to claim relationship to both, and to have the little one especially under her charge.

Tom had often caught glimpses of this little girl, for she was one of those busy, tripping creatures, that can be no more contained in one place than a sunbeam or a summer breeze, nor was she one that, once seen, could be easily forgotten.

Tom, who had the soft, impressible nature of his kindly race, ever yearning toward the simple and childlike, watched the little creature with daily increasing interest. To him she seemed something almost divine. Often and often she walked mournfully round the place where Haley's gang of men and women sat in their chains. She would glide in among them, and look at them with an air of perplexed and sorrowful earnestness; and sometimes she would lift their chains with her slender hands, and then sigh woefully, as she glided away. Several times she appeared suddenly among them, with her hands full of candy, nuts, and oranges, which she would distribute joyfully to them, and then be gone again.

Tom watched the little lady a great deal, before he ventured on any overtures towards acquaintanceship. But at last they got on quite confidential terms.

"What's little missy's name?" said Tom, at last, when he thought matters were ripe to push such an inquiry.

"Evangeline St. Clare," said the little one, "though papa and everybody else call me Eva. Now, what's your name?"

"My name's Tom; the little chil used to call me Uncle Tom, way back thar in Kentuck."

"Then I mean to call you Uncle Tom, because, you see, I like you," said Eva. "So, Uncle Tom, where are you going?"

"I don't know, Miss Eva."

"Don't know?" said Eva.

"No, I am going to be sold to somebody. I don't know who."

"My papa can buy you," said Eva, quickly, "and if he buys you, you will have good times. I mean to ask him, this very day."

"Thank you, my little lady," said Tom.

The boat here stopped at a small landing to take in wood, and Eva, hearing her father's voice, bounded nimbly away. Tom rose up, and went forward to offer his service in wooding, and soon was busy among the hands.

Eva and her father were standing together by the railings to see the boat start from the landing-place, the wheel had made two or three revolutions in the water, when, by some sudden movement, the little one suddenly lost her balance and fell sheer over the side of the boat into the water. Her father, scarce knowing what he did, was plunging in after her, but was held back by some behind him, who saw that more efficient aid had followed his child.

Tom was standing just under her on the lower deck, as she fell. He saw her strike the water, and sink, and was after her in a moment. A broad-chested, strong-armed fellow, it was nothing for him to keep afloat in the water, till, in a moment or two the child rose to the surface, and he caught her in his arms, and, swimming with her to the boat-side, handed her up, all dripping, to the grasp of hundreds of hands, which, as if they had all belonged to one man, were stretched eagerly out to receive her. A few moments more, and her father bore her, dripping and senseless, to the ladies' cabin, where, as is usual in cases of the kind, there ensued a very well-meaning and kind-hearted strife among the female occupants generally, as to who should do the most things to make a disturbance, and to hinder her recovery in every way possible.

译文：船上乘客中，有一位富有且有家室的年轻绅士，他家住新奥尔良，名叫圣克莱尔。跟他一起的，是一个五六岁的女儿，还有一位女士，似乎跟他们是亲戚，而且特别关照小女孩。

汤姆时常瞧见小女孩，因为她闲不住，四处走动，像一束阳光或一股夏日清风，不会在一个地方待着。凡是看见她的人，都不易将她忘掉。

汤姆有他和蔼民族的温柔和易打动人的性格，从来都渴望靠近小家伙和有童心的人。他望着小女孩，兴趣日增。对汤姆而言，她好像是一位天使。她经常忧愁地行走在哈里那群坐着的、被铁链铐住的男人和女人周围。她会从中间溜过去，带着疑惑的神情和真诚的悲伤看着他们；有时她用小手拿起他们的铁链，走开时悲痛地叹息。好几次她突然出现在他们中间，双手捧着糖果、核桃和橘子，高兴地分给大家，然后又离开了。

汤姆看了小女孩好久，才敢主动向前与她相识。但最后他们成了密友。

"小姐，你叫什么名字？"最终，汤姆认为时机成熟可以问这样的问题时，说道。

"伊万杰琳·圣克莱尔，"小女孩说，"虽然爸爸和其他每个人都叫我伊娃。那你叫什么名字呢？"

"我叫汤姆；在肯塔基那边，小孩们都叫我汤姆叔。"

"那我也叫你汤姆叔，因为，你看得出来，我喜欢你，"伊娃说，"你要去哪，汤姆叔？"

"我不知道，伊娃小姐。"

"不知道？"伊娃说。

"是的，我将被卖给别人。我不知道是谁。"

"我爸爸可以买你，"伊娃马上说道，"如果他买了你，你就会过得好。我今天就去叫他买。"

"谢谢，我的小小姐。"

船在一个小地方靠岸载木材。听到她爸爸的声音，伊娃敏捷轻快地跳着跑走了。汤姆起身,前去帮忙搬运木头,很快跟雇员们一起忙开了。

伊娃与爸爸一起站在护栏边,看着船从抛锚之处起航,涡轮在水中转了两三圈,一个突然的转动使小姑娘失去平衡,从船边径直掉入水中。她爸爸一下不知所措,正要扎入水中,背后有人把他拉住了,因为已有人先他采取更有效的营救落水孩子的措施了。

她落水时,汤姆正站在她下方的甲板上。他见她在水中挣扎下沉,马上就下水救她。他胸宽臂壮,浮在水上轻而易举,片刻之后孩子升到水面,他就用手臂抓住她,与她一起游到船边,将她举起,浑身滴水,上百只手抓住她。这些手好像全是一个人的手,急切地伸出来将她接住。不一会,她爸爸抱着浑身滴水、失去知觉的她送到女宾仓舱,女宾们会用尽一切办法来防止外界的打搅和妨碍她康复的行为,悉心照顾她。

Analysis of Major Characters

Uncle Tom: Uncle Tom is one of the most popular figures of nineteenth – century American fiction. But after its initial burst of sensational popularity and influence, the novel fell into neglect. Not until the early 1960s, when the Civil Rights Movement reawakened an interest in anti – slavery fiction, did the novel again become widely read. The values and attributes that seemed admirable in its characters in 1852 frequently appeared incomprehensible and even contemptible to twentieth – century readers. In particular, the passive acceptance of slavery practiced by Uncle Tom seemed horrendously out of line with the resolve and strength of modern black Civil Rights crusaders. The term "Uncle Tom" became an insult, conjuring an image of an old black man eager to please his white masters and happy to accept his own position of inferiority. Although modern readers' criticisms hold some validity, the notion of an "Uncle Tom" contains generalizations not found within the actual character in the novel. First, Tom is not an old man. The novel states that he is eight years older than Shelby, which probably places him in his late forties at the start of the novel. Moreover, Tom does not accept his position of inferiority with happiness. Tom's passivity owes not to stupidity or to contentment with his position, but to his deep religious values, which impel him to love everyone and selflessly endure his trials. Indeed, Tom's central characteristic in the novel is this religiosity, his strength of faith. Everywhere Tom goes, he manages to spread some of the love and goodwill of his religious beliefs, helping to alleviate the pain of slavery and enhance the hope of salvation. And while this religiosity translates into a selfless passivity on Tom's part, it also translates into a policy of warm encouragement of others' attempts at freedom. Thus, he supports Eliza's escape, as well as that of Cassy and Emmeline from the Legree plantation. Moreover, while Tom may not actively seek his own freedom, he practices resistance in his passivity. When Legree orders him to beat the slave girl, he refuses and stands firm in his values. He will submit to being beaten for his beliefs, but he will not capitulate or run away. Moreover, even in recognizing Tom's passivity and Stowe's approving treatment of it, one should note that Stowe does not present this behavior as a model of black behavior, but as a heroic model of behavior that should be practiced by everyone, black and white. Stowe makes it very clear that if the villainous white slaveholders of the novel were to achieve Tom's selfless Christian love for others, slavery would be impossible, and Tom's death would never have happened. Because Stowe believes that a transformation through Christian love must occur before slavery can be abolished successfully, she holds up Tom's death as nobler than any escape, in that it provides an example for others and offers the hope of a more generalized salvation. Through this death, Tom becomes a Christ figure, a radical role for a black character to play in American fiction in 1852. Tom's death proves Legree's fundamental moral and personal inferiority, and provides the motivating force behind George Shelby's decision to free all the slaves. By practicing selflessness and loving his enemy, Tom becomes a martyr and affects social change. Although contemporary society finds its heroes in active agents of social change and tends to discourage submissiveness, Stowe means for Tom to embody noble heroic tendencies of his own. She portrays his passivity as a virtue unconnected to his minority status. Within the world of the novel, Tom is presented as more than a black hero—he is presented as a hero transcending race.

Ophelia St. Clare: Probably the most complex female character in the novel, Ophelia deserves special attention from the reader because she is treated as a surrogate for Stowe's intended audience. It is as if Stowe conceives an imaginary picture of her intended reader, then brings that reader into the book as a character. Ophelia embodies what Stowe considers a widespread Northern problem: the white person who opposes slavery on a theoretical level but feels racial prejudice and hatred in the presence of an actual black slave. Ophelia detests slavery, but she considers it almost necessary for blacks, against whom she harbors a deep-seated prejudice—she does not want them to touch her. Stowe emphasizes that much of Ophelia's racial prejudice stems from unfamiliarity and ignorance rather than from actual experience-based hatred. Because Ophelia has seldom spent time in the presence of slaves, she finds them uncomfortably alien. However, Ophelia is one of the only characters in the novel who develops as the story progresses. Once St. Clare puts Topsy in her care, Ophelia begins to have increased contact with a slave. At first she tries to teach Topsy out of a sense of mere duty. But Stowe suggests that duty alone will not eradicate slavery—abolitionists must act out of love. Eva's death proves the crucial catalyst in Ophelia's transformation, and she comes to love Topsy as a human being, overcoming her racial prejudice and offering a model to Stowe's Northern readers.

Simon Legree: Although largely a uniformly evil villain, Simon Legree does possess some psychological depth as a character. He has been deeply affected by the death of his angelic mother and seems to show some legitimate affection for Cassy. Nonetheless, Legree's main purpose in the book is as a foil to Uncle Tom, and as an effective picture of slavery at its worst. Often associated with firelight and flames, Legree demonstrates literally infernal qualities, and his devilishness provides an effective contrast with the angelic qualities of his passive slave. Legree's demoniacally evil ways also play an important role in shaping the end of the book along the lines of the traditional Christian narrative. Above all, Legree desires to break Tom's religious faith and to see him capitulate to doubt and sin. In the end, although Tom dies and Legree survives, the evil that Legree stands for has been destroyed. Tom dies loving the men who kill him, proving that his faith prevails over Legree's evil.

Eliza: Eliza is a slave and personal maid to Mrs. Shelby who escapes to the North with her five-year old son Harry after he is sold to Mr. Haley. Her husband, George, eventually finds Eliza and Harry in Ohio and emigrates with them to Canada, then France and finally Liberia. The character Eliza was inspired by an account given at Lane Theological Seminary in Cincinnati by John Rankin to Stowe's husband Calvin, a professor at the school. According to Rankin, in February 1838 a young slave woman had escaped across the frozen Ohio River to the town of Ripley with her child in her arms and stayed at his house on her way further north.

Evangeline St. Clare (Eva): She is the daughter of Augustine St. Clare. Eva enters the narrative when Uncle Tom is traveling via steamship to New Orleans to be sold, and he rescues the 5 or 6 year-old girl from drowning. Eva begs her father to buy Tom, and he becomes the head coachman at the St. Clare house. He spends most of his time with the angelic Eva. Eva often talks about love and forgiveness, even convincing the dour slave girl Topsy that she deserves love. She even touches the heart of her Aunt Ophelia. Eventually Eva falls terminally ill. Before dying, she gives a lock of her hair to each of the slaves, telling them that they must become Christians so that they may see each other in Heaven. On her deathbed, she convinces her father to free Tom, but because of circumstances the promise never materializes.

Themes

Evil of Slavery: The novel was written after the passage of the Fugitive Slave Act of 1850, which made it illegal for anyone in the United States to offer aid or assistance to a runaway slave. The novel seeks to attack this law and the institution it protected, ceaselessly advocating the immediate emancipation of the slaves and freedom for all people. Each of Stowe's scenes also serves to persuade the reader—especially the Northern reader of Stowe's time—that slavery is evil, un-Christian, and intolerable in a civil society. Stowe explores the question of slavery in a fairly mild setting, in which slaves and masters have seemingly positive relationships. At the Shelbys' house, and again at the St. Clares', the slaves have kindly masters who do not abuse or mistreat them. Stowe does not offer these settings in order to show slavery's evil as conditional. She seeks to expose the vices of slavery even in its best-case scenario. Though Shelby and St. Clare possess kindness and intelligence, their ability to tolerate slavery renders them hypocritical and morally weak. Even under kind masters, slaves suffer, as we see when a financially struggling Shelby guiltily destroys Tom's family by selling Tom, and when the fiercely selfish Marie, by demanding attention be given to herself, prevents the St. Clare slaves from mourning the death of her own angelic daughter, Eva. A common contemporary defense of slavery claimed that the institution benefited the slaves because most masters acted in their slaves' best interest. Stowe refutes this argument with her biting portrayals, insisting that the slave's best interest can lie only in obtaining freedom. In the final third of the book, Stowe leaves behind the pleasant veneer of life at the Shelby and St. Clare houses and takes her reader into the Legree plantation, where the evil of slavery appears in its most naked and hideous form. This harsh and barbaric setting, in which slaves suffer beatings, sexual abuse, and even murder, introduces the power of shock into Stowe's argument. If slavery is wrong in the best of cases, it is nightmarish and inhuman in the worst of cases. In the book's structural progression between "pleasant" and hellish plantations, we can detect Stowe's rhetorical methods. First she deflates the defense of the pro-slavery reader by showing the evil of the "best" kind of slavery. She then presents her own case against slavery by showing the shocking wickedness of slavery at its worst.

Incompatibility of Slavery & Christian Values: Writing for a predominantly religious, predominantly Protestant reader, Stowe takes great pains to illustrate the fact that the system of slavery and the moral code of Christianity oppose each other. No Christian should be able to tolerate slavery. Throughout the novel, the more religious a character is, the more he or she objects to slavery. Eva, the most morally perfect white character in the novel, fails to understand why anyone would see a difference between blacks and whites. In contrast, the morally revolting, nonreligious Legree practices slavery almost as a policy of deliberate blasphemy and evil. Christianity rests on a principle of universal love. If all people were to put this principle into practice, it would be impossible for one segment of humanity to oppress and enslave another. Thus, not only are Christianity and slavery incompatible, but Christianity can actually be used to fight slavery. The slave hunter Tom Loker learns this lesson after his life is spared by the slaves he tries to capture, and after being healed by the generous-hearted and deeply religious Quakers. He becomes a changed man. Moreover, Uncle Tom ultimately triumphs over slavery in his adherence to Christ's command to "love thine enemy". He refuses to compromise his Christian faith in the face of the many trials he undergoes at Legree's plantation. When he is beaten to death by Legree and his men, he dies forgiving them. In this way, Tom becomes a Christian martyr, a model for the behavior of both whites and blacks. The story of his life both exposes the evil of slavery—its incompatibility with Christian virtue—and points the way to its transformation through Christian love.

Moral Power of Women: Although Stowe writes the novel before the widespread growth of the women's rights movement of the late 1800s, the reader can nevertheless regard the book as a specimen of early feminism. The text portrays women as more morally conscientious, committed, and courageous than men. Stowe implies a parallel between the oppression of blacks and the oppression of women, yet she expresses hope for the oppressed in her presentation of women as effectively influencing their husbands. Moreover, she shows how this show of strength by one oppressed group can help to alleviate the oppression of the other. White women can use their influence to convince their husbands—the people with voting rights—of the evil of slavery. Throughout the novel, the reader sees many examples of idealized womanhood, of perfect mothers and wives who attempt to find salvation for their morally inferior husbands or sons. Examples include Mrs. Bird, St. Clare's mother, Legree's mother, and, to a lesser extent, Mrs. Shelby. The text also portrays black women in a very positive light. Black women generally prove strong, brave, and capable, as seen especially in the character of Eliza. In the cases where women do not act morally—such as Prue in her drunkenness or Cassy with her infanticide, the women's sins are presented as illustrating slavery's evil influence rather than the women's own immorality. Not all women appear as bolsters to the book's moral code: Marie acts petty and mean, and Ophelia begins the novel with many prejudices. Nonetheless, the book seems to argue the existence of a natural female sense of good and evil, pointing to an inherent moral wisdom in the gender as a whole and encouraging the use of this wisdom as a force for social change.

Film Adaptations

Onkel Tom's Hütte (1965, a German – language version) was directed by Géza von Radványi, starring John Kitzmiller as uncle Tom, Herbert Lom as Simon Legree, Olive Moorefield as Cassy, O. W. Fischer as Saint – Clare, Catana Cayetano as Eliza, Michaela May as Little Eva. It was presented in the United States by exploitation film presenter Kroger Babb. Although well known in the whole world, *Uncle Tom's Cabin* has never been the subject of a major American motion picture, because the paternalistic side of the novel has grown unbearable to some people. The director made one masterpiece somewhere in Europe. It is more a European film than a German one. Eleonora Rossi Drago, who acted as Mrs. Saint – Claire was from Italy. Mylène Demongeot, who acted as Harriet was from France. There are many adaptations: Chaste old cousin Ophelia makes way for a vivacious gorgeous young Harriet. The deadly serious Saint – Clare goes to see a hostess in a bar. The slave trader at the beginning was Legree, instead of Mr. Haley. Topsy is a boy. Saint – Clare was killed on the National Day by Legree who hid himself with a rifle in a house and fired at him without being seen by anybody. A black boy was framed as the murderer and lynched to death. The end of the film becomes epic, as the slaves rise up against their "owners".

Fig 10.3 Legree and Arthur Shelby

Fig 10.4 Eliza crosses the half – frozen Ohio Rive

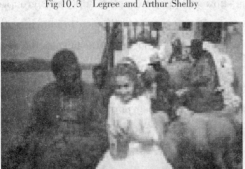
Fig 10.5 Uncle Tom and Eva

Fig 10.6 St. Clare and Ophelia

Uncle Tom's Cabin (1987) was directed by Stan Lathan, starring Avery Brooks, Phylicia Rashad, Edward Woodward, Jenny Lewis, Samuel L. Jackson and Endyia Kinney. This is a great film to know the reality of slavery in the antebellum South. Uncle Tom is placed into a world of slavery. He is benevolent and good nature, and with slavery as the back drop to his life. The viewer is given a glimpse into the depravity of slavery. The film does a great job of showing the extremes of slavery: a cruel slave master, an angelic little girl, and humane slave owner, a good slave…. Uncle Tom and Eliza's son Harry are both sold to Haley, but they respond to this news differently. Eliza takes Harry and runs away to Canada. Uncle Tom accepts slavery and is sold down South. The film doesn't tell the story very well. It leaves out some major scenes and changes some important facts. For example, Eliza crosses the river in the spring. There is no ice to jump across so she just swims. This is an important scene in the book and the entire essence of it is missing in the film. In addition, the Bird family is completely left out of the film! Their role is very important in the book. It shows slavery from the viewpoint of a senator's family. George Shelby is changed to Christopher Shelby in the film. The differences are very annoying and unnecessary.

Fig 10.7　A DVD Cover of the 1987 Film　　　　Fig 10.8　Simon Legree Chooses Slaves

A Wonderful Dialogue from the 1965 Film

Mrs. Shelby is writing a document on the table. After finishing it, she blows a breath on it. Eliza stands beside her.

Mrs. Shelby: Although it has not been verified by the sheriff, I'm sure it will serve the purpose. (*Standing up, folding the document and giving it to Eliza*) You are free, Eliza.

Eliza: Thank you, Mrs. Shelby (*Getting the document, folding it again*).

Mrs. Shelby: It's not the way they do things in the world outside, Eliza. You don't forget. For little Harry, the document I give you is useless. You have to be very careful. You belong to Mr. Legree at law. You'll be accused of kidnapping your own child. (*Going to a desk, opening a drawer, picking up some coins and a piece of paper money*) I haven't enough money. (*Giving them to Eliza*) Here, Eliza, here.

Eliza: No … You have given me what I need, Mrs. Shelby.

Mrs. Shelby: Take them, Eliza. I'm sure you need them before you are through. Tell old Jim to harness the fast horse in the stable and just leave him at the ferry.

Eliza: (*Bowing*) Oh, Mrs. Shelby, thank you.

Mrs. Shelby: Write when you find your husband and when you are safe. And you must have heard that Mr. Legree is a very dangerous man.

Mrs. Shelby leads Eliza out, closes the door and feels released.

 Discussions

1. The middle-aged Tom and the 6-year-old Eva become good friends. What do you think is the reason for them to get so close to each other and for Eva at her deathbed to ask her father to set Tom free?
2. Hoping to find freedom, Eliza takes her son Harry to cross the half-frozen Ohio River. What's your impression on her?
3. St. Clare decides to set Tom free after the death of Eva, but he is stabbed to death before he can act on his decision. Why does the author write the story like this? Can it be written in another better way?
4. In the novel, Mr. Haley buys Tom and sells him to Eva's father. And then after the death of St. Clare, Tom is sold to Simon Legree, who tortures Tom to death. But in the 1965 film, it is Simon Legree who buys Tom twice. How do you think of the change of the plot? Can you find some more changes in the film?
5. Besides Uncle Tom, there are some other literary images of African Americans, such as Lucas Beauchamp in Faulkner's *Intruder in the Dust* and Jim in Mark Twain's *The Adventures of Huckleberry Finn*. Which one do you prefer? Give your reasons.

Unit 11　Herman Melville and *Moby – Dick*

Herman Melville (1819—1891) was an American writer of novels, short stories and poetry. Around his twentieth year he was a schoolteacher for a short time, then became a seaman when his father met business reversals. On his first voyage he jumped ship in the Marquesas islands, where he lived for a time. His first book, an account of that time, *Typee* (1846), became a bestseller and Melville became known as the man who lived among the cannibals. After literary success in the late 1840s, the public indifference to *Moby – Dick* (1851) put an end to his career as a popular author. During his later decades, Melville worked at the New York Customs House and published volumes of poetry which are now esteemed but were not read in his lifetime. When he died in 1891, Melville was almost completely forgotten. It was not until the "Melville Revival" in the early 20th century that his work won recognition, especially *Moby – Dick*, which was hailed as one of the literary masterpieces of both American and world literature. He was the first writer to have his works collected and published by the Library of America.

Fig 11.1　Herman Melville　　　　Fig 11.2　A Book Cover of *Moby – Dick*

Plot

Ishmael, the narrator, announces his intent to ship aboard a whaling vessel. He has made several voyages as a sailor but none as a whaler. He travels to New Bedford, Massachusetts, where he stays in a whalers' inn. Since the inn is rather full, he has to share a bed with a harpooner from the South Pacific named Queequeg. At first repulsed by Queequeg's strange habits and shocking appearance (Queequeg is covered with tattoos), Ishmael eventually comes to appreciate the man's generosity and kind spirit, and the two decide to seek work on a whaling vessel together. They take a ferry to Nantucket, the traditional capital of the whaling industry. There they secure berths on the Pequod, a savage – looking ship adorned with the bones and teeth of sperm whales. Peleg and

Bildad, the Pequod's Quaker owners, drive a hard bargain in terms of salary. They also mention the ship's mysterious captain, Ahab, who is still recovering from losing his leg in an encounter with a sperm whale on his last voyage.

The Pequod leaves Nantucket on a cold Christmas Day with a crew made up of men from many different countries and races. Soon the ship is in warmer waters, and Ahab makes his first appearance on deck, balancing gingerly on his false leg, which is made from a sperm whale's jaw. He announces his desire to pursue and kill Moby-Dick, the legendary great white whale who took his leg, because he sees this whale as the embodiment of evil. Ahab nails a gold doubloon to the mast and declares that it will be the prize for the first man to sight the whale. As the Pequod sails toward the southern tip of Africa, whales are sighted and unsuccessfully hunted. During the hunt, a group of men, none of whom anyone on the ship's crew has seen before on the voyage, emerges from the hold. The men's leader is an exotic-looking man named Fedallah. These men constitute Ahab's private harpoon crew, smuggled aboard in defiance of Bildad and Peleg. Ahab hopes that their skills and Fedallah's prophetic abilities will help him in his hunt for Moby-Dick.

The Pequod rounds Africa and enters the Indian Ocean. A few whales are successfully caught and processed for their oil. From time to time, the ship encounters other whaling vessels. Ahab always demands information about Moby-Dick from their captains. One of the ships, the Jeroboam, carries Gabriel, a crazed prophet who predicts doom for anyone who threatens Moby-Dick. His predictions seem to carry some weight, as those aboard his ship who have hunted the whale have met disaster. While trying to drain the oil from the head of a captured sperm whale, Tashtego, one of the Pequod's harpooners, falls into the whale's voluminous head, which then rips free of the ship and begins to sink. Queequeg saves Tashtego by diving into the ocean and cutting into the slowly sinking head.

During another whale hunt, Pip, the Pequod's black cabin boy, jumps from a whaleboat and is left behind in the middle of the ocean. He goes insane as the result of the experience and becomes a crazy but prophetic jester for the ship. Soon after, the Pequod meets the Samuel Enderby, a whaling ship whose skipper, Captain Boomer, has lost an arm in an encounter with Moby-Dick. The two captains discuss the whale; Boomer, happy simply to have survived his encounter, cannot understand Ahab's lust for vengeance. Not long after, Queequeg falls ill and has the ship's carpenter make him a coffin in anticipation of his death. He recovers, however, and the coffin eventually becomes the Pequod's replacement life buoy.

Ahab orders a harpoon forged in the expectation that he will soon encounter Moby-Dick. He baptizes the harpoon with the blood of the Pequod's three harpooners. The Pequod kills several more whales. Issuing a prophecy about Ahab's death, Fedallah declares that Ahab will first see two hearses, the second of which will be made only from American wood, and that he will be killed by hemp rope. Ahab interprets these words to mean that he will not die at sea, where there are no hearses and no hangings. A typhoon hits the Pequod, illuminating it with electrical fire. Ahab takes this occurrence as a sign of imminent confrontation and success, but Starbuck, the ship's first mate, takes it as a bad omen and considers killing Ahab to end the mad quest. After the storm ends, one of the sailors falls from the ship's masthead and drowns—a grim foreshadowing of what lies ahead.

Ahab's fervent desire to find and destroy Moby-Dick continues to intensify, and the mad Pip is now his constant companion. The Pequod approaches the equator, where Ahab expects to find the great whale. The ship encounters two more whaling ships, the Rachel and the Delight, both of which have recently had fatal encounters with the whale. Ahab finally sights Moby-Dick. The harpoon boats are launched, and Moby-Dick attacks Ahab's harpoon boat, destroying it. The next day, Moby-Dick is sighted again, and the boats are lowered once more. The whale is harpooned, but Moby-Dick again attacks Ahab's boat. Fedallah, trapped in the harpoon line, is dragged overboard to his death. Starbuck must maneuver the Pequod between Ahab and the angry whale.

On the third day, the boats are once again sent after Moby-Dick, who once again attacks them. The men can see Fedallah's corpse lashed to the whale by the harpoon line. Moby-Dick rams the Pequod and sinks it. Ahab is then caught in a harpoon line and hurled out of his harpoon boat to his death. All of the remaining whaleboats and men are caught in the vortex created by the sinking Pequod and pulled under to their deaths. Ishmael, who was thrown from a boat at the beginning of the chase, was far enough away to escape the whirlpool, and he alone survives. He floats atop Queequeg's coffin, which popped back up from the wreck, until he is picked up by the Rachel, which is still searching for the crewmen lost in her earlier encounter with Moby-Dick.

Select Reading: Chapter 135

"Oh, lonely death on lonely life! Oh, now I feel my topmost greatness lies in my topmost grief. Ho, ho! from all your furthest bounds, pour ye now in, ye bold billows of my whole foregone life, and top this one piled comber of my death! Towards thee I roll, thou all-destroying but unconquering whale; to the last I grapple with thee; from hell's heart I stab at thee; for hate's sake I spit my last breath at thee. Sink all coffins and all hearses to one common pool! And since neither can be mine, let me then tow to pieces, while still chasing thee, though tied to thee, thou damned whale! Thus, I give up the spear!"

The harpoon was darted; the stricken whale flew forward; with igniting velocity the line ran through the grooves; ran foul. Ahab stooped to clear it; he did clear it; but the flying turn caught him round the neck, and voicelessly as Turkish mutes bowstring their victim, he was shot out of the boat, ere the crew knew he was gone. Next instant, the heavy eye-splice in the rope's final end flew out of the stark-empty tub, knocked down an oarsman, and smiting the sea, disappeared in its depths.

译文:"啊,生得孤独,死得凄凉呀! 现在,我感到我的至高的伟大就寓于我的至深的悲伤中。嗬,嗬! 我整整一生所经历过的惊涛骇浪呀,从最遥远的地方,汹涌过来吧,在我这死亡的波峰上再加上一层! 我要向你翻滚过去,你这毁灭成性而又无法征服的大鲸;我要与你扭斗到底,即便在地狱的中心,我也要捅你的刀子;为了泄恨,我要向你啐出我最后一口气息。把所有的棺材和灵柩都沉到大水塘里去吧! 既然两者都没有我的份儿,就让我给拖得粉身碎骨吧! 我虽然被捆在你的身上,但我还是在追击你,你这该死的大鲸! 因此,我就不用鱼矛了!"

标枪投出去了,中了枪的大鲸飞也似的向前游去,那根捕鲸索以火一般的速度穿过索槽,缠结在一起了。亚哈弯下身子去清理缠结,缠结倒是解开了,可是,那飞转着的线圈一下套住了他的脖子，他发不出任何声音，就像土耳其哑巴用坚实的细索勒死罹难者那样。亚哈被拖得像箭地一般射出了小艇，连水手们都还不知道他已经完了。接着，那根索端结成的沉重的索眼从空空如也的索桶里飞了出去，把一个桨手击倒，撞进大海，沉到海底，不见了。

Analysis of Major Characters

Ishmael: Despite his centrality to the story, Ishmael doesn't reveal much about himself to the reader. We know that he has gone to sea out of some deep spiritual malaise and that shipping aboard a whaler is his version of committing suicide—he believes that men aboard a whaling ship are lost to the world. It is apparent from Ishmael's frequent digressions on a wide range of subjects—from art, geology, and anatomy to legal codes and literature—that he is intelligent and well educated, yet he claims that a whaling ship has been his Yale College and his Harvard. He seems to be a self–taught Renaissance man, good at everything but committed to nothing. Given the mythic, romantic aspects of Moby–Dick, it is perhaps fitting that its narrator should be an enigma: not everything in a story so dependent on fate and the seemingly supernatural needs to make perfect sense. Additionally, Ishmael represents the fundamental contradiction between the story of Moby–Dick and its setting. Melville has created a profound and philosophically complicated tale and set it in a world of largely uneducated working–class men. Ishmael seems less a real character than an instrument of the author. No one else aboard the Pequod possesses the proper combination of intellect and experience to tell this story. Indeed, at times even Ishmael fails Melville's purposes, and he disappears from the story for long stretches, replaced by dramatic dialogues and soliloquies from Ahab and other characters.

Ahab: Ahab, the Pequod's obsessed captain, represents both an ancient and a quintessentially modern type of hero. Like the heroes of Greek or Shakespearean tragedy, Ahab suffers from a single fatal flaw, one he shares with such legendary characters as Oedipus and Faust. His tremendous overconfidence leads him to defy common sense and believe that, like a god, he can enact his will and remain immune to the forces of nature. He considers Moby–Dick the embodiment of evil in the world, and he pursues the White Whale madly because he believes it his inescapable fate to destroy this evil. As M. H. Abrams says about him, such a tragic hero "moves us to pity because, since he is not an evil man, his misfortune is greater than he deserves; but he moves us also to fear, because we recognize similar possibilities of error in our own lesser and fallible selves." Unlike the heroes of older tragic works, Ahab suffers from a fatal flaw that is not necessarily inborn but instead stems from damage, in his case both psychological and physical, inflicted by life in a harsh world. He is as much a victim as he is an aggressor, and the symbolic opposition that he constructs between himself and Moby Dick propels him toward a destined end.

Moby–Dick: In a sense, Moby–Dick is not a character, as the reader has no access to the White Whale's thoughts, feelings, or intentions. Instead, Moby–Dick is an impersonal force, one that many critics have interpreted as an allegorical representation of God, an inscrutable and all–powerful being that humankind can neither understand nor defy. Moby–Dick thwarts free will and cannot be defeated, only accommodated or avoided. Ishmael tries a plethora of approaches to describe whales in general, but none proves adequate. As Ishmael points out, the majority of a whale is hidden from view at all times. In this way, a whale mirrors its environment. Like the whale, only the surface of the ocean is available for human observation and interpretation, while its depths conceal unknown and unknowable truths. Furthermore, even when Ishmael does get his hands on a "whole" whale, he is unable to determine which part—the skeleton, the head, the skin—offers the best understanding of the whole living, breathing creature; he cannot localize the essence of the whale. This conundrum can be read as a metaphor for the human relationship with the Christian God: God is unknowable and cannot be pinned down.

Starbuck, Stubb, and Flask: The Pequod's three mates are used primarily to provide philosophical contrasts with Ahab. Starbuck, the first mate, is a religious man. Sober and conservative, he relies on his Christian faith to determine his actions and interpretations of events. Stubb, the second mate, is jolly and cool in moments of crisis. He has worked in the dangerous occupation of whaling for so long that the possibility of death has ceased to concern him. A fatalist, he believes that things happen as they are meant to and that there is little that he can do about it. Flask simply enjoys the thrill of the hunt and takes pride in killing whales. He doesn't stop to consider consequences at all and is "utterly lost ... to all sense of reverence" for the whale. All three of these perspectives are used to accentuate Ahab's monomania. Ahab reads his experiences as the result of a conspiracy against him by some larger force. Unlike Flask, he thinks and interprets. Unlike Stubb, he believes that he can alter his world. Unlike Starbuck, he places himself rather than some external set of principles at the center of the cosmic order that he discerns.

Themes

Limits of Knowledge: As Ishmael tries, in the opening pages of the novel, to offer a simple collection of literary excerpts mentioning whales, he discovers that, throughout history, the whale has taken on an incredible multiplicity of meanings. Over the course of the novel, he makes use of nearly every discipline known to man in his attempts to understand the essential nature of the whale. Each of these systems of knowledge, including art, taxonomy, and phrenology, fails to give an adequate account. The multiplicity of approaches that Ishmael takes, coupled with his compulsive need to assert his authority as a narrator and the frequent references to the limits of observation, suggest that human knowledge is always limited and insufficient. When it comes to Moby – Dick himself, this limitation takes on allegorical significance. The ways of Moby – Dick, like those of the Christian God, are unknowable to man, and thus trying to interpret them, as Ahab does, is inevitably futile and often fatal.

Deceptiveness of Fate: In addition to highlighting many portentous or foreshadowing events, Ishmael's narrative contains many references to fate, creating the impression that the Pequod's doom is inevitable. Many sailors believe in prophecies, and some even claim the ability to foretell the future. A number of things suggest that characters are actually deluding themselves when they think that they see the work of fate and that fate either doesn't exist or is one of the many forces about which human beings can have no distinct knowledge. Ahab clearly exploits the sailors' belief in fate to manipulate them into thinking that the quest for Moby – Dick is their common destiny. The prophesies of Fedallah and others seem to be undercut in Chapter 99, when various individuals interpret the doubloon in different ways, demonstrating that humans project what they want to see when they try to interpret signs and portents.

Exploitative Nature of Whaling: At first glance, the Pequod seems like an island of equality and fellowship in the midst of a racist, hierarchically structured world. The ship's crew includes men from all corners of the globe and all races who seem to get along harmoniously. Ishmael is initially uneasy upon meeting Queequeg, but he quickly realizes that it is better to have a "sober cannibal than a drunken Christian" for a shipmate. Additionally, the conditions of work aboard the Pequod promote a certain kind of egalitarianism, since men are promoted and paid according to their skill. However, the work of whaling parallels the other exploitative activities—buffalo hunting, gold mining, unfair trade with indigenous peoples—that characterize American and European territorial expansion. Each of the Pequod's mates, who are white, is entirely dependent on a nonwhite harpooner, and nonwhites perform most of the dirty or dangerous jobs aboard the ship. Flask actually stands on Daggoo, his African harpooner, in order to beat the other mates to a prize whale. Ahab is depicted as walking over the black youth Pip, who listens to Ahab's pacing from below deck, and is thus reminded that his value as a slave is less than the value of a whale.

Film Adaptations

Moby – Dick (1956) was directed by John Huston, starring Gregory Peck, Richard Basehart, and Leo Genn, distributed by Warner Brothers. Of the three film versions of *Moby – Dick* made between 1926 and 1956, this is the only one which is faithful to the novel and uses its original ending. But even down to the retention of Melville's original poetic dialogue, there are several slight changes:

(1) In the film, Elijah's prophecy: "A day will come at sea when you'll smell land and there'll be no land, and on that day, Ahab will go to his grave, but he'll rise again, and beckon, and all save one shall follow", foretells exactly what will happen to the Pequod and her crew in the film. In the novel, Elijah does not make a prophecy, but subtly hints that something will happen.

(2) In the film, Ishmael and Queequeg meet in and sail out of New Bedford while in the novel they meet in New Bedford but sail out of Nantucket.

(3) The demonic harpooner Fedallah is totally omitted from the film. In the novel, it is the dead Fedallah who ends up lashed to the back of Moby – Dick, but in the film, this happens to Ahab. In the novel, Ahab is merely dragged into the water by the harpoon rope and is never seen again.

(4) In the film, when the dead Ahab "beckons" to the crew (an incident caused by the whale rolling back and forth while Ahab is tied to its back), Starbuck, who had previously bitterly opposed Ahab's quest for vengeance, is so moved by the sight that he becomes like a man possessed, and orders the crew to attack Moby – Dick. This leads to the death of all except Ishmael, as the whale leaps on them in a fury.

In the novel, Starbuck does not participate in the final hunt and the ship and her crew are lost after the Pequod is rammed by Moby-Dick. In the film, the Pequod is also rammed by the whale, but only after Moby-Dick has killed the whole crew except Ishmael.

Fig 11.3　Ahab and the Three Mates

Fig 11.4　Ishmael and Queequeg

　　Moby-Dick (1997) is a television miniseries directed by France Roddam, starring Patrick Stewart as Captain Ahab, Henry Thomas as Ishmael, Gregory Peck as Father Mapple and Ted Levine as Starbuck, filmed in Australia, first released in the United States in 1998. Patrick Stewart makes his entrance late into this telefilm, stringy hair hanging from under his three-cornered hat, his peg leg tapping out his arrival on deck. This Captain Ahab is a hard, driven man. There's no question that he has the resolve and the mad devotion to complete his quest at all costs: kill the white whale that took his leg. This film manages its budget wisely: a judicious use of digital effects creates a terrifying vision of the great white whale. Henry Thomas' earnest performance as the young seaman Ishmael can't compete with Stewart's intensity, and Gregory Peck's cameo as Father Mapple is a hollow echo of his passionate Ahab from Huston's masterpiece. But the rest of the cast excels. The director's haunting imagery and horrific climax make this a compelling dramatic adventure. This version shows a consciousness of the factions that operate on the ship: Ahab's leadership emerges through the ways he unites these groups behind a common cause, forging close bonds between himself and his enemy. Ahab has often been portrayed as an aloof and distant leader who intimidates and dominates, whereas Stewart's version of Ahab emphasizes his desires for closeness with his crew even as he wants to bond them to his personal pursuit of Moby-Dick.

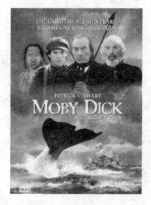

Fig 11.5　A DVD Cover of *Moby-Dick* (1997)

Fig 11.6　Death of Ahab

A Wonderful Dialogue from the 1956 Film

The sailors are cleaning the deck. Suddenly they see Captain Ahab who stands in front of them with a bone leg. The first mate Starbuck is beside him.

Voice – over: He didn't feel the wind nor smell the salt air. He only stood, starring at the horizon, with a mark of inner crucifixion in woe deep in his face.

Ahab: (*To Starbuck*) Starbuck.

Starbuck: Sir?

Ahab: Call everybody here.

Starbuck: (*Shouting to all*) All hands off! Down that stair! (*All men stop working or come down and gather in front of them.*)

Ahab: (*To all men*) What do you do when you see a whale, men? (*All men look at each other.*)

Man A: Sing out for him. (*Then all men "Yeah, sing out for him".*)

Ahab: Good, what do you do, next?

All men: Lower away, and after him.

Ahab: And what tune is it you pull to, men?

All men: A dead whale or a stove boat.

Ahab: All you mast – heads, now hear me. You will look for a white whale, as big and white as a mountain of snow. (*Taking out a gold coin*) See this Spanish gold ounce? (*To the carpenter*) carpenter, hand me a top – maul. (*The carpenter hands him the top – maul.*) Whoever of ye finds that white whale, he shall have this Spanish gold ounce, my boy. (*Hammering the coin unto the mast*). It's a white whale I say. Skin your eyes for him, men.

Tashtego: Captain Ahab, does he fan – tail a little before he goes down?

Daggoo: And he has a curious spout, sir, very bushy and mighty quick?

Queequeq: And he have iron in his hide, all twiske – tee like him?

Ahab: Aye, like corkscrew, all twisted. And his spout is like a whole shock of wheat. And his fantails like a split jib in a quall. Perhaps you have seen him. It's Moby – Dick.

Starbuck: Captain Ahab, was it Moby – Dick took off your leg?

Ahab: Aye. It's Moby – Dick that tore my soul and body until they bled into each other. Aye. I'll follow him around the Horn, around the Norway Maelstrom, and around perdition's flames before I give him up. This is what you have shipped for, men, to chase that white whale on both sides of the lands, over all sides of earth, till he spouts black and rolls dead out. What say ye men? I think you do look brave. Will you splice hands on it, now?

All men: Aye. Aye.

Discussions

1. Why is Ishmael used to narrate the story? What role does he play in the novel? How is he saved at the end of the story?

2. How do you think of Ahab's hate and revenge? What lesson can we draw from his tragedy?
3. We can never know the white whale's thoughts, feelings or intentions. He represents an impersonal force. What's your opinion of such a force?
4. The novel is called an encyclopedia of whaling industry, what have you got from it?
5. There are two films based on the novel, which do you prefer? Give your reasons.

Unit 12　Theodore Dreiser and *Sister Carrie*

Theodore Dreiser (1871—1945) was an American novelist and journalist of the naturalist school. His novels often featured main characters who succeeded at their objectives despite a lack of a firm moral code, and literary situations that more closely resemble studies of nature than tales of choice and agency. Dreiser's best known novels include *Sister Carrie* (1900) and *An American Tragedy* (1925). The former is a story of a working girl and her life as the mistress of a man who descends the social scale as she rises to success as an actress. The latter is a story of a youth of unstable character trapped by circumstances that lead to his execution for murder.

Fig 12.1　Theodore Dreiser

Fig 12.2　A Book Cover of *Sister Carrie*

Plot

Dissatisfied with life in her rural Wisconsin home, 18-year-old Caroline Meeber takes the train to Chicago, where her older sister Minnie and her husband Sven Hanson have agreed to take her in. On the train, Carrie meets Charles Drouet, a traveling salesman, who is attracted to her because of her simple beauty and unspoiled manner. They exchange contact information, but upon discovering the steady round of toil and somber atmosphere at her sister's flat, she writes to Drouet and discourages him from calling on her there.

Carrie soon embarks on a quest for work to pay rent to her sister and her husband, and takes a job running a machine in a shoe factory. Before long, she is shocked by the coarse manners of both the male and female factory workers and the physical demands of the job, as well as the squalid factory conditions. She also senses Minnie and Sven's disapproval of her interest in Chicago's recreational opportunities, particularly the theatre. One day, after an illness that costs her job, she encounters Drouet on a downtown street. Once again taken by her beauty and moved by her poverty, he encourages her to dine with him, where he persuades her to leave her sister and move in with him. He slips Carrie two ten dollar bills, opening a vista of material possibilities to her. The next day, he rebuffs her feeble attempts to return the money, taking her shopping at a Chicago department store and securing a jacket she covets and some shoes. That night, she writes a good – bye note to Minnie and moves in with Drouet.

Drouet installs her in a much larger apartment, and their relationship intensifies as Minnie dreams about her sister's fall from innocence. She acquires a sophisticated wardrobe and sheds her provincial mannerisms even as she struggles with the moral implications of being a kept woman. By the time Drouet introduces Carrie to George Hurstwood, the manager of Fitzgerald and Moy's, her material appearance has improved considerably. Hurstwood, unhappy with and distant from his social – climbing wife and children, instantly becomes infatuated with Carrie's youth and beauty. Before long they start an affair, communicating and meeting secretly.

One night, Drouet casually agrees to find an actress to play a key role in an amateur theatrical presentation of a melodrama. Upon returning home to Carrie, he encourages her to take the part of the heroine, Laura. Unknown to Drouet, Carrie long has harbored theatrical ambitions and has a natural aptitude for imitation and expressing pathos. The night of the production—which Hurstwood attends at Drouet's invitation—both men are moved to even greater displays of affection by Carrie's stunning performance.

The next day, the affair is uncovered: Drouet discovers he has been cuckolded, Carrie learns that Hurstwood is married, and Hurstwood's wife, Julia, learns from an acquaintance that Hurstwood has been out driving with another woman and deliberately excluded her from the theatre night. After a night of drinking, and despairing at his wife's financial demands and Carrie's rejection, Hurstwood stumbles upon a large amount of cash in the unlocked safe in Fitzgerald and Moy's offices. In a moment of poor judgment, he succumbs to the temptation to embezzle a large sum of money. Under the pretext of Drouet's sudden illness, he lures Carrie onto a train and escapes with her to Canada. Once they arrive in Montreal, Hurstwood's guilty conscience and a private eye induce him to return most of the stolen money, but he realizes that he cannot return to Chicago. Hurstwood mollifies Carrie by agreeing to marry her, and the couple move to New York City.

In New York, Hurstwood and Carrie rent a flat where they live as George and Carrie Wheeler. Hurstwood buys a minority interest in a saloon and, at first, is able to provide Carrie with a satisfactory standard of living. The couple grow distant, however, as Hurstwood abandons any pretense of fine manners toward Carrie, and she realizes that Hurstwood no longer is the suave, powerful manager of his Chicago days. Carrie's dissatisfaction only increases when she meets Robert Ames, a bright young scholar from Indiana and her neighbor's cousin, who introduces her to the idea that great art, rather than showy materialism, is worthy of admiration.

After only a few years, the saloon's landlord sells the property and Hurstwood's business partner expresses his intent to terminate the partnership. Too arrogant to accept most of the job opportunities available to him, Hurstwood soon discovers that his savings are running out and urges Carrie to economize, which she finds humiliating and distasteful. As Hurstwood lounges about, overwhelmed by apathy and foolishly gambling away most of his savings, Carrie turns to New York's theatres for employment and becomes a chorus girl. Once again, her aptitude for theatre serves her well, and, as the rapidly aging Hurstwood declines into obscurity, Carrie begins to rise from chorus girl to small speaking roles, and establishes a friendship with another chorus girl, Lola Osborne, who begins to urge Carrie to move in with her. In a final attempt to prove himself useful, Hurstwood becomes a scab driving a Brooklyn streetcar during a streetcar operator's strike. His ill-fated venture, which lasts only two days, prompts Carrie to leave him; in her farewell note, she encloses twenty dollars.

Hurstwood ultimately joins the homeless of New York, taking odd jobs, falling ill with pneumonia, and finally becoming a beggar. Reduced to standing in line for bread and charity, he commits suicide in a flophouse. Meanwhile, Carrie achieves stardom, but finds that money and fame do not satisfy her longings or bring her happiness and that nothing will.

Select Reading: Chapter I

When Caroline Meeber boarded the afternoon train for Chicago, her total outfit consisted of a small trunk, a cheap imitation alligator-skin satchel, a small lunch in a paper box, and yellow leather snap purse, containing her ticket, a scrap of paper with her sister's address in Van Buren Street, and four dollars in money. It was in August, 1889. She was eighteen years of age, bright, timid, and full of the illusions of ignorance and youth. Whatever touch of regret at parting characterized her thoughts, it was certainly not for advantages now being given up. A gush of tears at her mother's farewell kiss, a touch in her throat when the cars clacked by the flour mill where her father worked by the day, a pathetic sigh as the familiar green environs of the village passed in review, and the threads which bound her so lightly to girlhood and home were irretrievably broken.

To be sure there was always the next station, where one might descend and return. There was the great city, bound more closely by these very trains which came up daily. Columbia City was not so very far away, even once she was in Chicago. What, pray, is few hours—a few hundred miles? She looked at the little slip bearing her sister's address and wondered. She gazed at the green landscape, now passing in swift review, until her swifter thoughts replaced its impression with vague conjectures of what Chicago might be.

When a girl leaves her home at eighteen, she does one of two things. Either she falls into saving hands and becomes better, or she rapidly assumes the cosmopolitan standard of virtue and becomes worse. Of an intermediate balance, under the circumstances, there is no possibility. The city has its cunning wiles, no less than the infinitely smaller and more human tempter. There are large forces which allure with all the soulfulness of expression possible in the most cultured human.

Caroline, or Sister Carrie, as she had been half affectionately termed by the family, was possessed of a mind rudimentary in its power of observation and analysis. Self-interest with her was high, but not strong. It was, nevertheless, her guiding characteristic. Warm with the fancies of youth, pretty with the insipid prettiness of the formative period, possessed of a figure promising eventual shapeliness and an eye alight with certain native intelligence, she was a fair example of the middle American class—two generations removed from the emigrant. Books were beyond her interest—knowledge a sealed book. In the intuitive graces she was still crude. She could scarcely toss her head gracefully. Her hands were almost ineffectual. The feet, though small, were set flatly.

And yet she was interested in her charms, quick to understand the keener pleasures of life, ambitious to gain in material things. A half-equipped little knight she was, venturing to reconnoitre the mysterious city and dreaming wild dreams of some vague, far-off supremacy, which should make it prey and subject——the proper penitent, grovelling at a woman's slipper.

"That", said a voice in her ear, "is one of the prettiest little resorts in Wisconsin."

"Is it?" she answered nervously.

The train was just pulling out of Waukesha. For some time she had been conscious of a man behind. She felt him observing her mass of hair. He had been fidgetting, and with natural intuition she felt a certain interest growing in that quarter. Her maidenly reserve, and a certain sense of what was conventional under the circumstances, called her to forestall and deny this familiarity, but the daring and magnetism of the individual, born of past experiences and triumphs, prevailed. She answered.

He leaned forward to put his elbows upon the back of her seat and proceeded to make himself volubly agreeable.

"Yes, that is a great resort for Chicago people. The hotels are swell. You are not familiar with this part of the country, are you?"

"Oh, yes, I am," answered Carrie. "That is, I live at Columbia City. I have never been through here, though."

"And so this is your first visit to Chicago," he observed.

All the time she was conscious of certain features out of the side of her eye. Flush, colourful cheeks, a light moustache, grey fedora hat. She now turned and looked upon him in full, the instincts of self-protection and coquetry mingling confusedly in her brain.

"I didn't say that," she said.

"Oh," he answered, in a very pleasing way and with an assumed air of mistake, "I thought you did."

译文：当卡罗琳·米贝登上开往芝加哥的午班火车时，她的全部家当只有一只小手提箱、一个廉价的仿鳄鱼皮包、一个纸盒午饭和一个黄色皮制卡扣式钱包，里面装着她的车票，写有她姐姐在凡勃伦大街住址的小纸条和四块钱。1889年8月，她18岁，聪明，羞怯，满脑子充满年轻人幼稚的幻想。要是说她还有什么依依不舍的话，那也绝不是就要失去的居家所有的种种好处。和母亲吻别时，她突然流了泪，当火车哐当哐当地从她父亲白天工作的面粉厂开过去的时候，她有一阵哽咽之感。回头望去，那环抱村庄的绿野是一片凄楚的景象，对此她太熟悉了。她与她的少女时代和家庭之间纤弱的联系永远地断开了。

前方总有下一站，如果想要回家，下车也不迟。可是前面还有那座巨大的城市，正是天天开出的这些火车将它与哥伦比亚城紧密地联系在一起。芝加哥离哥伦比亚城不算太远，她甚至还去过一次。几小时的行程，不过几百里路，又算得了什么？她看了看记着姐姐地址的小纸条，有点儿惶惑。她看着眼前掠过的绿色田野，直到她那更为迅速的思绪进入对芝加哥的朦胧想象之中。

18岁的姑娘离家时，面临两种前途：要么，她幸遇劝善之人而变得更美好；要么，她迅速地顺从世俗的道德标准而堕落。在两种情形当中，欲取中间道路，绝无可能。城市生活自有其精巧的诡计，绝不亚于那些极其卑劣却人模人样的诱骗者。人世间有种种可怕的邪恶势力，他们利用最有教养的人类可能表现出的一切深情施展其诱骗的伎俩。

卡罗琳,或叫嘉莉妹妹(家人对她的昵称)只有初步的观察和分析事理的能力。她的利己之心不小,可也不算十分强烈,然而却是她性格的主导因素。她沉浸在青春的幻想之中,显现出成熟阶段那种尚待完善的质朴美。具有终能出落的优美身段和一双流露天生聪颖的眼睛,完全是美国中层社会,即美国移民第三代的样本。书籍对她来说,索然无味,学问对她是一部天书。她虽有外在的优雅,但尚待雕琢。她几乎还没有学会甩头的优美姿态。她那一双手还不能为她增姿添色,一双脚虽然小巧,却只会直挺挺地站着。不过她已经认识到自己的动人之处,能迅速感受强烈的生活乐趣,渴望获得物质财富。她是一位装备不良的小骑士,冒着风险去探索神秘的都市,疯狂般地梦想着某种虚无缥缈处的至尊地位:她要占领它,使其臣服,成为匍匐在女人脚下的一名规规矩矩的忏悔者。

"这一带是威斯康星州最美的景区之一。"话音传入她的耳朵。

"是吗?"她紧张不安地说。

火车正好驶出沃基肖。已经好一阵了,她觉察到身后有一个男人。她觉得他在注视她的一头浓密的头发,他有些骚动不安。凭着本能的直觉,她感到身后的男人对她产生越来越浓厚的兴趣。处于少女的矜持和传统的观念,她本该制止和拒绝这种意在亲近的行为。但是,那个男子老于此道,又频频得手,因此举止大方,充满魅力,占了上风。她回答了他。

他倾身向前,将胳膊肘靠在她的座背上,摆出一副善谈随和的样子。

"是的,对芝加哥的人来说,那可是了不起的景观。那里的饭店是第一流的。你对这地方还不太熟悉吧?"

"啊,不……我知道。"嘉莉说,"我的意思是……,我住在哥伦比亚城,不过我从未到这儿来过。"

"你这是第一次去芝加哥喽。"他说。

借助眼睛的余光,她已经注意到他的一些特征:生气勃勃,气色迷人,留着短髭须,戴一顶灰色浅顶呢帽。现在她转过身来面对着他,又要自重却又想卖弄,两种欲望在她脑海里交混成一团乱麻。

"我可没有说这是第一次嘛。"她说。

他立即承认自己听错了话,神态举止极讨人喜欢。"哦,我还以为你说过呢。"

Analysis of Major Characters

Carrie Meeber(Sister Carrie): She travels to Chicago to stay with her sister and her brother-in-law. The cosmopolitan consumer world of Chicago attracts her, and she constantly wants to buy things. Her first job is a low-paid, arduous position in a factory. When she loses her job, her sister and brother-in-law cannot support her, so she becomes Charlie Drouet's mistress. Afterward, she becomes infatuated with George Hurstwood. Carrie and Hurstwood run to New York, where they discover that married life is far less exciting than their affair. Carrie leaves Hurstwood because he fails to provide her with the lavish life she wants. She becomes a famous, high-paid actress in New York City.

Charlie Drouet: He is a charming, flashy salesman with a strong appetite for romance. Although he is warm-hearted, he never takes any of his romantic affairs seriously. He provides Carrie with a place to stay after she is forced to stop living with her sister. He also promises to marry her, but he never really makes it true. He loses Carrie to Hurstwood. Years later, after she has become a famous actress, he tries unsuccessfully to win her back.

George Hurstwood: He is the manager of Fitzgerald and Moy's, a saloon in Chicago. At the beginning, he is a wealthy, important man. He falls in love with Carrie after meeting her through Drouet. He tells Carrie that he loves her, but he fails to mention that he is married. After his wife discovers his affair with Carrie and files for divorce, he steals ten thousand dollars from the safe and flees with Carrie to Montreal. There, he marries her before his divorce with Julia is complete. Although he keeps his theft a secret from Carrie, he is discovered by an investigator and required to return most of the money in order to protect his reputation. In New York, Hurstwood slowly descends into apathy and poverty. After Carrie leaves him, he becomes a homeless beggar and eventually commits suicide.

Themes

Cost of Living: When Carrie arrives at her sister's apartment in Chicago, she is at once struck by the shabby economy of her sister's life. The four dollars she had in her possession mean nothing to Carrie before she gets off the train, because she has little sense of how much her cost of living will be in the big city. Her sister expects her to find a job for at least five dollars a week to help cover her room and board, but after one long, hard day searching for work and being coolly rejected, Carrie receives an offer of work for four – fifty a week. This shows Carrie's disillusionment—on this salary, she will not be going to restaurants or theaters, or out for any kind of fun. Four – fifty a week meant painstaking toil with little reward.

A Full Wallet, A New Outlook: Carrie's situation is gloomy until she runs into Drouet and he offers to take her under his wing. The first thing he does is to give her twenty dollars to buy a new hat—this represents a change in Carrie's attitude and a hint of change in her circumstances. Soon Carrie moves in with Drouet, leaving the discomfort of her sister's life behind. Her circumstances become pleasant if not lavish, and for a while she sails along wanting for little. The next change in her life comes when Hurstwood, who is wealthier and more impressive than Drouet, seduces her.

Declining Status: Before meeting Carrie, Hurstwood is a man with pride and personal dignity. Stealing the money is his first major lapse in ethical behavior, and represents a downward shift away from dignity and toward desperation. After they move to New York, Hurstwood is forced to work in a cheap saloon, and they have to rent a small flat and limit their expenses.

A Morality Tale: Hurstwood loses his job and fails to find another one, and eventually fails to try. He starts volunteering to handle all the household chores himself to save money. Then his doom is coming nearer and nearer. Carrie's eventual turn to wealth as a Broadway actress comes too late. The final image of Carrie's sitting alone depressed in a hotel room comes as no surprise.

Film Adaptation

Carrie (1952) was directed by William Wyler, starring Jennifer Jones in the title role and Laurence Olivier as Hurstwood, Eddie Albert as Charles Drouet. The film keeps many of Dreiser's themes in tact, namely, the realism of human nature in the face of Victorian morals, and the hardships of working – class America in the early 20th century. Yet there are several changes. The film's plot is like this: In South Chicago, Carrie stays with her sister, who is married and has one child. After losing her job, and then exhausting a fruitless day of job hunting, Carrie looks up Charles Drouet. He not only talks her into having dinner with him at Fitzgerald's, an upscale restaurant, but also gives her $10. Blamed by her sister, Carrie heads to Fitzgerald's to return the money to Drouet. While there she meets George Hurstwood, the manager of the restaurant, who is immediately smitten with her. Carrie ends up moving in with Drouet. He is a big talker but basically harmless. She pressures Drouet to marry her because the neighbors are talking about them. He tries to distract her and invites Hurstwood, whom he had run into by sheer coincidence, into their home. With Drouet's permission, Hurstwood takes Carrie to the theater while Drouet is on one of his many business trips. Hurstwood and Carrie end up spending every free minute together, and the two fall in love. Just before she is about to run off with Hurstwood, she finds out that he is married. She is distraught and confronts Hurstwood, who admits that he is married but terribly unhappy. At the restaurant, Hurstwood cashes up for the night and, by accidentally locking a safe, finds himself stuck with $10,000 of his boss's money. He goes home with the money and is initially pleased to find his boss there. He tries to give the money to his boss, but when he learns that his boss intends to give his salary directly to his wife because of his relationship with Carrie, he decides to take the money to run away with Carrie. He leaves an I – O – U intent on paying his boss back as soon as he made it on his own feet. He coaxes Carrie, who initially refuses to see him, out of the house by telling her that Drouet had injured himself and that he would take her to see him. On the train to Drouet, Hurstwood tells her that he loves her and that he wants to be with her, asking her to leave Drouet. Carrie is torn, but does love Hurstwood, so she decides to stay with him. The first few days are blissful, but then reality catches up with them. Hurstwood's boss sends an officer from the bond company after Hurstwood to collect the money Hurstwood took. Hurstwood, who has already been looking for work, finds out quickly that word of him stealing the money has gotten around. Unable to find a job, Hurstwood and Carrie soon find themselves living in poverty. When Carrie finds out that she is pregnant, the two think that things might take a turn for the better. But Hurstwood's wife shows up, wanting his signature and allowing her to sell the house they own jointly. Hurstwood wants his share of the proceeds but she says she will press charges against him for bigamy if he insists. Carrie is devastated. Hurstwood's wife refused to get a divorce and Hurstwood didn't know how to tell Carrie. Hurstwood tells his wife he will sign and will not ask for money if she'll grant him a divorce. She does, but it is too late. Carrie loses the baby and decides to try her luck at acting. Hurstwood reads in the newspaper that his son is due in New York after his honeymoon and decides to see him at the docks. While he is there, Carrie leaves him (even though she still loves him) because she thinks he will use this opportunity to re – enter his family's life. While Hurstwood drifts further and further into poverty and ends up living on the streets, Carrie's star in the theatre rises until she is a well – regarded actress on the cusp of fame. Hurstwood, entirely starved, visits her at the theatre stage door. She wants to take him back. She has found out from Drouet that Hurstwood has taken the money to start a life with her and blames herself for his predicament. She wants to make it up to Hurstwood but he won't take more than a quarter and disappears after toying with the gas burner in her dressing room.

From the plot of the film, we can see the differences between the film and the novel. In the old Hollywood rule, there is a high price to pay for those who lie, steal, cheat, or attempt to have sex outside of marriage. So the characters are punished for their misdeeds. So the film shows the audience that they have to live in squalid conditions and Hurstwood can't find a decent job after being blackballed from every good restaurant. Carrie has a miscarriage and learns that her marriage to George is illegal because Mrs. Hurstwood would never give him that divorce. In the end, they both search for a little absolution but neither of them finds it. We reap what we sew even if we're honest.

Fig 12.3   Drouet and Carrie

Fig 12.4   Hurstwood and Carrie

A Wonderful Dialogue from the 1952 Film

Hurstwood: (*Walking towards the Gaiety Theatre, seeing some people coming out of the stage door, hiding himself in the shade. Carrie comes out with two persons, who say good night to each other. Carrie passes him*) Excuse me, Carrie.

Carrie: (*Stopping walking and surprised*) George? (*Turning towards the shade*) Where are you? (*Seeing him*)

Hurstwood: I tried very hard not to do this.

Carrie: George, I've looked so for you.

Hurstwood: I need help, just tonight. I need a little help. I'm ⋯ hungry. Could you spare me a little something?

Carrie: Spare?

Hurstwood: Anything. I don't want to bother you. I won't again, but just tonight.

Carrie: Come with me. (*Taking Hurstwood's arm into hers and walking into the door, speaking to a man there*) John, get food. That Italian place at the corner will be open. Bring something hot right away. (*Making Hurstwood seated. Turning on the lights, taking off her coat and putting it on the chair, turning on the stove, and seeing Hurstwood in such a miserable condition*) George, what happened to you? In heaven's name, what happened?

Hurstwood: (*Very feebly*) I've ⋯ I've forgotten.

Carrie: Did I do this? Did I?

Hurstwood: Carrie, I'm here for a handout. Don't make me live through too much to get it. (*Pointing at her purse, which Carrie then puts on the table with a paper money bill beside, then pointing at the paper money*) This is very generous.

Carrie: I'll make it up to you. Will you let me?

Hurstwood: I have the trouble changing it.

Carrie: George, I left you to be safe and secure. Now that I can make it worth something to me, let me share it with you. George, look at me. I know a lot more now. I know what you did. I know how much you loved me. I want that again. Let me have it back. Let me bring you back. I can.

Hurstwood: Don't live in the past, remember.

Carrie: (*Crying*) I was too young. I didn't realize. Why didn't you tell me? Why didn't you make me understand?

Hurstwood: You still have time, Carrie. Move on now. Find some one to love. It's a great experience. (*Looking at the paper money*) Carrie, could you get that changed now?

Carrie: We'll need more money than that. I'll see if Mr. Amos is still in his office. (*Going towards the door, turning back*) You rest here. John will be right back with the food. Then I'll take you home with me. And tomorrow we'll get you some clothes.

Hurstwood: Thank you…. Carrie.

Carrie smiles and leaves. Hurstwood picks up a coin from the purse and puts the paper money inside the purse. He stands up, touching Carrie's coat on the chair, taking a look at himself in the mirror, turning off the stove, then slowly turning it on without setting the gas on fire, then turning it off, opening the door and disappearing. The film ends.

 Discussions

1. Carrie loses her job and encounters Drouet in a street, who slips her some money. She goes shopping and then writes a goodbye note to her sister and moves in with Drouet. How do you think of her behavior?
2. Infatuated with Carrie's youth and beauty and despairing at his wife's financial demand, Hurstwood takes a large sum of money and lures Carrie onto a train and then escapes. How do you think of his behavior?
3. As Hurstwood's savings are running out, Carrie finds it humiliating and distasteful to economize. His obscurity and ill-fated venture prompt her to leave him. How do you think of her behavior towards him?
4. If you are a male, what lesson can you draw from Hurstwood's tragedy? If you are a female, what can you learn or not learn from Carrie?
5. The 1954 film changes the original novel a lot. Do you think the changes make the story better and more acceptable or vise versa?

Unit 13 Scott Fitzgerald and *The Great Gatsby*

Scott Fitzgerald (1896—1940) was born in St. Paul, Minnesota. He went to Princeton in 1913 and entered the army in 1917. While being trained in the U.S. camps he wrote the initial draft of his first novel, *This Side of Paradise* (1920), set at his alma mater and an expression of a new generation and its jazz age. His book caught the flavor and the interests of the changing era. *The Great Gatsby* (1925), his finest work, was a sensitive and symbolic treatment of themes of contemporary life related with irony and pathos to the legendry of the "American dream". In *Tender Is the Night* (1934), he tried to express his view of the psychological and spiritual malaise of modern life. His personal life suffered the tragedies of his wife's nervous breakdown and his own loss of security as he became sick and saw his critical esteem and public reception deteriorate, leading him to write the touching essays posthumously collected by Edmund Wilson in *The Crack – Up* (1945).

Fig 13.1 Scott Fitzgerald

Fig 13.2 A Book Cover of *The Great Gatsby*

Plot

Nick Carraway, a young man from Minnesota, moves to New York in the summer of 1922 to learn about the bond business. He rents a house in the West Egg district of Long Island, a wealthy but unfashionable area populated by the new rich, a group who have made their fortunes too recently to have established social connections and who are prone to garish displays of wealth. Nick's next – door neighbor in West Egg is a mysterious man named Jay Gatsby, who lives in a gigantic Gothic mansion and throws extravagant parties every Saturday night.

Nick is unlike the other inhabitants of West Egg. He was educated at Yale and has social connections in East Egg, a fashionable area of Long Island home to the established upper class. Nick drives out to East Egg one evening for dinner with his cousin, Daisy Buchanan, and her husband, Tom, an erstwhile classmate of Nick's at Yale. Daisy and Tom introduce Nick to Jordan Baker, a beautiful, cynical young woman with whom Nick begins a romantic relationship. Nick also learns a bit about Daisy and Tom's marriage: Jordan tells him that Tom has a lover, Myrtle Wilson, who lives in the valley of ashes, a gray industrial dumping ground between West Egg and New York City. Not long after this revelation, Nick travels to New York City with Tom and Myrtle. At a vulgar, gaudy party in the apartment that Tom keeps for the affair, Myrtle begins to taunt Tom about Daisy, and Tom responds by breaking her nose.

As the summer progresses, Nick eventually garners an invitation to one of Gatsby's legendary parties. He encounters Jordan Baker at the party, and they meet Gatsby himself, a surprisingly young man who affects an English accent, has a remarkable smile, and calls everyone "old sport". Gatsby asks to speak to Jordan alone, and, through Jordan, Nick later learns more about his mysterious neighbor. Gatsby tells Jordan that he knew Daisy in Louisville in 1917 and is deeply in love with her. He spends many nights staring at the green light at the end of her dock, across the bay from his mansion. Gatsby's extravagant lifestyle and wild parties are simply an attempt to impress Daisy. Gatsby now wants Nick to arrange a reunion between himself and Daisy, but he is afraid that Daisy will refuse to see him if she knows that he still loves her. Nick invites Daisy to have tea at his house, without telling her that Gatsby will also be there. After an initially awkward reunion, Gatsby and Daisy reestablish their connection. Their love rekindled, they begin an affair.

After a short time, Tom grows increasingly suspicious of his wife's relationship with Gatsby. At a luncheon at the Buchanans' house, Gatsby stares at Daisy with such undisguised passion that Tom realizes Gatsby is in love with her. Though Tom is himself involved in an extramarital affair, he is deeply outraged by the thought that his wife could be unfaithful to him. He forces the group to drive into New York City, where he confronts Gatsby in a suite at the Plaza Hotel. Tom asserts that he and Daisy have a history that Gatsby could never understand, and he announces to his wife that Gatsby is a criminal—his fortune comes from bootlegging alcohol and other illegal activities. Daisy realizes that her allegiance is to Tom, and Tom contemptuously sends her back to East Egg with Gatsby, attempting to prove that Gatsby cannot hurt him.

When Nick, Jordan, and Tom drive through the valley of ashes, however, they discover that Gatsby's car has struck and killed Myrtle, Tom's lover. They rush back to Long Island, where Nick learns from Gatsby that Daisy was driving the car when it struck Myrtle, but that Gatsby intends to take the blame. The next day, Tom tells Myrtle's husband, George Wilson, that Gatsby was the driver of the car. George, who has leapt to the conclusion that the driver of the car that killed Myrtle must have been her lover, finds Gatsby in the pool at his mansion and shoots him dead. He then fatally shoots himself.

Nick stages a small funeral for Gatsby, ends his relationship with Jordan, and moves back to the Midwest to escape the disgust he feels for the people surrounding Gatsby's life and for the emptiness and moral decay of life among the wealthy on the East Coast. Nick reflects that just as Gatsby's dream of Daisy was corrupted by money and dishonesty, the American dream of happiness and individualism has disintegrated into the mere pursuit of wealth. Though Gatsby's power to transform his dreams into reality is what makes him "great", Nick reflects that the era of dreaming—both Gatsby's dream and the American dream—is over.

Select Reading: Chapter 9

After two years I remember the rest of that day, and that night and the next day, only as an endless drill of police and photographers and newspaper men in and out of Gatsby's front door. A rope stretched across the main gate and a policeman by it kept out the curious, but little boys soon discovered that they could enter through my yard, and there were always a few of them clustered open-mouthed about the pool. Someone with a positive manner, perhaps a detective, used the expression "madman" as he bent over Wilson's body that afternoon, and the adventitious authority of his voice set the key for the newspaper reports next morning.

I called up Daisy half an hour after we found him, called her instinctively and without hesitation. But she and Tom had gone away early that afternoon, and taken baggage with them.

"Left no address?"

"No."

"Say when they'd be back?"

"No."

"Any idea where they are? How I could reach them?"

"I don't know. Can't say."

I wanted to get somebody for him. I wanted to go into the room where he lay and reassure him: "I'll get somebody for you, Gatsby. Don't worry. Just trust me and I'll get somebody for you—"

…

A little before three the Lutheran minister arrived from Flushing, and I began to look involuntarily out the windows for other cars. So did Gatsby's father. And as the time passed and the servants came in and stood waiting in the hall, his eyes began to blink anxiously, and he spoke of the rain in a worried, uncertain way. The minister glanced several times at his watch, so I took him aside and asked him to wait for half an hour. But it wasn't any use. Nobody came.

About five o'clock our procession of three cars reached the cemetery and stopped in a thick drizzle beside the gate—first a motor hearse, horribly black and wet, then Mr. Gatz and the minister and I in the limousine, and a little later four or five servants and the postman from West Egg in Gatsby's station wagon, all wet to the skin. As we started through the gate into the cemetery I heard a car stop and then the sound of someone splashing after us over the soggy ground. I looked around. It was the man with owl-eyed glasses whom I had found marveling over Gatsby's books in the library one night three months before.

I'd never seen him since then. I don't know how he knew about the funeral, or even his name. The rain poured down his thick glasses, and he took them off and wiped them to see the protecting canvas unrolled from Gatsby's grave.

I tried to think about Gatsby then for a moment, but he was already too far away, and I could only remember, without resentment, that Daisy hadn't sent a message or a flower. Dimly I heard someone murmur, "Blessed are the dead that the rain falls on," and then the owl-eyed man said "Amen to that," in a brave voice.

译文：事隔两年，我回想起那天其余的时间，那一晚以及第二天，只记得一批又一批的警察、摄影师和新闻记者在盖茨比家的前门口进进出出。外面的大门口有一根绳子拦住，旁边站着一名警察，不让看热闹的人进来，但是小男孩们不久就发现，他们可以从我的院子里绕过来，因此，总有几个孩子目瞪口呆地挤在游泳池旁边。那天下午，有一个神态自信的人，也许是一名侦探，低头检视威尔逊的尸体时，用了"疯子"两个字，而他的语气偶然的权威就为第二天早上所有报纸的报道定了调子。

在我们发现他的尸体半小时后，我就打电话给黛西，本能地、毫不迟疑地给她打电话。但是她和汤姆那天下午很早就出门了，还随身带了行李。

"没留地址吗？"

"没有。"

"他们说了几时回来吗？"

"没有。"

"知道他们到哪儿去了吗？我怎样能和他们取得联系？"

"我不知道；说不上来。"

我真想给他找一个人来。我真想走到他躺着的那间屋子里去安慰他说："我一定给你找一个人来，盖茨比。别着急。相信我好了，我一定给你找一个人来"

……

快到三点的时候，路德教会的那位牧师从弗勒兴来了，于是我开始不由自主地向窗户外面望，看看有没有别的车子来。盖茨比的父亲也和我一样。随着时间过去，佣人都走进来站在门厅里等候，老人的眼睛开始焦急地眨起来，同时他又忐忑不安地说到外面的雨。牧师看了好几次表，我只好把他拉到一旁，请他再等半个钟头。但是毫无用处。没有一个人来。

五点钟左右我们三辆车子的行列开到墓地，在密密的小雨中在大门旁边停了下来，第一辆是灵车，又黑又湿，怪难看的，后面是盖茨先生、牧师和我坐在大型轿车里，再后面一点的是四五个佣人和西卵镇的邮差坐在盖茨比的旅行车里，大家都淋得透湿。正当我们穿过大门走进墓地时，我听见一辆车停下来，接着是一个人踩着湿透的草地在我们后面追上来的声音。我回头一看，原来是那个戴猫头鹰眼镜的人，三个月以前的一天晚上，我发现他看着盖茨比图书室里的书惊叹不已。

从那以后我没再见过他。我不知道他怎么会知道今天安葬的，我也不知道他的姓名。雨水顺着他的眼镜留下来，他只好把眼镜摘下擦一擦，再看着那块挡雨的帆布从盖茨比的坟上卷起来。

这时我很想回忆一下盖茨比，但是他已经离得很远了，我只记得黛西既没来电报，也没送花，然而我并不感到气恼。我隐约听到有人喃喃念道："上帝保佑雨中的死者，"接着那个猫头鹰眼睛的人用洪亮的声音说了一声"阿门！"

Analysis of Major Characters

Jay Gatsby: He is a young man, around thirty years old, who rose from an impoverished childhood in rural North Dakota to become fabulously wealthy. However, he achieved this lofty goal by participating in organized crime, including distributing illegal alcohol and trading in stolen securities. From his early youth, Gatsby despised poverty and longed for wealth and sophistication—he dropped out of St. Olaf's College after only two weeks because he could not bear the janitorial job with which he was paying his tuition. Though Gatsby has always wanted to be rich, his main motivation in acquiring his fortune was his love for Daisy Buchanan, whom he met as a young military officer in Louisville before leaving to fight in World War I in 1917. Gatsby immediately fell in love with Daisy's aura of luxury, grace, and charm, and lied to her about his own background in order to convince her that he was good enough for her. Daisy promised to wait for him when he left for the war, but married Tom Buchanan in 1919, while Gatsby was studying at Oxford after the war in an attempt to gain an education. From that moment on, Gatsby dedicated himself to winning Daisy back, and his acquisition of millions of dollars, his purchase of a gaudy mansion on West Egg, and his lavish weekly parties are all merely means to that end. Fitzgerald initially presents Gatsby as the aloof, enigmatic host of the unbelievably opulent parties thrown every week at his mansion. He appears surrounded by spectacular luxury, courted by powerful men and beautiful women. He is the subject of a whirlwind of gossip throughout New York and is already a kind of legendary celebrity before he is ever introduced to the reader. Fitzgerald propels the novel forward through the early chapters by shrouding Gatsby's background and the source of his wealth in mystery. As a result, the reader's first, distant impressions of Gatsby strike quite a different note from that of the lovesick, naive young man who emerges during the later part of the novel. Fitzgerald uses this technique of delayed character revelation to emphasize the theatrical quality of Gatsby's approach to life, which is an important part of his personality. Gatsby has literally created his own character, even changing his name from James Gatz to Jay Gatsby to represent his reinvention of himself. As his relentless quest for Daisy demonstrates, Gatsby has an extraordinary ability to transform his hopes and dreams into reality. His talent for self-invention is what gives Gatsby his quality of "greatness". As the novel progresses and Fitzgerald deconstructs Gatsby's self-presentation, Gatsby reveals himself to be an innocent, hopeful young man who stakes everything on his dreams, not realizing that his dreams are unworthy of him. Gatsby invests Daisy with an idealistic perfection that she cannot possibly attain in reality and pursues her with a passionate zeal that blinds him to her limitations. His dream of her disintegrates, revealing the corruption that wealth causes and the unworthiness of the goal, much in the way Fitzgerald sees the American dream crumbling in the 1920s, as America's powerful optimism, vitality, and individualism become subordinated to the amoral pursuit of wealth. Gatsby is contrasted most consistently with Nick. The former, passionate and active, and the latter, sober and reflective, seem to represent two sides of Fitzgerald's personality. Additionally, whereas Tom is a cold-hearted, aristocratic bully, Gatsby is a loyal and good-hearted man. Though his lifestyle and attitude differ greatly from those of George Wilson, Gatsby and Wilson share the fact that they both lose their love that Tom is interested in.

Nick Carraway: If Gatsby represents one part of Fitzgerald's personality, the flashy celebrity who pursues and glorifies wealth in order to impress the woman he loves, then Nick represents another part: the quiet, reflective Midwesterner adrift in the lurid East. A young man from Minnesota, Nick travels to New York in 1922 to learn the bond business. He lives in the West Egg district of Long Island, next door to Gatsby. Nick is also Daisy's cousin, which enables him to observe and assist the resurgent love affair between Daisy and Gatsby. As a result of his relationship to these two characters, Nick is the perfect choice to narrate the novel, which functions as a personal memoir of his experiences with Gatsby in the summer of 1922. Nick is also well suited to narrating the story because of his temperament. He is tolerant, open-minded, quiet, and a good listener, and, as a result, others tend to talk to him and tell him their secrets. Gatsby comes to trust him and treat him as a confidant. Nick generally assumes a secondary role throughout the novel, preferring to describe and comment on events rather than dominate the action. He functions as Fitzgerald's voice in his extended meditation on time and the American dream. Nick plays a role inside the narrative, he evidences a strongly mixed reaction to life on the East Coast, one that creates a powerful internal conflict that he does not resolve until the end of the book. On the one hand, Nick is attracted to the fast-paced, fun-driven lifestyle of New York. On the other hand, he finds that lifestyle grotesque and damaging. This inner conflict is symbolized throughout the story by Nick's romantic affair with Jordan Baker. He is attracted to her vivacity and her sophistication just as he is repelled by her dishonesty and her lack of consideration for other people. Nick states that there is a "quality of distortion" to life in New York, and this lifestyle makes him lose his equilibrium. After witnessing the unraveling of Gatsby's dream and presiding over the appalling spectacle of Gatsby's funeral, Nick realizes that the fast life of revelry on the East Coast is a cover for the terrifying moral emptiness that the valley of ashes symbolizes. Having gained the maturity that this insight demonstrates, he returns to Minnesota in search of a quieter life structured by more traditional moral values.

Daisy Buchanan: Partially based on Fitzgerald's wife, Zelda, Daisy is a beautiful young woman from Louisville, Kentucky. She is Nick's cousin and the object of Gatsby's love. As a young debutante in Louisville, Daisy was extremely popular among the military officers stationed near her home, including Jay Gatsby. Gatsby lied about his background to Daisy, claiming to be from a wealthy family in order to convince her that he was worthy of her. Eventually, Gatsby won Daisy's heart, and they made love before Gatsby left to fight in the war. Daisy promised to wait for Gatsby, but in 1919 she chose instead to marry Tom Buchanan, a young man from a solid, aristocratic family who could promise her a wealthy lifestyle and who had the support of her parents. After 1919, Gatsby dedicated himself to winning Daisy back, making her the single goal of all of his dreams and the main motivation behind his acquisition of immense wealth through criminal activity. To Gatsby, Daisy represents the paragon of perfection—she has the aura of charm, wealth, sophistication, grace, and aristocracy that he longed for as a child in North Dakota and that first attracted him to her. In reality, however, Daisy falls far short of Gatsby's ideals. She is beautiful and charming, but also fickle, shallow, bored, and sardonic. Nick characterizes her as a careless person who smashes things up and then retreats behind her money. Daisy proves her real nature when she chooses Tom over Gatsby, then allows Gatsby to take the blame for killing Myrtle Wilson even though she herself was driving the car. Finally, rather than attend Gatsby's funeral, Daisy and Tom move away, leaving no forwarding address. Like Zelda Fitzgerald, Daisy is in love with money, ease, and material luxury. She is capable of affection (she seems genuinely fond of Nick and occasionally seems to love Gatsby sincerely), but not of sustained loyalty or care. She is indifferent even to her own infant daughter, never discussing her and treating her as an afterthought. In

Fitzgerald's conception of America in the 1920s, Daisy represents the amoral values of the aristocratic East Egg set.

Themes

Honesty: Honesty does not seem to determine which characters are sympathetic and which are not. Nick is able to admire Gatsby despite his knowledge of the man's illegal dealings and bootlegging. Ironically, it is the corrupt Daisy who takes pause at Gatsby's sordid past. Her indignation at his "dishonesty" is less moral than class – based. Her sense of why Gatsby should not behave in an immoral manner is based on what she expects from members of her milieu, rather than what she believes to be intrinsically right. The standards for honesty and morality seem to be dependent on class and gender in this novel. Tom finds his wife's infidelity intolerable. However, he does not hesitate to lie to her about his own affair.

Decay: Decay is most evident in the so – called "valley of ashes". With great virtuosity, the novelist describes a barren wasteland which probably has little to do with the New York landscape and instead serves to comment on the downfall of American society. It seems that the American dream has been perverted, reversed. Gatsby lives in West Egg and Daisy in East Egg; therefore, Gatsby looks East with yearning, rather than West, the traditional direction of American frontier ambitions. The novelist portrays the chauvinistic and racist Tom in a very negative light, clearly scoffing at his apocalyptic vision of the races intermarrying. The novelist's implication seems to be that society has already decayed enough and requires no new twist.

Gender Roles: In some respects, the novelist writes about gender roles in a quite conservative manner. Men work to earn money for the maintenance of the women. Men are dominant over women, especially in the case of Tom, who asserts his physical strength to subdue them. The only hint of a role reversal is in the pair of Nick and Jordan. Jordan's androgynous name and cool, collected style masculinize her more than any other female character. However, in the end, Nick does exert his dominance over her by ending the relationship. None of the women are pure. Myrtle is the most obviously sensual. The fact that Jordan and Daisy wear white dresses only highlights their corruption.

Violence: Violence is most embodied by Tom. An ex – football player, he uses his immense physical strength to intimidate those around him. When Myrtle taunts him with his wife's name, he strikes her across the face. The other source of violence is car, which symbolizes the dangers of modernity and the dangers of wealth. The climax of the novel, the accident that kills Myrtle, is foreshadowed by the conversation between Nick and Jordan about how bad driving can cause explosive violence. The end of the novel consists of violence against Gatsby. It is his love affair, not his business life that kills him.

Class: The societies of East and West Egg are deeply divided by the difference between the noveau riche and the older moneyed families. Gatsby is aware of the existence of a class structure in America, because a true meritocracy would put him in touch with some of the finest people, but, as things stand, he is held at arm's length. Gatsby tries desperately to fake status, even buying British shirts and claiming to have attended Oxford in an attempt to justify his position in society. Ultimately, class gulf separates Gatsby and Daisy, and cements the latter in her relationship to her husband, who is from the same class as she is.

World War I: The war was crucial to Gatsby's development, providing a brief period of social mobility which quickly closed after the war. Gatsby only came into contact with a classy young debutante like Daisy as a result of the fact that he was a soldier and that no one could vouch for whether he was upper‐class or not. The war provided him with further opportunities to see the world, and make some money in the service of a millionaire. Gatsby's opportunities closed up after the end of the war, however, when he found upon returning to America that the social structure there was every bit as rigid as it was in Europe. Unable to convince anyone that he is truly upper‐class (although his participation in the war gave him some leeway about lying), Gatsby finds himself unable to break into East Egg society.

Film Adaptations

The Great Gatsby (1926) is a silent film, directed by Herbert Brenon and released by Paramount Pictures. Unfortunately it is a lost film.

The Great Gatsby (1949) is a feature film, directed by Elliott Nugent and released by Paramount Pictures.

The Great Gatsby (1974) is an American romantic drama film, directed by Jack Clayton, released by Newdon Productions and Paramount Pictures. The film was praised for its interpretation and staying true to the novel, but was criticized for lacking any true emotion or feelings towards the Jazz Age.

Fig 13.3　1949 Poster　　　　　　　　　　Fig 13.4　Gatsby and Daisy (1974)

The Great Gatsby (2000) is a drama film, directed by Robert Markowitz from a teleplay by John J. Mc Laughlin, released by the A&E Cable Network in the United States, and Granada Productions in Great Britain.

Fig 13.5　Gatsby and Daisy

Fig 13.6　Nick and Jordan

Fig 13.7　Tom Buchanan

Fig 13.8　George Wilson

The Great Gatsby (2013) film is Australian–American 3D drama film, directed by Baz Luhrmann. A granddaughter of Fitzgerald praised the style and music of the film. Some feel it a spectacle in search of a soul. Some others use the word "magnificent" to describe the performance. Still some comment that the film emphasizes visual splendor at the expense of its source material's vibrant heart.

Fig 13.9　Gatsby and Daisy

Fig 13.10　Nick and Jordan

Fig 13.11　Tom Buchanan

Fig 13.12　George Wilson

A Wonderful Dialogue from the 2013 Film

Tom: Mr. Gatsby, I understand that you're an Oxford man.

Gatsby: No, not exactly, no.

Tom: Oh, yes. I understand that you went to Oxford.

Gatsby: Well, yes, I went there.

Tom: (*With contempt*) Sure. The man in the pink suit went to Oxford.

Daisy: (*With displeasure*) Tom.

Gatsby: I said I went there, didn't I?

Tom: Yes, I heard that. I'd like to know when.

Gatsby: You'd like to know when? (*Walking to the window and drinking water*)

Tom: Well, Mr. Gatsby?

Gatsby: It was in 1919. I only stayed there five months. That's why I can't exactly call myself an Oxford man. You see, it was an opportunity they gave to some of us officers, who fought in the war.

Tom: Then you won't seem so stupid to yourself. Wait a minute. I want to ask Mr. Gatsby one more question.

Gatsby: Oh, please … please go on, Mr. Buchanan. Go on.

Tom: What kind of a row are you trying to cause in my house anyhow?

Daisy: (*To Tom angrily*) He isn't causing a row, you're causing a row. Please have a little self-control.

Tom: Self-control? Oh, I suppose the latest thing is to sit back and let Mr. Nobody from Nowhere make love to your wife. Well, if that's the idea you can count me out. See, nowadays people begin by sneering at family life and family institutions, and the next you'll know, we'll throw everything overboard. We'll have intermarriage between black ad white.

Gatsby: (*Going to Daisy and putting her hands into his. To Tom*) She never loved you. You see. She loves me.

Tom: You must be crazy.

Gatsby: No, old sport. No. You see. She never loved you. She only married you because I was poor and she was tired of waiting. It was a terrible terrible mistake, but in her heart, she never loved any one but me.

Daisy: (*Standing up*) Let's all go home.

Tom: Sit down, Daisy! Please, please take a seat.

Gatsby: Go on, Daisy. (*She sits down*)

Tom: Daisy, what's been going on? I want to hear about it.

Gatsby: I told you what's going on. It's been going on for five years.

Tom: You've been seeing him for five years?

Gatsby: No, no, no, not seeing. Not seeing, we couldn't. But both of us loved each other all that time. Didn't we?

Tom: Oh, that's all? (*Laughing*) You're crazy. I can't speak out what happened five years ago because I didn't know Daisy then. And I'll be damned if I see how you got within a mile of her unless you brought the groceries to the back door. But all the rest of that is a goddamn lie. Daisy loved me when she married me and she loves me now.

Gatsby: No, no. I'm sorry, Mr. Buchanan. No.

Tom: She does, though. She does. And what's more, I love Daisy too. No. I love you, Daisy. No. Once in a while I go off on a spree. I always come back.

Gatsby: (*Showing contempt*) A spree.

Tom: And in my heart I love her at all time.

Daisy: You're revolting. You know why we left Chicago? I'm surprised they didn't treat you to the story of that little spree!

Gatsby: That's all over now, Daisy, darling. That's all over. Just tell him the truth. Go on. That you never loved him and this will be wiped out forever.

Daisy: How could I love him possibly?

Gatsby: Remember or love our plans? (*Taking her hands into his*) You tell him that you never loved him and all this pain will be wiped out forever. Daisy, Daisy, tell him.

Daisy: I never loved him.

Tom: Never?

Gatsby: No (*Gesturing Daisy*).

Tom: Not at kapiolani? (*Daisy shakes her head*) Not that day I carried you down from the Punch Bowl to keep your shoes dry? (*Tears come out from her eyes and she lowers her head*) Never?

Daisy: Please don't.

Tom: Daisy.

Daisy: There, Jay. You want too much. I love you now. Isn't that enough? I can't help what's past. (*To Tom*) I did love him once, but I loved you too. (*Holding Gatsby's face with one hand*)

 Discussions

1. Why does the novelist arrange Nick Carraway to narrate the whole story? What role does he play?
2. Why does the novelist regard Gatsby "great"? What can we learn from his tragedy?
3. Is Daisy an ideal woman? Does she really love Gatsby? How do you think of her not sending a message or flower after Gatsby's death?
4. The 2013 film emphasizes the visual splendor. Do you think the film help you understand the novel better or misunderstand it? Give your reasons.
5. The novel is about the disillusionment of American dream. We are now pursuing our Chinese dream. To realize our own dream, what lesson can we draw from this tragic story?

Unit 14 Ernest Hemingway and *A Farewell to Arms*

Ernest Hemingway (1899—1961) was an American author and journalist. His economical and understated style had a strong influence on 20th-century fiction, while his life of adventure and his public image influenced later generations. He produced most of his work between the mid-1920s and the mid-1950s, and won the Nobel Prize for Literature in 1954. He published seven novels, including *The Sun Also Rises* (1926), *A Farewell to Arms* (1929), *For Whom the Bell Tolls* (1940) and *The Old Man and the Sea* (1952), six short story collections, and two non-fiction works. Three novels, four collections of short stories, and three non-fiction works were published posthumously. Many of his works are considered classics of American literature. *A Farewell to Arms* was based on his wartime experiences of a World War I ambulance driver in the Italian front.

Fig 14.1 Earnest Hemingway

Fig 14.2 A Book Cover of *A Farewell to Arms*

Plot

Lieutenant Frederic Henry is a young American ambulance driver serving in the Italian army during World War I. At the beginning of the novel, the war is winding down with the onset of winter, and Henry arranges to tour Italy. The following spring, upon his return to the front, Henry meets Catherine Barkley, an English nurse's aide at the nearby British hospital and the love interest of his friend Rinaldi. Rinaldi quickly fades from the picture as Catherine and Henry become involved in an elaborate game of seduction. Grieving the recent death of her fiancé, Catherine longs for love so deeply that she will settle for the illusion of it. Her passion, even though pretended, wakens a desire for emotional interaction in Henry, whom the war has left coolly detached and numb.

When Henry is wounded on the battlefield, he is brought to a hospital in Milan to recover.

Several doctors recommend that he stay in bed for six months and then undergo a necessary operation on his knee. Unable to accept such a long period of recovery, Henry finds a bold, garrulous surgeon who agrees to operate immediately. Henry learns happily that Catherine has been transferred to Milan and begins his recuperation under her care. During the following months, his relationship with Catherine intensifies. No longer simply a game in which they exchange empty promises and playful kisses, their love becomes powerful and real. They become tangled in their love for each other.

Once Henry's damaged leg has healed, the army grants him three weeks convalescence leave, after which he is scheduled to return to the front. He tries to plan a trip with Catherine, who reveals to him that she is pregnant. The following day, Henry is diagnosed with jaundice, and Miss Van Campen, the superintendent of the hospital, accuses him of bringing the disease on himself through excessive drinking. Believing Henry's illness to be an attempt to avoid his duty as a serviceman, Miss Van Campen has Henry's leave revoked, and he is sent to the front once the jaundice has cleared. As they part, Catherine and Henry pledge their mutual devotion.

Henry travels to the front, where Italian forces are losing ground and manpower daily. Soon after Henry's arrival, a bombardment begins. When word comes that German troops are breaking through the Italian lines, the Allied forces prepare to retreat. Henry leads his team of ambulance drivers into the great column of evacuating troops. The men pick up two engineering sergeants and two frightened young girls on their way. Henry and his drivers then decide to leave the column and take secondary roads, which they assume will be faster. When one of their vehicles bogs down in the mud, Henry orders the two engineers to help in the effort to free the vehicle. When they refuse, he shoots one of them. The drivers continue in the other trucks until they get stuck again. They send off the young girls and continue on foot toward Udine. As they march, one of the drivers is shot dead by the easily frightened rear guard of the Italian army. Another driver marches off to surrender himself, while Henry and the remaining driver seek refuge at a farmhouse. When they rejoin the retreat the following day, chaos has broken out: soldiers, angered by the Italian defeat, pull commanding officers from the melee and execute them on sight. The battle police seize Henry, who, at a crucial moment, breaks away and dives into the river. After swimming a safe distance downstream, Henry boards a train bound for Milan. He hides beneath a tarp that covers stockpiled artillery, thinking that his obligations to the war effort are over and dreaming of his return to Catherine.

Henry reunites with Catherine in the town of Stresa. From there, the two escape to safety in Switzerland, rowing all night in a tiny borrowed boat. They settle happily in a lovely alpine town and agree to put the war behind them forever. Although Henry is sometimes plagued by guilt for abandoning the men on the front, the two succeed in living a beautiful, peaceful life. When spring arrives, the couple moves to Lausanne so that they can be closer to the hospital. Early one morning, Catherine goes into labor. The delivery is exceptionally painful and complicated. Catherine delivers a stillborn baby boy and, later that night, dies of a hemorrhage. Henry stays at her side until she is gone. He attempts to say goodbye but cannot. He walks back to his hotel in the rain.

Select Reading: Chapter 30

Two carabinieri took the lieutenant – colonel to the river bank. He walked in the rain, an old man with his hat off, a carabinieri on either side. I did not watch them shoot him but I heard the shots. They were questioning some one else. This officer too was separated from his troops. He was not allowed to make an explanation. He cried when they read the sentence from the pad of paper, and they were questioning another when they shot him. They made a point of being intent on questioning the next man while the man who had been questioned before was being shot. In this way there was obviously nothing they could do about it. I did not know whether I should wait to be questioned or make a break now. I was obviously a German in Italian uniform. I saw how their minds worked; if they had minds and if they worked. They were all young men and they were saving their country. The second army was being re – formed beyond the Tagliamento. They were executing officers of the rank of major and above who were separated from their troops. They were also dealing summarily with German agitators in Italian uniform. They wore steel helmets. Only two of us had steel helmets. Some of the carabinieri had them. The other carabinieri wore the wide hat. Airplanes we called them. We stood in the rain and were taken out one at a time to be questioned and shot. So far they had shot every one they had questioned. The questioners had that beautiful detachment and devotion to stern justice of men dealing in death without being in any danger of it. They were questioning a full colonel of a line regiment. Three more officers had just been put in with us.

"Where was his regiment?"

I looked at the carabinieri. They were looking at the newcomers. The others were looking at the colonel. I ducked down, pushed between two men, and ran for the river, my head down. I tripped at the edge and went in with a splash. The water was very cold and I stayed under as long as I could. I could feel the current swirl me and I stayed under until I thought I could never come up. The minute I came up I took a breath and went down again. It was easy to stay under with so much clothing and my boots. When I came up the second time I saw a piece of timber ahead of me and reached it and held on with one hand. I kept my head behind it and did not even look over it. I did not want to see the bank. There were shots when I ran and shots when I came up the first time. I heard them when I was almost above water. There were no shots now. The piece of timber swung in the current and I held it with one hand. I looked at the bank. It seemed to be going by very fast. There was much wood in the stream. The water was very cold. We passed the brush of an island above the water. I held onto the timber with both hands and let it take me along. The shore was out of sight now.

译文：两个宪兵押着中校到河岸边去。中校在雨中走着，是个没戴军帽的老头儿，一边一个宪兵。我没看他们枪毙他，但是我听见了枪声。现在他们在审问另外一个人了。也是一个与他原来的部队失散的军官。他们不让他分辩。他们从拍纸簿上宣读判决词时，他哭了，他们把他带到河边去时，他一路大哭大喊，而当人家枪决他时，另外一个人又在受审问了。军官们的做法是这样的：第一个问过话的人在执行枪决时，他们正一心一意审问着第二个人。这样做表示异常忙碌，顾不到旁的事。我不知道要怎样做，是等待人家来审问呢，还是趁早拔脚逃走。我显然是个披着意军军装的德国人。我看得出他们脑子里是怎样想的;不过还要先假定他们是有脑子,并且这脑子是管用的。他们都是些年轻小伙子,正在拯救祖国。第二军正在塔利亚门托河后边整编补充。他们在处决凡是跟原来部队离散了的少校及以上军衔的军官。此外,他们对于披着意军制服的德国煽动者,也是从速就地枪决。他们都戴着钢盔。我们这边只有两人戴钢盔。有些宪兵也戴钢盔。其余的都戴着宽边帽子。我们叫这种帽子为飞机。我们站在雨中,一次提一人出去受审并枪决。到这时,凡是他们问过话的都被枪决了。审问者们本身全没危险,所以处理起生死问题来利索超脱,坚持严峻的军法。他们现在在审问一个在前线带一团兵的上校。他们又从撤退行列中抓来了三个军官。

"他的团兵在哪儿?"

我瞧瞧宪兵们。他们正在打量那些新抓来的。其余的宪兵则在看着那个上校。我身子往下一蹲,同时劈开左右两人,低着头往河边直跑。我在河沿上绊了一下,哗的一声掉进河里。河水很冷,我可竭力躲在水下不上来。虽然感觉到河里的急流在卷着我,我还是躲在下面,自以为再也不会上来了。我一冒出水面,便吸一口气,连忙又躲下去。潜伏在水里并不难,因为我穿着厚重的衣服和靴子。当我第二次冒出水面时,看见前头有一根木头,就游过去,一手抓住它。我把头缩在木头后边,连看都不敢往上边看。我不想看岸上。我逃跑时和第一次冒出水面时,他们都开枪。我快冒出水面时就听见枪声。现在却没人打枪。那根木头顺着水流转,我用一只手握着它。我看看岸上。河岸好像在很快地溜过去。河中木头很多。河水很冷。我随波逐流,从一个小岛垂在水面上的枝条下淌过去。我双手抱住那根木头,由它把我顺流漂去。现在已看不见河岸了。

Analysis of Major Characters

Frederic Henry: Henry portrays himself as a man of duty. He attaches to this understanding of himself no sense of honor. He does not expect any praise for his service. Even after he has been severely wounded, he discourages Rinaldi from pursuing medals of distinction for him. He distances himself from such abstract notions as faith, honor, and patriotism. Concepts such as these mean nothing to him beside such concrete facts of war as the names of the cities in which he has fought and the numbers of decimated streets. His reaction to Catherine Barkley is rather astonishing. His response to the game that Catherine proposes is only a hope for a night's simple pleasures. But an active sex drive does not explain why Henry returns to Catherine—why he continues to swear his love even after Catherine insists that he stop playing. In his fondness for Catherine, he reveals a vulnerability usually hidden by his stoicism and masculinity. The quality of the language that Henry uses to describe Catherine's hair and her presence in bed testifies to the genuine depth of his feelings for her.

Catherine Barkley: Her blissful submission to domesticity suggests a bygone era in which a woman's work centered around maintaining a home and filling it with children and her excessive desire to live a lovely life makes her more archetypal than real. She seems perfectly aware of the fact that she and Henry are, at first, playing an elaborate game of seduction. Even after Henry emphatically states that he loves her and that their living together will be splendid, Catherine exhibits the occasional doubt, telling him that she is sure that dreadful things await them and claiming that she fears having a baby because she has never loved anyone. Her loyalty to Henry is never doubtful. She is a loving, dedicated woman whose desire and capacity for a redemptive, otherworldly love makes her the inevitable victim of tragedy.

Rinaldi: He dominates an array of minor male characters who embody the kind of virile, competent, and good-natured masculinity. Rinaldi is an unbelievable womanizer. Since he frequently visits the local whorehouses, he has most likely succumbed to syphilis. There is no punishment for a man's bad behavior but rather the consequence of a man behaving as a man—living large, living boldly, and being true to himself.

Themes

Love as a Response to the Horrors of War and the World: Hemingway repeatedly emphasizes the horrific devastation of the war. The novel is among the most frank anti-war novels. But Hemingway does not merely condemn war. He indicts the world at large for its atmosphere of destruction. Henry frequently reflects upon the world's insistence on breaking and killing everysone. Whenever Henry and Catherine are blissful, something comes along to interrupt it—Henry's injury, his being sent back to the front, his impending arrest, or, finally, Catherine's death from childbirth. With such misery confronting them at every turn, the two turn to each other. Catherine plunges almost too easily into love when she first meets Henry. She admits she was "crazy" at first, most likely over the fairly recent death of her fiancé, but Henry, too, succumbs to the temptations of love. Love is a pleasurable diversion that distracts lovers from the outside world. The two often tell each other not to think about anything else, as it is too painful. The major problem with such escapist love is that one does not always know the "stakes" of love until it is over, or that one does not know about something until one has lost it. Henry hardly allows himself to think of life without Catherine while he is in love, and once he does lose her, it seems unlikely that he will recover.

Grace under Pressure and the Hemingway Hero: Chiefly, the "Hemingway hero" is a man of action who coolly exhibits grace under pressure while confronting death. Henry's narration is certainly detached and action—oriented—only rarely does he let us into his most private thoughts. Characters strive for this grace under pressure in an otherwise chaotic world. Even when the men eat spaghetti, they try to exercise mastery over a single skill to compensate for the uncontrollable chaos elsewhere. The Hemingway hero also avoids glory for a more personal code of honor. Henry is not greedy for any medals, nor is he stupidly sacrificial. He judiciously determines what is worth the sacrifice, and decides that the war is no longer worthwhile. Even after he makes his separate peace, he feels slightly guilty over letting his friends continue the battle without him.

Diversions: Nearly all the characters in the novel try to divert themselves with pleasurable activities from the horror of war. The soldiers play card games, drink heavily, and carouse in brothels; Rinaldi is the poster-boy for this hedonistic excess. Henry goes along somewhat, but his biggest diversion is love itself; he and Catherine treat it like a game at first, flirting and teasing each other. Above all, ignorance is prized during the war; if one does not think about the war, then one cannot be unhappy during the ongoing pursuit of games and diversions.

Abandonment: The novel deploys several instances of abandonment, intentional and forced, in the realms of love and war. After the death of her fiancé, Catherine understandably fears abandonment by Henry, and he makes every attempt to reunite with her when separated. In the war, there are several cases of abandonment: the engineering sergeants, who abandon Henry and the other drivers; the Italian retreat, a large - scale abandonment; and Henry's escape from army. But Henry's abandonment is completely justified (he was going to be executed if he did not). Ultimately, he decides that not abandoning Catherine is far more important than not abandoning the war, though he does feel guilty over leaving behind Rinaldi and the others at the front.

Film Adaptations

A Farewell to Arms (1932) was directed by Frank Borzage, starring Helen Hayes, Gary Cooper, and Adolphe Menjou, released by Paramount Pictures. It is noted that Hemingway was grandly contemptuous of Frank Borzage's version of this novel, but time has been kind to the film. It launders out Hemingway's pessimism and replaces it with a testament to the eternal love between a couple. The film is called "not only the best film version of a Hemingway novel, but also one of the most thrilling visions of the power of sexual love that even Borzage ever made. No other director created images like these, using light and movement like brushstrokes, integrating naturalism and a daring expressionism in the same shot. This is romantic melodrama raised to its highest degree." Criticism also says that there is too much sentiment and not enough strength in the pictorial conception of the novel. The film account skips too quickly from one episode to another and the hardships and other experiences of Lieutenant Henry are passed over too abruptly, being suggested rather than told.

Fig 14.3 A Poster

Fig 14.4 Henry and Catherine in love

Fig 14.5 Henry and Rinaldi

Fig 14.6 Henry and Catherine in her deathbed

A Farewell to Arms (1957) was directed by Charles Vidor, starring Rock Hudson, Jennifer Jones and Elaine Stritch, and released on December 14 by 20th Century Fox. It is called "an overblown Hollywood extravaganza that hasn't improved with age. The chief virtue of this hollow epic is the stupendous color photography of the Italian Alps. It is also described as an "inflated remake" with "surplus production values and spectacle".

Fig 14.7　A Poster

Fig 14.8　Rinaldi and the Father

Fig 14.9　Catherine and Henry in Italy

Fig 14.10　Catherine and Henry in Switzerland

Wonderful Dialogues from the 1957 Film

(1) Henry and Catherine Are Rowing a Boat

Henry: Hold your nose when you jump.

Catherine: (*Jumping into the water with her nose held by the hand, swimming, then turning towards Henry*) How many people have you loved?

Henry: Nobody.

Catherine: except me, of course.

Henry: You're the first and only.

Catherine: Oh, come. How many others, really?

Henry: None.

Catherine: You're lying to me.

Henry: (*Laughing*) A little.

Catherine: It's all right. That's what I want you to do. Keep right on lying to me. (*Swimming away, then turning towards Henry again*) When does a girl say how much it costs?

Henry: I don't know.

Catherine: (*Chuckling*) Of course, not. Does she say she loves him? Tell me that. I want to know that.

Henry: Yes, if he knows her to.

Catherine: Does he say he loves her? Tell me, please. It's important.

Henry: He does if he wants to.

Catherine: But you never did. (*He laughs*) Tell me the truth, please.

Henry: (*Laughing*) No.

Catherine: You wouldn't. I know you wouldn't. Oh, I love you, darling. (*Falling back into water and swimming away happily. He laughs*) The girl just says what the man wants her to.

Henry: Well, not always. But, uh—

Catherine: But I will. I'll say just what you wish and I'll do what you wish. Then you'll never want other girls, will you?

Henry: Never.

Catherine: I'll do what you want and I'll say what you want. Then I'll be a great success, won't I?

Henry: You're lovely and wonderful.

Catherine: There isn't any "me" any more. Just what you want, ask for it.

Henry: You. (*Helping her out of the water into the boat. They embrace.*)

(2) A Deserter

Henry escapes the Italian army and comes to where Catherine lives. He knocks at the door. Catherine opens it.

Catherine: (*Gasping*) Oh, darling. (*He enters and they embrace.*) Oh, darling. My darling. Darling, what's wrong? What's the matter?

Henry: I'll tell you about it. (*Falling down on the floor*)

Catherine: Oh, darling. You're ill. I'll get a doctor.

Henry: No, I don't need a doctor. I'm not sick, at least not that way.

Catherine: Then, what is it? I don't understand.

Henry: It's just that I'm through. I'm through with the war. It made a separate peace.

Catherine: You mean you…you deserted?

Henry: Yes, I'm a deserter.

Catherine: It's not your army or your country. Tell me what happened.

Henry: All kinds of hell. Rinaldi's dead. They killed him. A firing squad. I better not tell you about it.

Catherine: No, no. I want to hear.

Henry: He was sick, talking like a madman and the firing squad blew his brains out. I was next. You can't win an argument with a firing squad.

Catherine: Oh, of course you can't and you're not going to try. You're not going back.

Henry: I'm not against them. They're the good ones, the brave ones. I wish them all the luck. They deserve it. But it's not my show any more.

Catherine: Of course it isn't. We're together. That's all that matters. The rest is something else far away. Just us. Us.

Discussions

1. How does Henry and Catherine's relationship develop from a game of exchanging empty promises and playful kisses to a powerful and real love?
2. Rinaldi is a good physician, but he frequently visits the local whorehouses and is not afraid of being executed by the battle police. What's your opinion about this character?
3. If Henry hadn't broken away and dived into the river, he would have been executed like the other officers. But he is then wanted as a deserter in the press. How do you think of it?
4. Catherine is overly submissive confection. Is she an ideal woman? How do her desire and capacity for a love make her the victim of tragedy?
5. The story is about both love and war. What are the author's attitudes towards the war and love?

Unit 15　Ernest Hemingway and *The Old Man and the Sea*

The Old Man and the Sea is a novella written by Ernest Hemingway in 1951 in Cuba, and published in 1952. It was the last major work of fiction to be produced by Hemingway and published in his lifetime. As one of his most famous works, it centers upon Santiago, an aging fisherman who struggles with a giant marlin far out in the Gulf Stream. The novella reinvigorated Hemingway's literary reputation and prompted a reexamination of his entire body of work. It restored many readers' confidence in Hemingway's capability as an author.

Fig 15.1　Hemingway's Home at Key West

Fig 15.2　A Book Cover of *The Old Man and the Sea*

Plot

For eighty-four days, Santiago, an aged Cuban fisherman, has set out to sea and returned empty-handed. So conspicuously unlucky is he that the parents of his young, devoted apprentice and friend, Manolin, have forced the boy to leave the old man in order to fish in a more prosperous boat. Nevertheless, the boy continues to care for the old man upon his return each night. He helps the old man carry his gear to his ramshackle hut, secures food for him, and discusses the latest developments in American baseball, especially the trials of the old man's hero, Joe DiMaggio. Santiago is confident that his unproductive streak will soon come to an end. And he resolves to sail out farther than usual the following day.

On the eighty-fifth day of his unlucky streak, Santiago sails his skiff far beyond the island's shallow coastal waters and ventures into the Gulf Stream. He prepares his lines and drops them. At noon, a big fish, which he knows is a marlin, takes the bait that Santiago has placed one hundred fathoms deep in the waters. The old man expertly hooks the fish, but he cannot pull it in. Instead, the fish begins to pull the boat.

Unable to tie the line fast to the boat for fear the fish would snap a taut line, the old man bears the strain of the line with his shoulders, back, and hands, ready to give slack should the marlin make a run. The fish pulls the boat all through the day, through the night, through another day, and through another night. It swims steadily northwest until at last it tires and swims east with the current. The entire time, Santiago endures constant pain from the fishing line. Whenever the fish lunges, leaps, or makes a dash for freedom, the cord cuts Santiago badly. Although wounded and weary, the old man feels a deep empathy and admiration for the marlin, his brother in suffering, strength, and resolve.

On the third day the fish tires, and Santiago, sleep-deprived, aching, and nearly delirious, manages to pull the marlin in close enough to kill it with a harpoon thrust. Dead beside the skiff, the marlin is the largest Santiago has ever seen. He lashes it to his boat, raises the small mast, and sets sail for home. While Santiago is excited by the price that the marlin will bring at market, he is more concerned that the people who will eat the fish are unworthy of its greatness.

As Santiago sails on with the fish, the marlin's blood leaves a trail in the water and attracts sharks. The first to attack is a great mako shark, which Santiago manages to slay with the harpoon. In the struggle, the old man loses the harpoon and lengths of valuable rope, which leaves him vulnerable to other shark attacks. The old man fights off the successive vicious predators as best he can, stabbing at them with a crude spear he makes by lashing a knife to an oar, and even clubbing them with the boat's tiller. Although he kills several sharks, more and more appear. And by the time night falls, Santiago's continued fight against the scavengers is useless. They devour the marlin's precious meat, leaving only skeleton, head, and tail. Santiago chastises himself for going out too far, and for sacrificing his great and worthy opponent. He arrives home before daybreak, stumbles back to his shack, and sleeps very deeply.

The next morning, a crowd of amazed fishermen gathers around the skeletal carcass of the fish, which is still lashed to the boat. Knowing nothing of the old man's struggle, tourists at a nearby café observe the remains of the giant marlin and mistake it for a shark. Manolin, who has been worried sick over the old man's absence, is moved to tears when he finds Santiago safe in his bed. The boy fetches the old man some coffee and the daily papers with the baseball scores, and watches him sleep. When the old man wakes, the two agree to fish as partners once more. The old man returns to sleep and dreams his usual dream of lions at play on the beaches of Africa.

Select Reading: Dreaming and Waking up the Boy

He was asleep in a short time and he dreamed of Africa when he was a boy and the long golden beaches and the white beaches, so white they hurt your eyes, and the high capes and the great brown mountains. He lived along that coast now every night and in his dreams he heard the surf roar and saw the native boats come riding through it. He smelled the tar and oakum of the deck as he slept and he smelled the smell of Africa that the land breeze brought at morning.

Usually when he smelled the land breeze he woke up and dressed to go and wake the boy. But tonight the smell of the land breeze came very early and he knew it was too early in his dream and went on dreaming to see the white peaks of the Islands rising from the sea and then he dreamed of the different harbours and roadsteads of the Canary Islands.

He no longer dreamed of storms, nor of women, nor of great occurrences, nor of great fish, nor fights, nor contests of strength, nor of his wife. He only dreamed of places now and of the lions on the beach. They played like young cats in the dusk and he loved them as he loved the boy. He never dreamed about the boy. He simply woke, looked out the open door at the moon and unrolled his trousers and put them on. He urinated outside the shack and then went up the road to wake the boy. He was shivering with the morning cold. But he knew he would shiver himself warm and that soon he would be rowing.

The door of the house where the boy lived was unlocked and he opened it and walked in quietly with his bare feet. The boy was asleep on a cot in the first room and the old man could see him clearly with the light that came in from the dying moon. He took hold of one foot gently and held it until the boy woke and turned and looked at him. The old man nodded and the boy took his trousers from the chair by the bed and, sitting on the bed, pulled them on.

The old man went out the door and the boy came after him. He was sleepy and the old man put his arm across his shoulders and said, "I am sorry."

"Que va," the boy said. "It is what a man must do."

They walked down the road to the old man's shack and all along the road, in the dark, barefoot men were moving, carrying the masts of their boats.

译文： 他不多久就睡熟了，梦见小时候见到的非洲，长长的金色海滩和白色海滩，白得耀眼，还有高耸的海岬和褐色的大山。他如今每天夜里都回到那道海岸边，在梦中听见拍岸海浪的隆隆声，看见土人驾船穿浪而行。他睡着时闻到甲板上柏油和填絮的气味，还闻到早晨陆地上刮来的风带来的非洲气息。

通常一闻到陆地上刮来的风，他就醒来，穿上衣裳去叫醒那孩子。然而今夜陆地上刮来的风的气息来得很早，他在梦中知道时间尚早，就继续把梦做下去，看见群岛的白色顶峰从海面上升起，随后梦见了加那利群岛的各个港湾和锚泊地。

他不再梦见风暴，不再梦见妇女们，不再梦见伟大的事件，不再梦见大鱼，不再梦见打架，不再梦见角力，不再梦见他的妻子。他如今只梦见一些地方和海滩上的狮子。它们在暮色中像小猫一般嬉耍着，他爱它们，如同爱这孩子一样。他从没梦见过这孩子。他就这么醒过来，望望敞开的门外边的月亮，摊开长裤穿上。他在窝棚外撒了尿，然后顺着大路走去叫醒孩子。他被清晨的寒气弄得直哆嗦。但他知道哆嗦了一阵后会感到暖和，要不了多久他就要去划船了。

孩子住的那所房子的门没有上锁，他推开了门，光着脚悄悄走进去。孩子在外间的一张帆布床上熟睡着，老人靠着外面射进来的残月的光线，清楚地看见他。他轻轻握住孩子的一只脚，直到孩子给弄醒了，转过脸来对他望着。老人点点头，孩子从床边椅子上拿起他的长裤，坐在床沿上穿裤子。

老人走出门去，孩子跟在他背后。他还是昏昏欲睡，老人伸出胳臂搂住他的肩膀说："对不起。"

"哪里！"孩子说，"男子汉就该这么干。"

他们顺着大路朝老人的窝棚走去，一路上，黑暗中有些光着脚的男人在走动，扛着他们船上的桅杆。

Analysis of Major Characters

Santiago: Santiago embodies the "Hemingway Code", which means that a man is defined by will, pride and endurance: the endurance to accept pain, even loss—when the loss cannot be avoided; the pride of knowing that one has done one's best, with the courage to act truly according to one's own nature; and the will to face defeat or victory without whining on one hand or boasting on the other. Santiago suffers terribly throughout the story. In the opening part, he has gone eighty – four days without catching a fish and has become the laughingstock of his small village. He then endures a long and grueling struggle with the marlin only to see his trophy catch destroyed by sharks. Yet, the destruction enables the old man to undergo a remarkable transformation, and he wrests triumph and renewed life from his seeming defeat. After all, Santiago is an old man whose physical existence is almost over, but he will persist through Manolin, who, like a disciple, awaits the old man's teachings and will make use of those lessons long after his teacher has died. Thus, Santiago manages the most miraculous feat of all: he finds a way to prolong his life after death. Santiago's commitment to sailing out farther than any fisherman has before, to where the big fish promise to be, testifies to the depth of his pride. It also shows his determination to change his luck. Later, after the sharks have destroyed his prize marlin, he chastises himself for his hubris, claiming that it has ruined both the marlin and himself. True as this might be, it is only half the picture, for Santiago's pride also enables him to achieve his most true and complete self. It helps him earn the deeper respect of the village fishermen and secures him the prized companionship of the boy—he knows that he will never have to endure such an epic struggle again. Santiago's pride is what enables him to endure. And it is perhaps endurance that matters most in Hemingway's conception of the world—a world in which death and destruction, as part of the natural order of things, are unavoidable. Hemingway seems to believe that there are only two options: defeat or endurance until destruction. Santiago clearly chooses the latter. His stoic determination is mythic, nearly Christ – like in proportion. For three days, he holds fast to the line that links him to the fish, even though it cuts deeply into his palms, causes a crippling cramp in his left hand, and ruins his back. This physical pain allows Santiago to forge a connection with the marlin that goes beyond the literal link of the line: his bodily aches attest to the fact that he is well matched, that the fish is a worthy opponent, and that he himself, because he is able to fight so hard, is a worthy fisherman. This connectedness to the world around him eventually elevates Santiago beyond what would otherwise be his defeat. Like Christ, to whom Santiago is unashamedly compared at the end of the novella, the old man's physical suffering leads to a more significant spiritual triumph.

Manolin: Manolin is present only in the beginning and at the end of the story, but his presence is important because Manolin's devotion to Santiago highlights Santiago's value as a person and as a fisherman. Manolin demonstrates his love for Santiago openly. He makes sure that the old man has food, blankets, and can rest without being bothered. Despite Hemingway's insistence that his characters were a real old man and a real boy, Manolin's purity and singleness of purpose elevate him to the level of a symbolic character. Manolin's actions are not tainted by the confusion, ambivalence, or willfulness that typify adolescence. Instead, he is a companion who feels nothing but love and devotion. Hemingway does hint at the boy's resentment for his father, whose wishes Manolin obeys by abandoning the old man after forty days without catching a fish. This fact helps to establish the boy as a real human being—a person with conflicted loyalties who faces difficult decisions. By the end of the story, the boy abandons his duty to his father, swearing that he will sail with the old man regardless of the consequences. He stands as a symbol of uncompromised love and fidelity. As the old man's apprentice, he also represents the life that will follow from death. His dedication to learning from the old man ensures that Santiago will live on.

Themes

Endurance: The old man's battle with the fish is not only a battle of strength, but a battle of wills. The old man makes up for his old age with incredible endurance, willing to withstand hunger, physical pain, and isolation from the rest of the world as he battles the fish. Endurance becomes a way to connect the old man and the fish he fights, as they share a determination that separates them from other people and creatures.

Suffering: The ability to withstand physical pain is one of Santiago's defining characteristics. Suffering is a necessary step in his battle with the fish. It adds intensity to the struggle, and commands a respect from the reader. The mental anguish of losing the fish to the sharks is underplayed. Such pain can be controlled by sheer willpower.

Memory and the Past: Because of his age, the old man can recall a strength and prowess of his youth. Readers at first wonder if such elements have faded from his character over time, but are left with a suspicion that the old man in his strength and abilities has lived up to heroic image readers see portrayed in his memories of his younger self. Memory is overlaid with current action. The past can be used to comment on the present. The old man's memory of the lions is a constant motif, as he implicitly compares his own abilities to their prowess and pride.

Defeat: Whether the old man is defeated or not is a persistent question. Readers are asked to define defeat, to struggle with what it really means to be beaten. Santiago draws a distinction between being destroyed and being defeated. It seems that "destruction" carries a physical connotation (the old man identifies something broken in his chest), but defeat implies the breaking of one's spirit, a psychological or spiritual act.

Isolation: The old man is a character isolated from people—and in fact from the world of humans entirely—in his time on the sea. This isolation defines who he is, and emphasizes the unique nature of his character. Isolation becomes both a weakness (he suffers from loneliness), and a necessary element to his battle with the fish.

Man and the Natural World: The old man is unique in his relationship to and understanding of the natural world. He talks about the sea as though it were a woman, the birds as friends, the sharks as personal enemies. He examines the relationship between turtles and jellyfish, between fish and birds. The creatures and the natural world become a lens through which readers examine the old man.

Respect and Reputation: The old man derives respect from others with displays of strength and prowess. Santiago himself feels great awe and respect for the marlin, repeatedly emphasizing this during his struggle and after he has killed the fish. Additionally, the old man's friendships are based on mutual respect.

Friendship: The old man's relationship with the boy is characterized as "love", and Manolin expresses deep admiration for the old man's fishing abilities. The old man also finds brotherhood with certain creatures on the sea. This type of relationship is based on similar characteristics such as nobility or determination. This story draws no distinction between friend and enemy. In fact, the two are repeatedly associated. The marlin is both the old man's friend and his enemy. The two roles are tied together, again, with the idea of respect.

Film Adaptations

The Old Man and the Sea (1958) was directed by Peter Viertel, starring Spencer Tracy. It was released by Warner Bros. The screenplay was the most literal, word-for-word rendition of a written story ever filmed. Hemingway said it had a wonderful emotional quality and he was very grateful and pleased with the transference of his material to the screen. He thought Tracy was great. The photography was excellent, the handling of the fishing and mechanical fish very good. Among the film's short-comings, it is noted that though there are some lovely long shots of Cuban villages and the colorful coast, the main drama is played in a studio tank, and even some fine shots of a marlin breaking the surface and shaking in violent battle are deflated by obvious showing on the process screen. The actor was never permitted to catch a marlin while on location, so the director must cross-cut so interminably—fish, Tracy, fish, Tracy. The film loses the lifelikeness, the excitement, and above all the generosity of rhythm that the theme requires.

Fig 15.3 A Poster of the 1958 Film

Fig 15.4 Santiago and Manolin

Fig 15.5 Hand wrestling with a negro

Fig 15.6 Santiago and the Fish

The Old Man and the Sea (1990) was directed by Jud Taylor, starring Anthony Quinn, Gary Cole, Patricia Clarkson. Besides the story of Santiago, the film adds how Tom Pruitt, writer, and his wife Mary are there in the village, witnessing Santiago's going out and coming back with a skeleton of a big fish. Pruitt is having trouble writing anything of substance. He does not want to leave the village immediately. She wants to know what he's thinking, so she can better understand his motivations. He tells her he's thinking about the old man, about his not having caught a fish for 84 days, and how someone deals with something like that. More than three days later, it's Sunday. People are coming out of church. Manolin is on the beach, watching and waiting. He's the first to see Santiago's boat. He runs and tells Tom Pruitt, who is in his room and wakes his wife and tells her. Angela, the old man's daughter, goes down to the beach and watches. The old man comes back at last very physically exhausted. Angela calls him a stubborn old man and invites him to come to see his grandchildren soon. So this film is neither like the original novella nor the 1958 film. With how a writer is there and how the old man's daughter is worried about her father, audience can know more behind the original story.

Fig 15.7 A Poster of the 1990 Film

Fig 15.8 Santiago and the Fish

Fig 15.9 Manolin and Angela

Fig 15.10 Tom Pruit and Mary

The Old Man and the Sea (1999) was directed by Aleksandr Petrov, starring Gordon Pinsent. Petrov's animation technique involves oil painting on glass. When combined with IMAX, the result is stunning. There is one shot near the end of the film which shows the Cuban fishing village at night with the stars in the background. The stars shimmer like diamonds set into dark blue velvet.

Fig 15.11 A DVD Cover of the 1999 Film   Fig 15.12 Santiago and the fish

Wonderful Dialogues from the 1958 Film

(1) At the Terrace

Manolin: Santiago, can I go out and get the sardines for you tomorrow?

Santiago: No, no. You play ball. I can still row. And I can still throw the net.

Manolin: I know where I can get your fresh fish baits.

Santiago: I still have nine for today.

Mandolin: Let me get four fresh ones.

Santiago: One.

Manolin: Two.

Santiago: (*Nodding his head*) Two. You didn't steal them, did you?

Manolin: I would. But I bought these.

Santiago: Thank you.

Manolin: If I cannot fish with you. I'll serve in some way.

Santiago: You bought me a beer. You are already a man.

They both drink.

(2) Fighting Sharks

Voice – over: He couldn't talk to the fish any more because the fish had been ruined too badly. Then something came into his head. "Half fish," He said, "Fish that you were. I'm sorry I went out too far. I ruined us both. But we have killed many sharks, you and I, and ruined many more. How many have you ever killed, old fish? You do not have that spear on your head for nothing." "What will you do now if they come in the night? I'll fight them. I'll fight them until I die. Oh, but I hope I do not have to fight again," he thought, "I hope so much I do not have to fight again." (*More sharks come. He fights again.*). And this time, he knew the fight was useless. "Come on, galanos, come on …"(*He fights hard and becomes very exhausted.*). He knew he was beaten now, finally and without remedy.

Santiago: I'm sorry, fish.

Voice – over: He could feel he was inside the current now. And he could see the lights of the beach colonies along the shore. He knew where he was now. And it was nothing to get home. "The wind is our friend, anyway," he thought, then he added, "sometimes, and the great sea with our friends and our enemies. And bed. Bed is my friend, just bed. Bed will be a great thing."

Santiago: It is easy when you are beaten. What beat you? Nothing, I just went out too far. Man is not made for defeat. Man can be destroyed, but not defeated.

(3) At the Shack

Santiago comes home exhaustedly and lies in bed. Mandolin comes to him, gives him some coffee, and squats at the bed.

Santiago: They beat me, beat me, Manolin. They truly beat me.

Mandolin: He didn't beat you, not the fish. Did you suffer much? Now we'll fish together again.

Santiago: Now, no. I'm not lucky with me.

Manolin: The hell with luck. I'll bring the luck with me.

Santiago: What will your father say?

Manolin: I don't care what he says.

Santiago: We'll ⋯ we will have to get a killing lance and keep it on board at all time. It must be very sharp and not tempered so it will break, like my knife broke.

Manolin: I'll get another knife. How many days of heavy wind have we?

Santiago: Oh, maybe three, maybe more.

Manolin: I'll have everything in order. You get your hands well, old man.

Santiago: They will be all right in a couple of days. I know how to care for them. During the night, I spat up something strange. I felt like something in my chest was broken.

Manolin: Get that well too. Drink your coffee. I'll get you something to eat.

Santiago: And⋯ and bring me the papers from the time I was away.

Manolin: I will. (*Going out of the room*)

 Discussions

1. Santiago is called a "tough guy". How does he earn such an honor?
2. Santiago says that he loves the fish, but he must kill him. Is there contradiction in his words? What does he really want to express?
3. Manolin is Santiago's best friend and a helping hand. He is considerate of the old man from the beginning to the end. What is the purpose of the author to put the boy in the story?
4. The old man says that man can be conquered, but can never be defeated. How do you explain it?
5. Generally, a film based on a classic work puts aside some plot and details of the original. Yet the 1990 film adds something beyond the original work. Is it good or bad? Compared with other film adaptations, is this one preferable or less interesting?

References

[1] Ackerman, Robert. Thomas Hardy's *Tess of the D'Urbervilles*. 北京:外语教学与研究出版社,1996.
[2] Blackburn, Ruth H. Charlotte Brontë's *Jane Eyre*. 北京:外语教学与研究出版社,1996.
[3] Brontë, Emily. *Wuthering Heights*. New York: Pocket Books, 2004.
[4] Cooperman, Stanly F. Scott Fitzgerald's *The Great Gatsby*. 北京:外语教学与研究出版社,1996.
[5] Ernest Hemingway. *The Old Man and the Sea*. 北京:外语教学与研究出版社,1996.
[6] Fitzpatrick, William J. Jane Austen's *Pride and Prejudice*. 北京:外语教学与研究出版社,1996.
[7] Gilbert E L. Emily Brontë's *Wuthering Heights*. 北京:外语教学与研究出版社,1996.
[8] Hemingway, Ernest. *A Farewell to Arms*. 北京:外语教学与研究出版社,1992.
[9] Mark Twain. *The Adventures of Huckleberry Finn*. 北京:外语教学与研究出版社,1992.
[10] Melville, Herman. *Moby–Dick*. Wordsworth Classics, Great Britain, 1993.
[11] Ochojski, Paul M. Charles Dickens' *David Copperfield*. 北京:外语教学与研究出版社,1996.
[12] 艾米丽·勃朗特.呼啸山庄[M].宋兆霖,译.石家庄:河北教育出版社,1996.
[13] 笛福.鲁滨孙漂流记[M].徐霞村,译.北京:人民文学出版社,2000.
[14] 德莱塞.嘉莉妹妹[M].裘柱常,译.上海:上海译文出版社,1990.
[15] 菲茨杰拉德.了不起的盖茨比[M].巫宁坤,译.上海:上海译文出版社,1997.
[16] 费尼莫·库柏.最后的莫西干人[M].陈兵,刘建成,周瑛,译.合肥:安徽文艺出版社,1996.
[17] 哈代.苔丝[M].孙法理,译.南京:译林出版社,1994.
[18] 海明威.海明威作品集[M].唐永宽,等,译.杭州:浙江文艺出版社,1991.
[19] 赫尔曼·梅尔维尔.白鲸[M].杨善录,蒋勤荣,译.合肥:安徽文艺出版社,1997.
[20] 简·奥斯汀.傲慢与偏见[M].孙致礼,译.南京:译林出版社,1994.
[21] 马克·吐温.赫克儿贝里·芬历险记[M].许汝祉,译.南京:译林出版社,1998.
[22] 斯托夫人.汤姆叔叔的小屋[M].刘瑾,等,译.北京:中国致公出版社,2005.
[23] 夏洛蒂·勃朗特.简·爱[M].宋兆霖,译.石家庄:河北教育出版社,1996.
[24] The Adventures of Huckleberry Finn (DVD). Turner Entertainment Co. and Warner Bros. Entertainment Inc, 2003.
[25] The Great Gatsby (DVD). A&E Television Networks, 2000.
[26] Carrie (DVD). Paramount Pictures, 2005.
[27] Wuthering Heights(DVD), Paramount Pictures, 2009.
[28] Pride and Prejudice(DVD). BBC Worldwide Limited, 2006.
[29] David Copperfield (DVD). BBC Worldwide Limited, 2006.
[30] Jane Eyre (DVD). BBC Worldwide Limited, 2008.
[31] A Tale of Two Cities (DVD). BBC Worldwide Limited, 2006.
[32] Moby Dick (DVD), Artisan Entertainment Inc, 1998.
[33] The Last of the Mohicans(DVD). Twentieth Century Fox Home Entertainment, 2010.
[34] Tess(Film). Renn Productions, 1979.
[35] Moby Dick(DVD),广州中凯文化发展有限公司,1999.
[36] Robinson Crusoe (DVD),福建音像出版社,2003.
[37] 海明威作品电影精选藏集(DVD).潇湘电影制片厂音像出版社,2005.
[38] http://wikipedia, the free encyclopedia.
[39] http://www.sparknotes.com/lit/.
[40] http://novel.tingroom.com/shuangyu/453/(英文小说网).
[41] http://www.tianyabook.com/waiguo2005/d/digengsi/dwkb/index.html(天涯在线书库).